THE GOLDE

Dead Winter Bones

ANNA PENROSE

First published 2023 by Mudlark's Press

First paperback edition 2023
Cover design by Deranged Doctor Design

ISBN 9781913628109

Also by Anna Penrose

The Golden Murders Series

Prologue

The storm howled. There was no rain yet, but the wind was fierce, punching through sheds and whipping up waves in the sheltered harbour. Boats slammed against each other as many lost their moorings. Up at Liggan Hall, the trees groaned in protest; branches tore from their trunks and crashed onto the ground below. The storm was turning into a gale as it picked up speed. Clouds raced in front of the moon, plunging the scene of devastation into darkness. Shadows flickered on and off in stroboscopic flashes of light; illuminating the chaos then plunging back into darkness and the blind roar of the winds.

An explosive *crack* roared across the sky as a gigantic oak finally succumbed to the unrelenting pressure and, slowly at first then with monstrous speed, fell. Animals quaked in their burrows as the reverberations of its impact shuddered through the woods. Birds huddling in its canopy flew up in alarm, their wings battering against the winds.

In a world turned upside down, the great oak's anchor thrust out of the earth, a semicircular crown of mud and roots, and a hollowed-out crater beneath. Amongst the debris, the moon shone briefly on a small collection of pale white bones before the clouds once again drew a veil over the scene.

There would always be storms in Golden. And every now and then, there would be bodies.

Chapter One

Barry Whitchurch put down his mug and slapped his thighs. The sky was light enough that he could go and inspect the damage to the gardens. As head groundsman, he was responsible for the grounds of Liggan Hall. He oversaw both the family and public gardens, along with the lower arboretum. The farms and outer woodlands were managed separately. Truth be told, man and boy, he'd been a gardener rather than a farmer or an arboriculturist.

Ironically, Fred, the man in charge of the woodlands, was unable to get in due to fallen trees, so Barry had said he would go and see the extent of the damage before returning to the gardens.

'Are we going to open today, boss?' asked one of the junior gardeners, a young girl with piercings and blue hair.

Barry wondered what Emily's pain was. A lot of troubled souls were drawn to gardening, but she worked hard and maybe he was just an old dinosaur.

'Did you drive or walk to work this morning?' he asked.

'I walked.'

'So you won't have seen the big old tree lying across the entrance to the car park, then?'

The staff that had made it to work had had to park on the verge before they went and picked up the chainsaws.

'We'll be closed today, and depending on what we find now, we might be closed for a few days.' He studied the small team that had made it in. They would have to do. 'You've all got your radios. Call in to the office with details of damage. Sheila will be keeping note of everything. Don't bother with the small stuff. We know there's lots of that.'

'What about broken glass?' Emily asked.

'Yes, if the greenhouses are damaged, call it in. Do *not* enter them.' He paused and thought about it. 'Also, don't stand too close to any brick walls.'

'Do you think it's going to be that bad, Barry?' That was Sheila, looking concerned. Sheila was an excellent administrator, but would sometimes drive him potty with her adherence to matters around health and safety.

'Don't know, but I don't want to find out that a wall has collapsed and one of you is under it. If you see anything that looks off, call it in, and we'll get the building team down for an assessment.'

He stood up. 'Now, you've all got your areas. I'm starting with the lower woods and making my way back up. I'll have my radio on at all times. Let's go.'

After leaving the office shed, Barry threw himself into one of the electric buggies. He made it as far as the entrance to the formal gardens, then the path became unpassable. Broken terracotta pots and branches were strewn across the path. He jumped out and walked along a cobbled cut-through that doubled as a water channel, and slipped down to the lower paths between two large yew hedges. The garden had been designed to weave visitors slowly through the various areas of the estate; most workers knew plenty of shortcuts, but Barry knew them all.

At nine o'clock, the clouds had all but lifted, showing the extent of the damage. Large ornate wrought-iron gates led from the formal gardens into the arboretum, and the lower woods below that framed the river valley. Looking over the canopy, Barry could see gaps that hadn't been there before.

He spoke into the radio, 'Lots of damage in the lower woods. Looks like someone has been playing dominoes. A few trees down in the arboretum. Just going to check on the Old Man.'

The Old Man was an oak that stood on a prominent ridge overlooking the surrounding estate. It was a feature of Liggan and appeared on a lot of their publicity. It also marked the border between the public grounds and the farmland beyond.

As Barry walked up the path towards it, he realised he should have seen its crown already, and sadness enveloped him. The Old Man had been a feature of his life. As nippers, he and his mates would race up the hill to slap the trunk. They would climb its branches, claiming that they could see the north coast from the top. That wasn't feasible, of course. From that angle, they could barely see their own coastline, but that never stopped kids from boasting of their prowess.

When they'd finished climbing and playing on the rope swing, they would roll and tumble down the hill before The Beast would come shouting at them about trespass.

'The Beast' was the name they'd given Mr Haverstock, owner of Liggan. He would come roaring out, firing his shotgun into the sky. Mikey swore The Beast had once nicked his ear, but everyone knew that'd happened when he tried to vault some barbed wire and got tangled up in it instead.

But now, Mikey had moved away—might even be dead—and Barry was head groundsman, The Beast was his boss, and as Barry reached the top of the hill, he could see the Old Man was no more.

The giant oak was lying on one side, its roots having torn up a huge crater of earth, with the canopy lying a hundred feet away. Leaves were still fluttering in the wind, making a mockery of life. The entire tree had simply tipped over. The trunk was unbroken, and Barry knew the wood would be highly prized. For the moment, though, he felt only pity. Pulling out his radio, he set it to Open Broadcast.

'The Old Man has gone.'

After a moment of silence on the airwaves, Barry heard muffled cursing from the other gardeners. No one there didn't love that old tree.

Switching the chatter off, he went to inspect the roots. As he approached, he noticed something tangled at the edge, fluttering in the breeze. It looked like a bit of cloth and struck Barry as odd. As he got closer, he squinted. The fabric seemed to be wrapped around a slender section of white roots. But every part of Barry's mind told him it wasn't a root. He had seen enough animal carcasses before to know when he was looking at bones.

Maybe someone had once buried a beloved pet up there. He got to the lip of the crater and looked down at a small skull nestled in the earth. Nobody could mistake that domed shape and those wide eye sockets. This was no pet. A child's face had once laughed out of those bones.

Chapter Two

Malachite Peck stretched carefully and sat up. It was a poor consolation that with age came confidence and wisdom, but left you with wrinkles and creaking bones. The fact was that, in a society where getting old was a crime, she was a confirmed criminal—in more ways than one.

She removed her earplugs and heard the wind outside still going strong. The previous night, as the storm picked up, she'd given up and put them in and promptly slept like a baby. At the foot of the bed were her patio table and chairs, which neighbours had advised she either bring inside or tie down. She'd thought they were exaggerating. Her little rooftop patio was sheltered by other buildings on three sides. She felt her neighbours were worrying needlessly, but she'd humoured them. Despite having experienced lots of foul weather since her arrival, this was the first time anyone had said it would be a rough night. After wrapping her kimono around herself, she opened the French doors and stared in amazement at the wreckage on her patio. She wondered how on earth she'd slept through that.

The few potted plants she'd accrued were gone. They hadn't been very big and had no doubt blown off the edge of the roof. She would have to apologise to her various neighbours, but that was the least of her issues by a very long shot. Completely engulfing her patio and blocking her view of the sea was a mangled trampoline. It looked to be ten feet across and must once have been a very fine plaything. Now, it was a battered mess.

The wind was still whipping along, so she pulled her kimono tight and stepped out onto the patio. The roofing felt was cold and wet under her feet, and she stepped carefully. Bits of terracotta and slate tiles were smashed on the floor. As she leant over the balustrade, she could see some of her plastic pots clogging her neighbours' drainpipes. The netting from the trampoline cage was slapping against her legs, making her kimono wet, and she headed back into the warmth of her bedroom.

Mac jumped off the bed and rubbed against her ankles. Not a stray as such—he appeared to be the village cat, if such a thing was possible—but for the past few months, since Malachite's arrival in the village, he'd adopted her and was allowing her to feed him every day. He also slept on her bed in order to ensure she never forgot her duties. He was pacing back and forth, aware that she was failing to provide him with breakfast.

'Well, Mac, a trampoline. Have you ever seen the like?'

Chuckling, she headed downstairs. Once she fed the cat, she would grab a photo of the trampoline and add it to her Instagram account. Life in the village was full of unexpected images. Sights that were no doubt mundane to the locals caught her eye, but she was certain no one had seen that before; a trampoline three floors up, trapped on a patio and wedged between the various roofs.

After a quick coffee, she got dressed and headed out to see if anyone was looking for it. It was the dead days between Christmas and New Year, and holidaymakers had left their bins outside. Along the debris-strewn lane, amongst the wine bottles and ready-meal cartons, were fishing nets and seaweed. A cold wind was sending loose items tumbling along the lane; the sound of a drinks can rattled by.

Mal nipped back into her bookshop and headed to the back of the building, where she kept the bin bags. Returning to the street, she started picking up the debris. Life in Golden seemed to revolve around bins, she thought, and smiled as she noticed other residents performing similar tasks. Some were locals, whilst others were unfamiliar, and she decided either they were here on holiday or visiting their second homes.

'Morning, Mal!'

Mal turned and saw Bob Yates walking towards her. He was wearing a big fluorescent jacket and carrying a heavy broom. Bob was one of the local fishermen and in summer ran pleasure rides on his boat, a high-speed inflatable. The only time Mal had been on it was far from pleasurable, as the pair of them chased a murderer who was shooting at them. They'd literally dodged a bullet, and since then had become firm friends.

'Morning, Bob. It's a bit of a mess. Is everyone okay?'

'No flooding. Storm hit at low tide, thank the Lord, but a couple of properties on The Heights have lost their roofs; some boats broke free of their moorings and sank; and one car went over the jetty. But no deaths. Think we got lucky. It's worse inland. Loads of trees down. Liggan lost a few specimen trees. The A391 is closed, as are many minor lanes. Hope you weren't planning on going anywhere today.'

Mal listened in astonishment to the list of damages. She walked with Bob down to the harbour and gasped as she saw the state of the place. The Christmas lights were hanging from poles, ripped off their supports. A bench was jutting out of the front window of the Cat and Fiddle, with broken glass hanging in shards around it. People were picking up shop hoardings and stacking them against the wall as they swept the seaweed back into the harbour. Two women hauled a collection of tangled fishing nets into a pile by the pub wall. Over by the jetty, a group of men were looking down at the bumper of a white pickup truck—the rest of the van was below the rising tide.

'Oh dear, I think my issue will have to wait,' said Mal, as she tried to take in the devastation.

'What's that, maid?' Bob looked at her in concern. 'Is your roof alright?'

'Do you know I haven't even checked? No, I've gained a trampoline. Up on the top terrace.' Mal's hair was playing in the wind, causing her repeatedly to tuck it behind her ears in frustration. 'Bloody hell. How much longer will this wind last?'

'It's almost done,' said Bob, looking at the clouds racing overhead. 'Forecast says rain tomorrow, so we might have enough time to tidy up in the dry. Small mercies, hey? Anyway, come with me. I think I can solve your trampoline issue.'

They walked towards the harbour master's office, and Bob called out to a man busy talking into a handheld mic.

'Alright, Bill, did you say you had lost your trampoline? Think I may have found it.'

William Hunt was Golden's harbour master and had juggled the concerns of fishermen, sailors, and water users for years. A local lad who'd spent years in the navy, he'd been pleased to retire home and find a position had opened up for harbour master. Many had applied, but none could compete with his local knowledge and years of maritime experience. His beard was nearly as white as Mal's hair, but his was at a sensible length and stayed as a dense cloud around his jaw.

'Hang on, Bob.' He spoke into the walkie-talkie again. 'Tell them to make for our outer harbour. I'll send a pilot out to help them in. But if Fowey can accommodate them...' As he listened to the reply, he shook his head in dismay. 'Understood. Send them our way, then.'

Bob cocked an eyebrow as Bill disconnected his call.

'Fowey pretty smashed up as well?'

'Yes, they have a yacht sunk in the channel. The mast is going to cause issues.'

'Nasty business. Who's trying to come in?'

12

'Some Londoner. Bloody fool thought he could outrun it. He's limping in for repairs.'

'Lucky not to go down.'

'Agreed,' said Bill. He clipped the radio set back onto his waistband and looked at the pair of them, giving Mal a quick nod of the head. 'Now, what's this about my trampoline?'

'You have a trampoline?' asked Mal, blinking. Looking at his stocky figure and serious countenance, she couldn't quite picture him bouncing up and down.

'Well, strictly speaking, it's my grandchildren's.' He shook his head. 'Their mother thought it would be a good idea to have one in case they got bored when they come to stay.'

His tone of voice made clear what he thought about children needing to be constantly entertained. Privately, Mal agreed. Boredom encouraged creativity and mischief. A lot of people thought that was a bad thing, but Mal liked the chaos and energy it stirred up. Boredom was good for the brain. God knows, after five years in prison, she knew all about boredom. The wardens also knew the dangers of boredom amongst a contained group of women with flexible attitudes towards law and order; activities were always laid on in a desperate attempt to exhaust any stirrings of sedition. Mal had used the time to read and learn. She also helped some of the younger women who'd become her friends. But that was prison. Little children shouldn't be treated like convicts, constantly distracted and mollified.

'Well, you are welcome to come and retrieve it,' said Mal, with a twinkle in her eye. 'But it's a mangled wreck and three floors up on my roof patio.'

Bill growled and thrust his hands into his pockets. 'God damn it. I told her to tether it properly. Should have done it myself.'

Mal wondered who he was referring to—possibly the daughter-in-law. From the way he'd called her *their mother*, he probably wasn't talking about his own daughter.

'They don't learn if you always do it for them,' suggested Bob. 'Mind you, bet she's not the one that will have to go get it.'

Bill snorted. 'Chance would be a fine thing.'

Clearly, Bob also knew the woman in question. As Mal had no inkling of the family politics, she decided not to get involved.

She cleared her throat. 'Well, it's not going anywhere, and I'm not using the patio in this weather, so it can wait.'

That wasn't strictly true. Mal enjoyed taking her morning coffee outside; wrapped up in a blanket, watching the sunrise over the water, the gulls drifting overhead as they greeted the dawn.

'Just call me when you're free. I think today you have your hands full.'

Turning, she left the two men with a smile as she retraced her steps, bending down to put a plastic bottle into the bag. As she slowly worked her way along the harbour front, she also retrieved a washing line, a tattered coat, and a broken bucket. All went into the bag as the gulls swept down on the food waste strewn across the lanes. Ahead of her were two children, racing after crisp packets and Coke cans as they clattered along the concrete road, their mother shouting warnings as they went.

Despite the chaos, the village was pulling together.

Chapter Three

Barry turned his back to the bones and switched his radio to a private channel. He knew Sheila would be busy coordinating all the damage reports, but this had to take priority.

'Sheila, there's a skeleton up here, buried in the roots of the Old Man.'

He paused as she processed his words and responded to her flurry of questions.

'No, long dead, I'd say. Leastways, I couldn't see any flesh. I need to go speak to Mr Haverstock, but I need to stop anyone from coming up here. Do we have anyone spare?'

He listened to her reply and grimaced.

'No one else? Okay, send him up and tell him to hurry. Don't tell him what it's about, and I need you to keep this to yourself as well.'

Switching the radio off, he sat down on the grass and waited for Lachlan Jones. Truth be told, Lachlan was a pleasant lad in his early twenties, longer than a bean pole and just as skinny. He was one of life's dreamers, drifting away from the simplest of instructions. But once something caught his fancy, Lachlan would work like a machine until the task was done. He particularly liked cleaning the clay pots that everyone else put off until there was nothing left to do. He did the best job as well. One year, he'd scrubbed off all the moss from the pots that the

16

publicity team had put together for a photo shoot. Lachlan just shrugged and said moss indicated poor horticultural management and walked away, leaving the PR department fuming. Barry had laughed and set Lachlan to another task well away from the staged photoshoot areas.

Now he watched as Lachlan ambled up the hillside towards him.

'Morning, Barry. That's a bloody sad sight.'

'That it is, lad.' Barry got to his feet. 'Now, I need you to do me a favour.'

He showed the bones to Lachlan, who looked suitably curious, then stepped away respectfully.

'I'll be back in an hour, but we need to inform the police—'

'Call in the feds!'

Barry stared at Lachlan patiently. 'We are not in America.'

'I know, but feds sounds way cooler. *Gangsta style.*'

Barry shook his head and scowled. Why did the youth today have to Americanise everything?

'Whatever. Wait here. Don't allow anyone else to approach. And don't tell anyone about the bones. Is that clear?'

Lachlan thought about it. 'How close can they come?'

'What?'

'Well, what if someone is walking by, down there, along the path, and they see me up here and think,

"What's Lachlan doing up there by himself? I'll go and keep him company." How close can they come?'

Barry ground his teeth. 'No one will be walking by this morning.'

'So who am I stopping?'

'Well, just in case.'

'In case…'

Lachlan tipped his head, trying to understand the contradictory instructions.

'I just need you to secure the site. You know…' Barry faltered, wondering if he should've got Sheila to send someone else.

'You want me to keep the bones company?'

'What?'

'Reckon they'll be feeling unsettled right now. They were used to the dark and had mice and moles for company. Now, it's all sunshine and birds. Must be a bit disconcerting, like.'

Barry stared at Lachlan and wondered if the boy had the makings of a poet. He certainly looked at the world oddly.

'Let's go with that. Stay here, do not leave for any reason, and I'll be back as quick as I can.'

Moderately convinced that Lachlan wouldn't wander off, Barry headed downhill as quickly as he could and back to Liggan Hall itself. Using a set of keys, he passed through a garden door into the private gardens and smiled again at how beautiful they were, if somewhat battered that morning.

Liggan Hall had been opening their gardens to the public for decades, just small charity events. Then, twenty years ago when Henry Haverstock started to run the estate instead of his father, he had made a business of the gardens. Now the gardens wrapping around the house were the only private area of the estate. Henry's parents had initially disagreed with their son's plans, but as the money and the accolades poured in, his mother, at least, came around to the idea.

Strictly speaking, Barry should've reported to Henry, but Mr Lionel Haverstock had been his boss first, and he still viewed the old man as his gaffer. He'd come a long way since the days he thought of his boss as The Beast. Besides, he had no time for Henry. A man who couldn't tell a bluebell from a primrose was bad enough, but plenty of other reasons existed to despise Lionel's heir.

Chapter Four

It wasn't so much that Lionel Haverstock felt life had let him down, so much as his family had. He was the sole heir to the Haverstock Estate, and when his parents mercifully spared him their further existence, he inherited the lot. With their passing, he experienced neither joy nor sadness. His wife, Imogen, twenty years his junior, made more of a fuss than he, but it was a big day for her. Finally, she was lady of the manor, and by elevating their deaths into notable events, she cast more shine on herself.

Imogen had been a millstone from the day he married her. Over the decades, whilst he'd done nothing to confront her, he'd also ensured that days spent in his company were neither welcome nor pleasurable. That arrangement seemed to suit her as well. As long as someone was there to pick up the bills, along with a house suited to entertaining and impressing her friends, she appeared content.

Lionel leant back in his chair and looked out from his study to the grounds beyond. The storm had ravaged the garden and any plans to have drinks on the terrace after his birthday celebrations were now on hold. He wasn't disappointed. Eighty-five was just a figure. He wondered if anyone was celebrating the fact that he'd survived so long. He was certain his wife wasn't, and he doubted his sons were, either.

Both boys were equally disappointing. The elder, Henry, was a braggart, the younger son was craven, and both were fools. Henry spent his life hanging around with people impressed by his wealth, of which he frequently reminded them. Lionel wondered when his son would actually start earning the wealth he spent so freely. Liggan Estate was more than just some gardens for tourists. When Lionel complained about the expenses, Henry explained they were what was necessary to impress people. Public relations had to be earned, and a business was nothing without an excellent reputation. Lionel felt that a business was nothing without sound financial planning, prudent budgeting, and long-term resilience. Those three tenets made his eldest son yawn.

His younger son, Algernon, spent his days in disappointment, for which he blamed his parents. Despite his lifestyle, he was missing a title. Lots of boys at school had titles and an attitude that Algernon hadn't quite mastered. In the company of the aristocracy, he was unctuous; with everyone else, he was superior. He'd married Daisy because of her wealth—that choice had been between her and a Lady Felicity. With the latter, he would've eventually gained a title but also a shedload of debt and some dreadful run-down property. Following Daisy's father's bankruptcy, it seemed Algernon had chosen unwisely, and was forever running back to his father for loans that never got repaid.

Lionel wondered whether, if Algernon and Daisy divorced, he would still see his grandchildren. As long as he had money, he imagined he would. He had five grandchildren, but only one of them was worth anything. Algernon had twins—ugly, grasping little things, Fred and Fenella. Through his first marriage, Henry had Jasper, Lionel's eldest and most promising grandson. Then, with his second wife, Henry had Persephone and Percy. Lionel was convinced his daughters-in-law were competing for the daftest children's names available.

A knock on the door shook him out of his bad mood, and he called out that whoever it was should enter— anything to distract him from his own company. When the door opened, he saw the caller was Barry, the estate manager. Normally, Barry would deal directly with Henry—as Henry was in charge of the public side of the estate—but his company was welcome, nonetheless.

'Morning Barry, I see the garden has had a bit of a battering this morning. Can I help with anything?'

The younger man walked in and closed the door behind him, seeming to be in no hurry to speak. Thinking of Barry as a younger man was amusing. Lionel remembered chasing Barry and his friends out of the orchards. The village lads had always taken a perverse pride in scrumping from the Liggan kitchen gardens. Barry was always the fastest up over the walls. Lionel couldn't imagine Barry climbing much of anything anymore without the help of a ladder. And as for himself, his days of running anywhere were long past.

'Is everything okay? No one's been hurt, have they?'

Falling trees were an absolute nightmare for public liability, but this storm had come at night, so the grounds and woods should've been empty.

Barry scratched his beard. 'Not as such, but we have made a discovery. The Old Man has fallen over.'

Lionel's shoulders slumped. 'Ah, now that's a crying shame. I thought he would outlast me, outlast all of us, if it came to that.'

Barry rubbed his face again.

'Actually, there's more to it than that.'

Just as he was about to speak again, the door was flung open, and Lionel's eldest son stormed in. 'What the hell is this about a body being found on the estate?' He glared angrily at the two men then addressed Barry directly. 'I'm in charge. You should have come to me directly. What the hell do you mean by pestering my father about it?'

Barry took a step back from the onslaught and cleared his throat. 'But your father is the actual landowner, and I just thought—'

He was cut off by Lionel, who stared at the two men. 'What body? What are you talking about?' His voice was harsh. 'Barry, you said no one was injured.'

'These are old bones, father, up by the big tree on the hill.'

'The Old Man.'

'Yes, whatever. Sheila told me. She made me look a right fool. I didn't know what the hell she was talking about.' He was snapping at Barry again, having dismissed his father's comment.

'Sorry, sir. As I said, I wanted to inform your father first. I was then coming to find you. I tried you on the walkie-talkie, but there was no reply.'

'Bloody hell, man. I'm not wedded to that thing. You should have come and looked for me.'

'Well, as I said, I needed to tell someone. We'll need to call the police.'

'The police!' said Henry.

Lionel looked at his son, surprised that he should sound so worried. 'Henry, if a body has been found, we have to inform the police immediately.'

'But they'll close us down until they're satisfied.'

'With all due respect,' Barry told Henry, 'we won't be opening for the next day or two anyways. The garden isn't safe for visitors.'

'What? Bloody hell. Surely the storm hasn't caused that much damage. Can't we just rope sections off?'

Lionel shook his head. 'Henry, you're focusing on the wrong thing. We have a death on the grounds.' Turning his gaze back to Barry, he carried on. 'How long do you think the body has been there? You're sure it wasn't hit by the tree falling?'

Barry was fiddling with his cap, uncomfortable at being caught in the middle of another father-and-son row.

24

'No, Mr Haverstock.' Formality was his refuge. 'These are bones. Looks like the body was buried under the tree. When the roots pulled up, it brought the bones with it.'

'Christ,' said Henry. 'Who the hell buries a body on our land? Father, do you know anything about this?'

'Of course I don't.' Lionel glared at his son as Barry cleared his throat.

'I'm afraid there's a bit more,' said Barry. 'Given the size of the bones, it's pretty clear that this is a child's grave.'

Both of the Haverstocks stared at Barry in horror. An unknown burial on their land was bad enough, but a child's body was a nightmare scenario.

'Right, well, I guess that's ruined our Spring Festival plans. And what about your birthday celebrations?' Henry was speaking quickly, trying to assess how much damage this would cause. 'I bet we can't keep this out of the papers. Who's guarding the site?'

'Lachlan—'

'Lachlan Jones! That idiot? It will be all over the village by lunch.'

Barry clenched his jaw and shoved his cap into a coat pocket. 'No, it won't. Lachlan's a good lad. Might not see the world the same way as the rest of us, but he won't say a word.'

'If he does, I'm holding you responsible.'

Lionel slammed a hand on the table, making both men jump. 'Is that all you can think?' A tear slid down his face.

'Your first thought is money. Your second thought is blame.' Lionel shuddered to his feet, his whole body shaking. 'I'm a foolish old man, and I should have changed my will years ago.'

Barry and Henry stared at the older man as he glared at his son, unaware of the tears on his face. His hands flapped furiously as he waved at them to leave.

'Get out of my sight, and when the police arrive, let me know.'

'Father, I—'

'Get out!' roared Lionel, in a voice breaking through his tears.

As the men left the study, Henry turned around and jabbed Barry in the chest. 'You will not repeat that conversation to anyone. My father was clearly overcome with shock. Which, by the way, wouldn't have happened if you had come to me first.' He drew a deep breath and straightened the sleeves on his jumper before continuing. 'I'm going to call the police now. When they arrive, my father is *not* to be disturbed. I don't want him distressed any further. And if I find Lachlan has talked to anyone, it will be your head on the block.'

As he stormed off towards the estate offices, Barry could see two gardeners out on the lawn talking excitedly and pointing in the direction of the Old Man. He shook his head. Some secrets could stay buried for years, but others would be public knowledge before the sun set.

Chapter Five

Mal stretched her back and looked around the harbour as the dying wind gently tugged at her hair. The bench had been removed from the pub window and the section boarded up. The glass had been swept up, as had most of the other debris. It was amazing how quickly things could be sorted when an entire community came out with buckets and brooms.

She'd been on her feet for the past three hours, bending, picking, and sweeping, and was fit to collapse.

'Hello, would you like some soup?'

Mal turned to see a young woman smiling at her, holding a stack of cardboard cups with lids on.

'I've got broccoli and blue, or mixed veg.'

Mal was embarrassed to feel herself salivating, but a warm bowl of fresh soup was exactly what she needed right then. The young woman smiled at her, her red curls tied up into a bun on her head. She was wearing dungarees, white fisherman's wellies, and a big smile. Sensing Mal's confusion, she hurried on.

'I'm Holly. I run Forget-Me-Nots.' She pointed at one of the little shops on the harbour front. 'Ice cream in summer, and soup in winter. I wasn't too badly affected by the storm, so I thought I'd rustle up some soup for everyone out working today.'

Mal groped in her pockets, annoyed that she had no change to hand. The soup smelled delicious.

'No charge,' Holly said quickly. 'The food would have gone off, anyway.'

'Well, thank you,' said Mal warmly. Village life was still a new concept to her, and whilst it often felt claustrophobic, at times like this, she could see the appeal. 'That's very generous of you.'

'Just us locals pulling together.'

'You're not a local, though, are you?' said a new voice, and Mal turned to see an old woman walking towards them. She was the most old-fashioned woman Mal had ever laid her eyes on. She looked as though she'd stepped out of a pre-war movie wearing sturdy navy shoes with a small solid heel; tights and a brown woollen skirt; brown woollen jumper under a darker-brown woollen coat; a neat little navy hat protected her permed grey hair; and hanging off one arm was a handbag with a brass clasp— like the Queen used to favour—held tightly against the woman's chest.

Holly narrowed her eyes. 'I've lived here all my life, Mrs Kitto. I was born here, for God's sake. So was my mother. I reckon that makes me local.'

Mal winced. What made someone local was a thorny issue for some Cornish people, but normally, being born in the county was good enough.

'I remember when your grandmother arrived with her up-country attitude. Selling ice creams to fishermen...' The old woman scoffed at the notion. 'She wasn't local then, and you're not local now.'

'Give over,' snapped Holly, 'you remember Methuselah being born, you do. I may not be as local as you, but I reckon I'll do.'

The younger girl's voice didn't carry much humour, and Mal felt the situation was turning unpleasant. The older woman's expression showed she was also ready for a fight.

'Morning, ladies,' said a fresh voice. 'Although if Holly is passing out the soup, I guess it must be afternoon.'

Mal turned, smiling at the sound of salvation. Sophie Taphouse was the village police officer and Mal's first friend in Golden. Although she wasn't actually assigned to the village—no police officer was in these days of cuts and fresh thinking—the fact that Sophie lived in the village meant she was everyone's first port of call when problems arose. The situation seemed to work well. Sophie had pride in her village and would do anything to support it and put her residents' needs first.

'Everything alright, Mrs Kitto?' she asked the older woman.

'Not by a long shot, but nothing more than we can handle.' Mrs Kitto rearranged her handbag. 'You'll be needing to know that the chapel has lost several tiles, and the gutter has come off.'

Sophie pulled a little notepad from the breast pocket of her stab jacket. She flipped it open and nodded. 'Yes, I have that noted.'

'The Harbour Watch has had its window smashed in. Although you can see that for yourselves.'

Sophie nodded again.

'Someone best have a word with the harbour master,' Mrs Kitto continued. 'Shoddy work that was, not securing the bench properly.' From her tone, nothing short of twenty lashes would be appropriate. 'There's a wall of ivy down on Priory Hill.'

Sophie checked her notes again, nodding once more as Mrs Kitto ran through a list of issues in the village.

'And finally, Ben Gothers has parked on the double yellow lines outside the surgery again.'

'The surgery car park is flooded this morning, and Mr Gothers was probably in picking up prescriptions,' said Sophie in a placating voice. 'I think on days like this, we have to give and take a bit. Besides which, old Harry's car is there as well.'

Mrs Kitto scoffed and clasped her bag against herself, her skin taut across her knuckles. 'He don't count. He's been parking there long before there were ever yellow lines.'

'Wow.' Holly laughed. 'It really is one rule for locals, and another one for outsiders with you, isn't it?'

Sophie jumped in quickly to cut off Mrs Kitto's response, giving Holly a pleading frown, then smiled at Mrs Kitto again. 'That's a very comprehensive list and matches everything I have.'

Mal watched in amusement as the older woman seemed mollified by the praise.

'Well, some things can't be taught, Officer Taphouse. Those of us that go back know what needs to be done in times like this. It takes more than a bowl of soup to fix things when proper work is called for.'

Mal had been watching the three women jibing and jostling, but felt the older woman had landed a blow Holly would not ignore.

'Well, at least I know about the missing trampoline.' Holly jutted her jaw out. 'Seems like you don't know everything.'

Mal winced. She didn't want to get pulled into this argument. She just wanted to sit down and enjoy her lunch, which was rapidly cooling down.

'A trampoline?' asked Mrs Kitto.

'Aye, that's right,' said Holly. 'Bill told me he'd lost his. Told me when I delivered him his soup.' She grinned tightly at the older woman.

'Well now, that's news to me as well,' said Sophie quickly, as she wrote it up in her notebook. 'Looks like us locals, *all* us locals,' she stressed towards Mrs Kitto's direction, 'have something to add on days like this. I'm very grateful, Holly. I'll go and have a word with Bill about it now.'

She was about to leave and Mal felt she should speak up and save her a mission, but she was loath to draw the attention of a woman who appeared to be the village harridan. She had never seen her before, but that wasn't surprising. Bookshops weren't for everyone, and this one in particular didn't strike Mal as a reader.

If Mrs Kitto judged Holly, who'd been born in town, as an incomer, then God knows what she thought of Mal. She wasn't concerned about the woman's poor opinion, but she just didn't wish to engage with her.

As Sophie turned to leave, Holly piped up again. 'Is it true about up at Liggan? The dead body.'

Sophie stepped back towards the three women, her face severe. 'Now, Holly. I don't know who you've heard that from, but can I ask you not to repeat it?'

'So, it's true then?'

'Holly!' Looking cross, she glared at both Mal and Mrs Kitto. 'Whatever is going on up there isn't helped by people gossiping about it down here. Is it?'

'Death comes to Golden again,' said Mrs Kitto, ominously.

'Please,' said Sophie, with a slight pleading tone. 'And it's not a body. It's old bones.'

'I heard it was a child!'

'Holly Champlain, I thought I made myself clear. Everything is under control, and there's nothing to be alarmed about,' she told Mrs Kitto, 'or excited about.' she continued, glaring at Holly. Then she looked at Mal. 'Honestly, we're not always like this.'

'If you'll excuse me,' said Mrs Kitto, flustered at having been reprimanded by an officer of the law. Pulling her coat around her, she left the other three women, taking one of the narrow lanes heading uphill towards the chapel.

'She is such a witch,' said Holly, as the woman moved away. Mrs Kitto was close enough to have heard Holly but paid her no attention and continued to limp uphill, her back bowed against the wind and her age.

'Holly, how many times do I have to tell you?'

'Sorry, Mum.'

'I'm your godmother, not your mum!' But Sophie was laughing. 'I know Margaret Kitto is difficult, but if you can't show some respect, at least show some manners. Or should I mention this to your mother?'

'She'd say the same. She was being rude about Nan. About how she was an incomer selling ice cream to fishermen.'

'And what would your Nan say?'

'She'd laugh and tell her to get over herself.'

Sophie smiled. 'That she would. So take a lesson from your Nan, and rise above it. Now, if you'll excuse me...'

Mal cleared her throat. She'd felt like an awkward bystander in the interplay between the three women, but at least now she could offer something. 'I have the trampoline.'

The two women stared at her.

'It's on my roof terrace.'

They both laughed.

'Bloody hell, woman,' laughed Holly. 'What some people will do for a sea view. How high do you have to jump?'

The silly joke dispelled the tension that had formed around Mrs Kitto's presence.

'I've already spoken to the harbour master. He'll come and sort it out when he's free. And now, if you'll excuse me, I am dying to sit down.'

Holly looked alarmed and suddenly held out an arm to Mal whilst trying to balance her soup pots.

Mal glared at her. 'My hair may be the same colour as Mrs Kitto's, but that's where any similarities stop. I'm perfectly fine, and after my soup, I shall play on my new trampoline.'

As the two women laughed, Mal headed back towards her shop, smiling. Her pot of soup was warm in her hands, and she was looking forward to putting her feet up. She'd been curious about the bones up at Liggan, but Sophie had been quite firm that topic of conversation was out of bounds, so she would just have to enjoy her new copy of Elly Griffiths instead. *Enough old bones in there for anyone.*

As Mal turned down her lane, she saw a man standing outside the door of her shop. Dressed in laced tan leather boots and a wax jacket, he seemed more suited to the countryside than a fishing village. She wondered if he was hoping to do some shopping, and her heart sank a little. She knew she had to make money whilst she could, but she was so looking forward to her soup. Still, he was very easy on the eyes. Mal chided herself, noting he was easily half her age.

'Hello. I'm afraid I'm not open today.' She headed towards the door, balancing the soup pot and her keys.

The man turned and looked at her, relieved. 'Are you the owner? Only I was asked to fetch you.'

Chapter Six

Mal raised her eyebrows as she stepped past him and unlocked the door. Heading into the shop, she switched on the lights, then looked back at him. 'Fetch me?'

He looked uncomfortable and somewhat apologetic. 'If it's convenient, of course,' he stammered. 'My boss, Mrs Haverstock, wonders if you are free to have a word. I can take you up?'

Mal placed the soup on the counter and stared at him, then shook her head. 'I'm sorry. I have no idea what you are talking about.'

'Mrs Haverstock. Owns Liggan Hall. I'm sorry. She's in quite a state and hoped that you would be free to visit as soon as possible.' The man looked over his shoulder as though, just by saying her name, he might somehow summon her.

Mal was tired and in no mood to be called upon by a total stranger.

Clearly, the younger man saw that on Mal's face. 'Please. She'll make my life hell. She's already in a foul temper. Preparations for the birthday aren't going to plan, and she's like a bear with a sore head. I'll drive you up there and bring you down again afterwards.'

A gull flew overhead, laughing, and Mal shrugged.

'Very well. I imagine missing lunch won't kill me. What's your name?'

'Dougie. And I'm so grateful for this. I can let Mrs Haverstock know you haven't eaten yet. Maybe you can eat together?'

Having lunch with the lady of the manor? Mal couldn't think of anything worse, and honestly, she was so dog-tired that all she wanted was a cheeky nap in front of the television. Only when they got into the little car and were heading up a back lane, did she realise she was still wearing her new boots. She was too tired by far.

'We have to go back! I'm in wellies.'

Dougie looked down at her footwear. 'She won't mind. Half the staff are in boots. Besides, we're pretty much here.'

Mal wanted to point out that she wasn't staff, but her retort died off as the lane turned into a proper driveway leading past formal lawns. Clearly, this was a private road between the village and the estate and not encumbered by tree falls.

'The emergency services use this route when the main road is closed,' Dougie said. 'The air ambulance also uses that lawn.'

He stopped the car and jumped out to open a heavy gate with Private Property plastered across it, then returned to the car. After they drove through, Mal insisted on closing the gate. It was heavy but well oiled, and she got the sense of an estate in excellent working order. She returned to the car, questions playing in her mind.

If it's this easy to walk into Liggan, what stops the general public from traipsing in this way and avoiding the charge?

Over the past few months of working in the bookshop, Mal had become very aware of the *general public* and had even come to think of them in italics. In fact, the *general public* was made up of many factions, and one faction was particularly disinclined to pay the full price for anything. They would wander around the shop, then loudly inform Mal that they could buy the same book for fifty pence at the car boot. Mal had never attended a car boot but thought Waterstones had best watch out. Apparently, every single book ever published could be found lying on a tarpaulin in a field somewhere. And yours for just a few pennies.

She remembered staring at the first customer who'd mentioned this until she realised the wretched woman expected her to drop her prices. Mal's laugh had been short but loud, and the woman had left in a huff. Mal had lost little sleep over the loss of fifty pence. Talking to a few other shopkeepers, she soon discovered this was par for the course with some of the visitors.

Dougie grinned at her. 'The dogs see to that. This entrance is to the private grounds. There are instructions on how to get to the open gardens, and there's a sign at the bottom of the hill as well. Still, every year, people try to pretend that they somehow missed both signs. Then Max and Milo have the last word.'

As he spoke, two large black dogs ran across the lawn towards the car, barking loudly and wagging their tails as they ran alongside.

'Will they bite?' said Mal in alarm. She was wearing boots but had never had a dog, and had no idea how to calm one down.

'No. Not a bit. No need to worry. They recognise the engine noise.'

'What if we were trying to pull a fast one?'

'Then they would follow the car until it stopped and bark at it. That usually draws the attention of someone who then redirects them accordingly, or they leave via the main drive, never to darken our shores again.'

The car headed between a collection of small brick buildings and around a bend towards the back of a very large estate house.

'Liggan Hall,' declared Dougie. 'It's much prettier from the front, but Mrs Haverstock doesn't like staff cars pulling up around the front of the property.'

'Staff entrance it is, then,' said Mal with a smile.

'Indeed.' After pulling on the handbrake, he opened the door, called to the dogs to sit, then leant back into the car. 'Come and meet two of the dopiest guard dogs this side of the Tamar.'

Mal ventured out and walked carefully around the back of the car. She didn't want to alarm the hounds. Both dogs were sitting to attention, their tongues lolling out of their mouths as their tails lashed back and forth on the gravel.

'Let them have a smell of your hand, and then they'll know you're a friend.'

Dougie seemed very relaxed about the idea of her going anywhere near their jaws, but bracing herself, she approached them and held out a hand for them to sniff.

'Milo likes having his ear scratched.'

Mal tentatively scratched his ear while the other dog slumped to the ground and rolled on his back.

'And Max is a fan of the old belly rub.' Dougie crouched down and duly obliged. The large dog rolled onto his back and pedalled his legs in the air in pure joy.

'They're just big softies, aren't they?'

'For friends, absolutely. Woe betide anyone else.' He turned to the dogs and clapped his hands. 'Off, now.'

Max sprang up from the floor, and he and Milo raced off, no doubt to terrorise some squirrels.

'Right, let's wash our hands, and I'll introduce you to Mrs Haverstock.'

They walked through a large wooden door, along a corridor paved with terracotta tiles, and into a cloakroom lined with coats, boots, and a bank of large white Belfast sinks, whose taps also looked original. Mal felt she'd walked into the eighteen hundreds. She hung her coat but was certain her socks had holes in them, so she kept her boots on. The lady of the manor would just have to cope.

Then she followed Dougie along the corridors as they moved from terracotta tiles and flagstones to carpets and into the family part of the house. Mal wondered what Mrs Haverstock wanted with her. Dougie had explained that she was in the middle of preparations for her husband's eighty-fifth birthday party, and tensions were running high. The guest list was already up in the hundreds. And tomorrow, Liggan would have a free firework display and food for everyone attached to the estate; which was practically the entire village, according to Dougie.

Mal knew that would require an enormous amount of planning, and the storm couldn't have helped, but she didn't know what on earth Mrs Haverstock thought Mal could do? She knew nothing about party planning or storm damage.

The whole house was tastefully furnished in a way that indicated considerable sums of money spent on interior designers. Mal had spent time in lots of homes like this and was curious to see how this summons would play out. Dougie opened a white painted door flanked by two side tables that had various ornaments on them. She followed him through the door and into a large, bright drawing room with views over rolling parkland. Two sofas faced each other across a low buttoned footstool. To one side stood a grand piano covered in photo frames. At the other end of the room, a large log fire was crackling in the hearth, and a woman was sitting, reading a book. As Mal and Dougie entered, she put down her book and stood up, smoothing her skirt. She wasn't how Mal had imagined. For a start, she was clearly her husband's junior. Mal suspected maybe a little bit of surgery, but the rest seemed the result of a lifetime of rigorous control over her body. Slim, mid-sixties, blonde hair—she could have been one of Mal's contemporaries.

'Thank you, Dougie.' She gave him a flirtatious smile, but Mal detected no serious intent in the gesture, just that of a woman who liked male attention. Glancing at Mal, she splayed her fingers in mock horror. 'Douglas! She's still in her wellies. Whatever were you thinking? You could at least have let her change. I'm sure you wanted to, my dear.'

As she had finally addressed Mal directly, she decided to speak and get on with this pantomime. 'Actually, what I wanted was my soup. Now, your driver said you needed my help?'

Mal had always been, if not abrupt, then straight to the point. She would rather step back and watch than rush in full of chatter. She was not good at dissembling. Now her host was wrong-footed and Mal wondered if she had expected someone like herself, a socialite. Or maybe she had been hoping for someone in awe of her—the big house and the money. Time would tell. The woman was flustered for less than a second, and with practiced ease, she waved towards the sofa, indicating that Mal should join her by the fire. Then she dispatched Dougie with a request for tea and biscuits. She also offered Mal a bite of lunch, which Mal hurriedly dismissed. It was a little tic of hers, but she disliked eating in front of strangers.

As the door closed, Mrs Haverstock looked across at her. 'Mrs Peck, I hope you can help me with a delicate matter.'

Mal bristled. No matter how many times someone called her *missus*, it still grated, and she cut the woman off. 'Please, just Malachite or Mal.'

Mrs Haverstock smiled warmly. 'Of course, and please call me Imogen. I can see we're going to be friends.'

Mal smiled in return, but failed to agree. 'A delicate matter?'

'Ah, yes. Well, the thing is, this morning, the wind brought down one of our trees, and some human bones were revealed in its roots.' She waited for Mal's astonished reaction, and when none came, her face tightened.

'For heaven's sake. Do you already know? This wretched estate. Liggan is like a sieve. Nothing stays in, and all news trickles down to the village faster than tabloid gossip. The paparazzi have nothing on the Golden rumour mill.'

A knock came at the door, and a young woman walked in with a tea tray, placed it on the footstool between the two women, then left without being introduced. She hadn't expected to be thanked and gave Mal a quick smile when she did so.

Imogen poured Mal a cup of tea and offered her a biscuit, but waited for the door to close before continuing.

'You never know what tales they tell. Anyway, these bones. I need you to prove they have nothing to do with the estate.'

Mal stopped drinking, placed the dainty cup back on its saucer, and looked at Imogen carefully. 'I imagine this is a matter for the police.'

'Pah, they're up there now, securing the scene.' She air-quoted her disdainful words before continuing. 'Obviously, the bones have nothing to do with us.'

'Which the police will quickly establish.'

'They didn't with Malcom Jago and that whole business. From what I heard, that was down to you.'

Mal sighed. Finding a dead body in her shop had been an unwelcome introduction to village life. It was hardly something she had sought. She'd got dragged into the mystery and barely made it out with her life intact.

'I was just in the wrong place at the right time and happened to put a few clues together before the police did.'

'Nonsense. You're being modest. Young Sophie Taphouse speaks highly of you.'

'And I think highly of her. If she's involved with your bones, then all will be well.'

Imogen settled back in her armchair and studied Mal carefully. 'They are not my bones, and we both know that she's in uniform and doesn't have the influence or skills that you clearly have. Plus, you have a unique insight, what with your time spent—how shall we say—observing the criminal element at close quarters.'

Mal laughed dryly. That was the most euphemistic description yet.

'You mean my time spent inside as a prisoner?'

Chapter Seven

The other woman blinked quickly, then recovered. 'Well, yes, but I wasn't sure if you liked to talk about it.'

In which case, why bring it up? thought Mal. 'No point pretending it didn't happen. It's not as if I was innocent of the offence. I was guilty and served my time.'

Imogen put her cup and saucer on the tray, placed her hands on her knees, and stared directly at Mal. 'Can I just say that I think you should have been rewarded? Not imprisoned.' She placed a hand theatrically on her own chest. 'Saving the life of a child, using a criminal's money to do so… It's your company that should have gone to jail for laundering drug money like that.'

'Not laundering,' said Mal. 'Our business did everything by the book. That our client had money in other institutions that may have had a dubious provenance was not part of our concern.'

That was the party line, and it stank, but when your client regarded millions as loose change, the stench was apparently bearable.

'I still think you did the right thing.' Imogen shook her head. 'The way you were treated was deplorable. I was in Cucina's last month for lunch with some girlfriends, and they all agreed you should have been given a medal.'

Being the subject of gossip irked Mal. She'd always been talked about, usually in a business sense, but having her private life discussed felt wrong. *Shouldn't have stolen hundreds of thousands, then gone to jail, then been released, and then solved a murder if you didn't want to be talked about,* her inner voice said waspishly, sounding remarkably like her sister.

'Is that Cucina on Sloane Square?' asked Mal, trying to change the subject.

'Yes!' exclaimed Imogen. 'Do you know it?'

'It's just around the corner from my nephew's flat. I would often pop in there for lunch. Is it still owned by Pepe?'

Pepe made the best *bagna cauda*, and just thinking about it made Mal smile.

'It is. Do you remember Caterina?'

'Of course. She used to do her homework in the corner.'

'I know!' Imogen laughed. 'Such a funny sight. He had a waiting list as long as your arm, and yet he always had a table for little Kitty Cat.' She shook her head at the father's indulgence. 'Anyway, she just got a double first from Cambridge!'

Mal's smile was broad and unreserved.

'But she's still a child. Well, in my eyes, anyway. I must write and congratulate them.' She frowned in annoyance. 'Oh, I have missed so much.'

It was a rare display of annoyance, and she immediately regretted her outburst. The truth was that whilst Mal had lingered in jail, time had bent out of shape. For her, it elongated, but for the rest of the world, it had sprinted forward, and she wondered if she would ever find herself back in sync with the world around her.

'I'm sure they would love that,' said Imogen, in a moment of compassion. 'Do you remember Darcy's?'

For the next few minutes, the two women fell into an idle chat about shops and venues. Mal knew Imogen was building a picture of her and deeming her to be the right sort, as though shopping and eating at certain places made people part of the same tribe. Which she supposed it did. In another lifetime, Mal and Imogen could have been, if not friends, then at least acquaintances. Mal had many friends that didn't work, but every one of them would have introduced the girl that brought the tea in.

'If you don't mind me asking, what did you miss the most whilst you were inside?'

Mal knew that Imogen wasn't asking for anything deep and meaningful, like her freedom or the privacy of silence. She wanted to know about hairdressers and skiing in St. Moritz. Which was fine. Mal didn't want to talk about serious stuff with this woman.

'I suppose the worst of it was missing out on Anna Netrebko singing at La Scala.'

Imogen clapped her hands in delight. 'I went! It was a triumph. Lionel treated me to a box. We spent the weekend shopping in Milan, and I met Netrebko afterwards. The woman is incredible. Lionel has all her albums, but some of them do go on. I said she should record an album of more popular tunes. She'd make so much money.'

'I believe she has done just that.'

'I know. And I like to think that she listened to me.'

You can think what you like, thought Mal. *No doubt, her manager had been thinking the same for years.*

'Well, I am very envious. What a wonderful performance to have witnessed. Your husband must love you very much.'

Imogen picked up her teacup again. 'Well, of course he does, but truth be told, this was more a present to himself. I was just there for the shopping.' She laughed, delighted at her own observation.

Mal smiled politely. Imogen didn't seem to notice the difference as she regaled Mal with a list of her purchases. Mal just wanted to know how Anna Netrebko's voice had sounded in the venue. A live performance could never be captured on vinyl. Maybe she could ask Lionel Haverstock. Clearly, he was the one interested in opera, not Imogen.

'You are lucky to have such a caring husband.' Mal helped herself to a biscuit.

Imogen shrugged. 'I suppose. I was a child bride, just twenty. He was in his forties. I should have thought it through a bit more, but I suppose I was overcome with the estate, his dashing looks and aloof manner. Over time, I realised his silence did not hide a burning passion but a weary disdain. The country estate was a lifetime away from London, and good looks eventually count for little.'

She paused, and for a moment, Mal glimpsed a young girl, bored, lonely, and out of her depth. *Who knows what a person becomes when they grow up in the shade?*

'Personally, I suspect he's gay. You know the sort— only touches his wife in order to get an heir and spare.' She paused. 'Oh, listen to me go on. I think the bones this morning have shocked me into excessive candour. I feel I can trust you. You're so quiet. I have a girlfriend like you—very clever, always watching. I must introduce you.'

Mal listened to this torrent of confessions and sipped her tea again, unsure what to make of such personal statements. She was about to speak when the door was flung open and banged against a small footstool.

'Mother!'

Where Mal was sitting, she was partially obscured by a large fern, and the male voice continued.

'What the bloody hell is father on about, changing his will? Do you know—' He was cut off as Imogen jumped to her feet.

'Henry, darling, have you met Malachite Peck? She's recently moved into the area. Used to work in the City. And imagine this: she knows Darcy.'

Henry Haverstock strode into the room, his glare rapidly smoothing into a polite smile as Mal rose and shook his hand. 'Which firm did you work for?'

When Mal announced the name, he nodded. As he'd heard of them, they were clearly of interest.

'Do you know Oliver Carter?' he asked.

'Over at Blue Light Holdings?'

'That's the chap. Mind like a ferret.'

'Indeed,' Mal said generously. *If that ferret had been run over and then mounted.*

Oliver Carter was a bore of the first order and not too bright, but he seemed honest enough, which in the City was quite the accolade and more than she could say for herself.

'Well, I had better leave you to it.' She turned to Imogen. 'It was lovely to meet you, and I'm sure your situation will quickly be resolved.'

'Well, if it isn't, I'll be calling for your help.' Imogen laughed. 'Henry, could you find someone to run Mal back home?'

Mal waved away the suggestion and said she would be happy to walk home. The route was downhill, and she could do with the fresh air. Sitting by the fire in a pair of wellies was giving her hot flushes, and she'd had enough of those the first time around.

After only two wrong turns, she found her way to the row of sinks and the outdoors. For such a large house, it was uncomfortably empty. Ghosts of previous servants seemed to rush past on their way to various errands, all trying to get on with their work. Now, she could walk around unchallenged by a single living soul. Mal shuddered and stepped out into the sunshine.

Almost immediately, Max and Milo bounded up, scaring the life out of her. After discovering she had no treats, they settled for a tummy rub each, then ambled off.

Saying goodbye to the dogs, she walked down the drive and wondered how soon Imogen had told her son exactly who she was. *Or would she? And would he care?* He seemed to have greater issues on his mind. Thankfully, all Mal had to worry about was whether there was enough hot water in the cistern for a bath and if she should have her soup before or after her soak. However, she couldn't help but wonder what connected the discovery of a pile of bones and the changing of a will.

Chapter Eight

With a deep sigh, Mal sank into her sofa. The bath had eased her back and, having reheated Holly's soup, she felt an afternoon nap creeping up on her. Today had been exhausting, but first things first: she had some letters to catch up on, and if she fell asleep then, she would very likely sleep on till morning.

She eyed her writing paper and fountain pen over on the table. Try as she might, she couldn't make the items levitate towards herself, and with another grumble, she heaved herself out of her sea of cushions and settled onto the firmer dining chair.

Dear Barney,

Well, you will never guess what I have on my roof terrace. I have a trampoline. It's ten feet wide, and I believe that if you could get a big enough jump, you could dive off it into the harbour! Imagine what the fishermen would say. It's bad enough being dive-bombed by seagulls. Now, it's the turn of the woodpeckers.

Happily, the fishermen can relax as the trampoline is broken. We had a terrible storm here, and the wind picked this trampoline up from someone's garden and then dumped it on my terrace.

Now, I have to thank you for my lovely thermometer. It was brilliant of you to think I would need to know how cold it was outside. At the moment, it's twelve degrees Celsius. It doesn't get very cold in Cornwall. I took it to the sea when I got home, and the

53

water was seven degrees. Your aunt Charlotte gave me an incredible wetsuit for Christmas, and it kept me wonderfully warm. (ish)

Finally, here's a puzzle for you.

Is it more correct to say, 'The yolk of an egg are white,' or 'The yolk of an egg is white'?

Lots of Love,

Yaffle

Mal smiled as she signed her family nickname. It was a childhood name that had stayed with her all her life but was only used by the younger family members like her godson. Now she needed to thank his aunt. Charlotte was her sister Opal's daughter and the eldest of her nieces and nephews.

Dear Charlotte,

The first thing I did when I came back to Golden was to get into the sea in your lovely present. I felt insane going into the sea on the 28th. Talk about freezing. But please tell your friend Ted that I am very impressed with his company's wetsuit. It went on like a glove. The plastic-bags suggestion was a great tip, and I actually managed a small swim. I can't tell you how good it felt to be back in the water again, but dear God almighty, it was cold, so I only managed a short session by the steps in case I should have a heart attack. Yesterday, there was a big storm, so I couldn't go into the sea, which was probably just as well as the suit is still wet. I've currently set it up over the bath to dry out. I must say bathing under

54

a neoprene canopy is not something I ever envisaged. Maybe it will become all the rage?

I have posted a photograph of myself in the suit and popped it up on Instagram. Try not to laugh. I took the photo afterwards as I thought the cold water would make my skin look less wrinkled. I think I need an iron for that, though, and some bulldog clips in my hairline!

You mentioned calling in sometime, and I wanted to reiterate that you are all most welcome anytime. I would love it. Just give me some notice, and I'll get everything in place. I have two spare bedrooms here, but no outside space. The dogs would be very welcome, too, but you might find it a bit confining.

Anyway, let me know. I should love to see you.
Much love,
Mal

Putting down her pen, Mal yawned and looked at the clock. Too late for an afternoon nap, too early for bed, yet as she yawned again, that was where she was heading. Grabbing a book, she climbed upstairs. Today had been eventful and she couldn't help but think about her meeting with Imogen and her son's annoyance with his father. Why did Lionel Haverstock want to change his will? Clearly, Henry was furious about the prospect. Did this mean he was losing out? And if so, who was winning?

Chapter Nine

Imogen was sitting at the breakfast table as her grandchildren entered the room. The merry chatter of Percy and Persephone mobbing their half-brother, Jasper, as they were reunited brought life into the silent room.

Percy and Persephone spent most of their time in London with their mother, whilst Jasper and Henry ran the estate. Presently, they were all together for Lionel's birthday celebrations. Algernon, her younger son, had also arrived with his family the previous day, and the house was full. The party that night would be spectacular, and the whole village would be involved. The morning was just for the family, though.

'Hey Jasper,' said Persephone, 'I got a B in French. Told you I could do it.'

'You said you'd get an A.'

'Well, if I lived down here, I would have. But there's so much going on in London. It's so alive!'

'Yes,' drawled Jasper, ruffling his sister's hair, 'there's absolutely no life in the countryside. It's known for it.'

'That's not what I meant, smart-arse.'

Jasper was a funny sort of boy—*man*, Imogen corrected herself—but he never seemed to have the gumption that she felt an alpha male required. Still, he was her first grandchild, so that counted for something, even if his mother had filled his head with strange nonsense. Henry's second wife was much more her own sort of woman, and her two children, whilst tiresome, were just at that tricky age.

'Good morning, Granny. Did you sleep well?'

Jasper leant down and kissed her on the cheek before heading over to the sideboard to fill his plate.

'Persephone, behave yourself or I'll tell Fenella that you fancy that lead singer you're always watching.'

Imogen winced. Persephone adored her older cousin and was always trying to emulate her. At this age, the six-year age gap was painful. Persephone was all too aware that she came across as a child and could never be as cool as Fenella, but that wasn't going to stop her from trying.

Imogen smiled, thinking Persephone had nothing to worry about. Her granddaughter frowned to herself under Jasper's teasing. Fenella was unlikely to surface for breakfast. She and her brother had rolled in from a party at around three in the morning. The sound of a car had woken Imogen, and she'd realised a taxi must've dropped them off.

'Jasper, stop teasing your half-sister. Percy, Persephone, stop messing about, and eat your breakfast like well-behaved children, not farmyard animals.'

Silence settled for a second, but was then disrupted as Fred thundered into the breakfast room. His rugby shirt looked like he might have slept in it. Wet hair dripped onto his shoulders as he ran his fingers back through the curls. He could be quite good-looking, thought Imogen, if he made more of his looks. At twenty-two, he presented more like little Percy, a haphazard child, than his other cousin. Jasper was only two years older, but was decades ahead of him in terms of maturity. Fred was all impulse and chaos, while Jasper was quiet and methodical.

'Pig pen!'

Jasper looked across at his cousin and rolled his eyes. 'Morning, Freddie. Good party last night?'

Fred looked blank. 'Only me in the bed last night. Not much of a party, more's the pity.'

'Jesus. Mind your language,' snapped Jasper, trying to defend his siblings' modesty.

Jasper was a bit straight-laced for Imogen's taste, but he was right to admonish his cousin.

'I thought I heard you and Fenella coming in from a party last night, darling,' Imogen said, attempting to steer the conversation away from the gutter. This generation was so frank about their sex lives that she found it bewildering.

'After yesterday's drive?' said Fred. 'Do you know we were stuck on the A30 for a solid hour? Dad was determined to beat the record for the slowest journey ever, and Fenella, constantly live streaming to her followers, was doing my head in.'

Algernon entered the room, followed by his wife. He greeted Imogen, then poured Daisy a cup of coffee.

As though summoned by their voices, Henry joined the family. Imogen frowned at the mud on his shoes, but said nothing. He was always up and out first thing, seeing to the estate. She could hardly complain if occasionally he brought some of it back in. She would mention it to the cleaners later.

'Fen has over a million followers now, you know,' her father said, laughing. 'I should post some of the videos we have of her with braces on.'

'Uncle Algernon,' gasped Persephone, 'you can't do that! She curates her content very carefully.'

'I know, sweetie. I was just joking.' He ruffled his niece's hair, and she angrily tied it back behind her ears.

'So was it Fenella out partying last night?' Imogen asked again.

'Not that I'm aware of,' said Fred. 'She said she was doing several posts today about country living, so she wanted an early night. Besides, no one's around. Everyone's skiing except for us.'

'Complaining that your grandfather had the temerity to have his birthday in the middle of the ski season?' asked Henry, as he tucked into a full breakfast.

'That's not what he said, and you know it,' Algernon said, leaping to his son's defence.

Imogen clattered her teaspoon onto her saucer. 'Do you think we could at least have breakfast in peace without you two bickering? Today is about your father, and tomorrow, we will have a house full of guests. It would be good if, for the next forty-eight hours, you could stop jumping down each other's throats.'

As each of her sons mumbled an apology, she looked around the table. 'Is Jocasta not joining us?'

'She said she had a bad night,' Henry said. 'Will come down later.'

'Oh, poor thing,' said Daisy as she sipped her coffee. 'Has she tried meditation? Maybe it's her age?'

'You must mention it to her,' suggested Imogen, wondering if her daughters-in-law would ever stop putting each other down. Out in the corridor, she heard her granddaughter talking to someone in a one-sided conversation and wondered what fresh drama was unfolding.

'Family breakfasts are always so special. There's no better way to start the day.'

Fenella walked into the room, her phone aloft as she tapped the screen and recorded the room. Persephone sat up straight and laughed at something her brother hadn't said. He, in turn, pretended to pick his nose, much to the annoyance of his aunt, who immediately reprimanded him. Fred yawned and winked at the camera. He featured in many of his sister's campaigns and had quite the following himself.

'Be a dear, and switch that off,' said Imogen. 'No one needs to see how we spread our butter.'

Fenella tapped the screen and pulled a face for her followers, then shut the phone off.

'Granny, that was live!'

'Until you have everyone's permissions to be broadcast to millions of people, no recording without our agreement. You know how annoyed your grandfather gets.'

'Ugh, Granny—'

'I understand—you know I do—but your grandfather doesn't, and as this is his weekend, let's not film breakfast.' Imogen took a sip of tea and smiled at her glamorous granddaughter. 'But I loved your post about scarves last week. Maybe we could do something with my collection of Hermès scarves if you'd like.'

'Can I help?' asked Persephone, desperate to be involved.

'Oh, I love it,' said Fen. 'I could make it all about vintage fashion and generations.'

'So, where is Grandad? Out with the dogs?'

Imogen frowned. 'Not down yet. I'll tell him everyone is up.'

As she rose, Jasper jumped out of his seat. 'Stay there, Granny, I'll get him.'

As he left the room, Daisy smiled over at Henry. 'He's always so attentive.'

'Don't know what he's doing, hanging around the estate,' sniped Algernon. 'Lad his age should be out having fun, getting a proper career behind him. Look at Freddie. Already worked out in Africa, established some good contacts, and currently working in the city.'

'I'm going to Sandhurst, aren't I, Dad?' said Fred between mouthfuls of bacon.

Imogen sipped her tea as she listened to her family trying to outdo each other with their achievements. They were such a talented bunch, but they could be quite demanding and competitive. Jasper came back into the room and headed straight for his father. Something in his manner raised the hairs on the back of Imogen's neck. The two of them looked across at her, and her son stood up and followed Jasper back out.

And, just like that, she knew.

Lionel was never late for breakfast. The fact was that Lionel would never join them for breakfast ever again. No more complaints about noise. Excessive spending. The heating on. Radio 2. The shopping bills. The children. The grandchildren.

The criticisms and disappointments had come to an end. Imogen's husband was finally dead.

Chapter Ten

Mal peered into her fridge and swore. In all of yesterday's excitement, she'd forgotten to get more milk. If there was one drink she couldn't abide, it was black coffee. Placing a saucer of water on the floor for Mac, he padded over, took one sniff, and turned his back on the paltry offering. It would appear the cat was not a fan either.

'You sir, are a fuss-arse. You know cats aren't supposed to drink milk. That's what it says on Google. Don't you read the internet?'

Mac began to groom himself, and Mal realised she would never win an argument with a cat. Grabbing her coat, she headed downstairs and out through the shop. It would be impossible to spend a day working without a coffee, so she would grab some milk before she opened.

Only the newsagents were open that early, so Mal reluctantly grabbed the first pint of milk and left fifty pence on the counter, telling Phyllis to put the change in the charity pot.

'A whole tuppence. They'll name a lifeboat after you.'

Mal turned, ready to engage, then took a deep breath. She'd lost an argument with a cat already—no point running the risk of losing to a shrew as well.

Out on the street, she stepped aside as a delivery van trundled down the narrow street, and she smiled at her self-restraint.

'Alright, Mal?'

Mal turned to see Sophie coming out of the pub opposite. She was in full uniform, her stab vest making her appear the size of a small planet. How she walked in that lot was beyond Mal. Running in it must be a nightmare. She imagined the criminals took off like a rocket whilst the police lumbered behind, dragged down by all the trappings on their belt and vest.

Sophie popped her notebook back into her pocket and nodded at Mal. 'You're looking happy.'

'I am! The weather looks good. I have milk. Today is going to be a good one. What about you? Isn't it a little early for a tipple?'

Sophie grinned. 'That would be very old-school, wouldn't it? No, I'm checking up on all the local businesses. See how much damage they sustained.'

The two women walked towards the harbour.

'No need to call in on me. The shop is fine. The slates on my patio are from next door, and the trampoline is firmly wedged. Damage, but all under control.'

'Good to hear it.'

'Tell me.' Mal knew she was pushing, but she was curious. 'The child's bones up at Liggan. Is anything more known?'

Sophie stopped walking and gave Mal an old-fashioned look, then sighed.

'You are like a dog with a bone. But...' she paused as Mal tried not to hold her breath, '... it turns out the bones are ancient. Which is no doubt a relief for the family as

64

Lionel Haverstock died last night. Poor sod, just before his eighty-fifth birthday.'

Mal winced. 'That's a shame. I remember an old song called "My Grandfather's Clock." Do you know it?'

When Sophie shook her head, Mal briefly paused, reflecting on the fact that she was getting old herself. 'Well, it goes that when the old grandfather clock stopped ticking, then the old man died as well. It feels like the tree and the owner both bowed out at the same time.'

Sophie looked at Mal again. 'Malachite Peck, I never had you down as an old romantic. But yes, end of an era. The villagers had a lot of respect for Lionel.'

She paused, and sensing Sophie's discomfort, Mal moved the conversation back to the old bones.

As they reached the shop door, Sophie turned down Mal's offer of a drink and headed on her way.

Back upstairs, Mal poured some milk for Mac, who was currently out of sight, and switched the kettle on whilst she caught up on the rest of her letters, the one to her sister being the most pressing. Two full days had passed since she had left after Christmas, and she still hadn't written.

Dear Opal,

Thank you again for the most wonderful Christmas. Yes, it was a little overwhelming, but in a good way. I have so many precious memories that I have hoarded them all up, and I keep opening each memory like a reverse advent calendar, but one that will last me a whole year.

I see Pete's bagpipe playing hasn't improved much in the five years I've been away. You have to admire his tenacity, if not his actual skill. But his charades were on point as ever. I am still laughing over Great Expectations. And trust Will to get it. Always one for the chocolates.

Life in the village is a lot quieter now, especially after such a manic Christmas, but Golden still manages its own level of drama. We had a big storm passing through last night that did quite a bit of damage. A nightmare for the insurance bods, but us analysts have been saying for years that these once-in-a-lifetime storms are now annual events and premiums need to be brought in line with current projections. Anyway, off topic.

There's a big house here that overlooks the village, called Liggan. You may have visited? Its gardens are apparently special. Anyway, a whole slew of trees fell over, and in the roots of one were the bones of a child. Of course, everyone got very worked up, and I have to confess my heart sank. But Sophie Taphouse, the local police officer, has just said that the forensic team confirmed that it was an ancient burial.

It was a young child, buried with a bead necklace and the bones of a small dog. Both skeletons showed evidence of fire damage. Apparently, there's going to be a TV show about it. It's very rare to find anyone buried with an animal, and it looks, in this case, that the child was buried with either their pet or their guard dog. Funny, isn't it? A thousand years later, and we haven't changed a bit.

Typical, I've made myself maudlin. What a fool I am. I suspect this is as good a time as any to open the port you gave me, but it's morning, and I need to open the shop instead. I shall write more later.

Mal pushed away from the table and made herself a coffee instead. Sophie's words had moved her, and she needed to lighten her spirit before starting work. After making a coffee, she returned to the table and picked up her pen again, smiling. At her age, making new friends felt silly, but she'd certainly found herself enjoying the company of Jacques Peloffy, a French fisherman who lived in Golden but returned to France every winter. With his help, she'd discovered the tunnel leading from her shop, and he also loaned her his battered old Land Rover from time to time. When she first met him, she'd considered him arrogant and aloof, but she'd learnt that was simply his way with strangers.

Dear Jacques,

How funny it is to be writing a French address and yet not use one of those thin blue airmail letter-envelopes. Do you remember them? I'm sure every European pen friend has flashbacks to when we would try to curl our sentences around the edges of the paper. Or, if the language was not one of our favourites, using every other line and writing in big letters with ridiculous gaps between the words. I had a Maltese pen pal and was bewildered by the language. I know the English have a poor reputation for languages, but I swear even the Maltese struggle.

It's just as well that I have sheets and sheets of paper to write a long letter as I don't have the skill or time to write a short one. (I was going to claim that witty observation as my own, but I imagine you are well versed with the sayings of Mark Twain).

I have been down to the harbour and can confirm that your boat still rests above the water. For a more accurate assessment of her condition, I'm sure others can inform you. You may wonder at my wishing to reassure you about your boat, and indeed you may know by now, but we have endured a tremendous storm. A belter, in fact. Roofs were lost, trampolines were gained, and boats were sunk. But not yours.

I have been up to your house. Your table and chairs are still in place. I can now see the appeal for cast iron over wood, but some of the panes in your greenhouse are broken. I have left things as they are but can ask a glazier to call if you would like. I swept the debris off your patio, much less seaweed than on my street, but far more twigs and leaves. Each to their own, the peasant in her hovel, the king in his palace. The back road from your house heading towards Truro was also closed by a fallen tree. I was sorry to see its passing. It framed the skyline beautifully.

Speaking of trees, there was some excitement at Liggan Hall as one of the old oaks fell, and the bones of a small child were revealed within the roots. The police were called, and for a ghastly moment, I thought there was about to be another 'incident'. However, it turns out the bones are ancient. Sadly for the family, the owner also died last night, a Mr Lionel Haverstock. It occurs to me as I write this *that you may have known him, and if so, I am sorry for the sudden announcement.*

Mal put her pen down. Her letters were all turning gloomy. It was no good. She would open the shop and finish them after work. It was time to go and try to make some money.

Chapter Eleven

The family had all gathered in the sitting room. Henry had insisted on an immediate reading of the will, and despite the firm of solicitors being closed for the holiday season, he got his way. The rush was unseemly. Lionel's body had only just been removed by the undertakers and Imogen would've preferred some time to get used to the situation, but Henry was adamant. However, his obstinacy on the matter made it easier for her to get her way with her own demands.

'Mummy, why don't you stay with friends for the next few days? This party is ridiculous,' said Algernon, as he came and sat by her side. 'I don't know what Henry is thinking,' he continued, patting her hand.

'This isn't his decision,' she said firmly. 'It's mine. We are going to treat the fireworks as a celebration of your father's life. Besides which, the villagers were looking forward to it. A bit of goodwill in the community goes miles.'

'Fair pay goes further,' said Jasper from an armchair in the corner of the room.

As requested, the entire family was gathered for the reading of the will, even the twins. It was right that they should witness how family matters were handled.

'Really, Jasper,' said Imogen.

'What? If we really wanted to honour grandfather, we'd give all the staff the pay rise they deserve.'

'You know full well that after your father took charge, he had to reduce the wages. Your grandfather was too generous.'

'That's a laugh,' said Algernon. '*Generous* is not a word I'd use to describe Daddy.'

'Is this because he failed to write off your ski season when you were in your thirties, or buy you that house in Antigua, or when you had to pay for the twins' school trip to South Africa?'

Suddenly Jasper was the centre of a lot of shouting as his aunt and uncle yelled at him and his father and step-mother sprang to his defence. His siblings giggled to themselves, and his cousins stared in shock.

'Enough!' snapped Imogen, and was then interrupted by a knock at the door.

Dougie ushered Mr Blythe in. Gerald Blythe was the family solicitor and had worked at Blythe and Sons for decades. Nearing retirement, he walked into the room and shook hands with Imogen, Henry, and Algernon, then offered his condolences to the rest of the room.

'I wasn't expecting the whole family,' he said nervously.

'It's the Haverstock way. We all pull together,' said Imogen, as she waved him towards a chair at the front.

'Very well, but this won't actually take long. As you are aware, Lionel was a straightforward man, and his will is very simple. I—'

'When was this will made?' said Henry, cutting him off. Imogen narrowed her eyes. The boy could be a fool at times. No one else knew Lionel had mentioned changing his will, but Henry had just brought it into the open. He hadn't said as much, but Algernon was bound to pounce on the question. Even as a child, he'd counted every slight and discrepancy. Being the spare was a hard job, and whilst Imogen had always tried to console and indulge him, she may have encouraged his slightly grasping manner.

'This is the same will that Lionel drew up decades ago. As you know, every year, the estate would have an annual review of holding and investments, and the will was reviewed as well. He never once changed it.'

Silence fell around the room. Then Persephone whispered excitedly to her brother, who quickly slapped her down.

'How can he have left you a pony if his will hasn't changed in decades, stupid? You weren't alive,' mocked her brother.

Their mother leant across the sofa and tapped both of them on a knee, glaring at them, then mouthing an apology towards Imogen.

'Mr Blythe, maybe you could proceed?' said Imogen, keen to get on with the task in hand. In the past few hours she had had to manage the removal of her husband's body; discuss funeral arrangements; cancel their guests and caterers; and inform the firework company that the

72

display would go ahead. Henry had sent the grounds staff home, argued with the catering company about their bill, and called the insurance company and the solicitors. In Imogen's mind, it all felt a bit grubby, but Henry seemed to come alive. He was now truly in charge of Liggan, and he wasn't wasting a minute.

The solicitor cleared his throat and removed a document from his briefcase. 'As I said, the will is very simple. It reads as follows:

'"I, Lionel Anthony Haverstock of Liggan Hall, being of sound mind and body, do hereby leave all my worldly goods to my firstborn child or, should their death precede mine, the heirs of their line."'

Mr Blythe paused and looked around the room, then handed the will to Henry, who received the document.

After taking a deep breath, Henry cleared his throat. The moment had come; he was now the owner of the Liggan Estate, the lord of the manor. 'Thank you, Gerald. My family and I are grateful for your attendance today. I hope you have a safe—'

'Hang on a minute,' said Algernon, jumping to his feet and snatching the will out of Henry's hands. 'Is that it? What about Mummy? What about me? And what the hell did Daddy mean by *firstborn child*?'

'He meant me, obviously.'

'So why not name you?'

Henry stared at his brother in confusion. 'Why would he? You heard the will—lots of archaic phrases, no point in saying my name when we all know it's me. And as for Mother, you know I shall always look after her.' He looked at Imogen, who was still trying to recover from the shock of not being mentioned in the will at all. 'Mother, you shall carry on living your life as before. I will always take care of you.'

'And me?' Algernon snapped.

Henry looked at him quizzically. 'You're a grown man. Surely, you can take care of yourself?'

'You little shit. You know exactly what I mean. He was my father, too. Am I to be written out without so much as a farthing?' His face mottled in anger as he turned towards Blythe. 'Is this even legal? Apparently, Daddy said he was going to change his will. Is this the new one or the old one?'

Gerald Blythe hadn't bothered to stand up. He knew the reading of the will was going to be controversial. 'This will hasn't changed in over four decades. Your father called yesterday to make an appointment, but that was for next week. As I said, this will was reviewed annually, and each year, we advised your father that it might cause issues.'

'I'll bloody say it does.'

Imogen watched her younger son and wished she could heal his pain. This rejection was monstrous. On the sofa, Daisy was wiping tears from her face, and their children were sitting as still as statues. Finally, an event had occurred that Fenella didn't want to share on

Instagram. Imogen didn't think they understood the full implication. But as the holidays dwindled to a halt and they were forced to change schools, everything would soon become horribly clear. She would speak to Henry later and insist that he at least provide for his niece and nephew. Maybe she could do something?

'Darling,'—she stretched an arm out to him, entreating him to sit down again—'I can sell the house in London or sign it over to you. If Henry is going to look after me, I can help you out now. No need to wait for my will. Which I suppose I'd better write. Gosh. What a mess this is.'

Blythe cleared his throat. 'Mrs Haverstock, I hate to remind you at a time like this, but you don't own Liggan Hall in London. That belongs to the estate. We have always advised you to have an independent financial review.'

'Of course Little Liggan is mine. Lionel gave it to me as a wedding present.'

'According to our records, it is an estate asset. Do you have any savings plans or properties in your own name?'

Imogen blinked. 'I don't follow you. I have lots of investments. Every year after the financial review, I would ask Lionel how we were doing, and he said everything was in order. I don't understand.' Her voice broke.

Algernon sat back down, throwing an arm around her shoulder. 'Now see here, Gerald. You can't be suggesting that Mummy has no independent money or property?'

Gerald Blythe remained calm. 'I'm afraid, Algernon-'

'Mr Haverstock.'

'I'm afraid, Mr Haverstock, that that is exactly what I am saying. Your mother entered the marriage with no independent assets and, over the course of her lifetime, gained none either.'

'There you go, Algernon,' snapped Henry 'It's crystal clear. You get nothing, and I'll take care of Mother.'

'Boys!' Imogen rose slowly to her feet, her whole body shaking as the blood drained from her face. 'Mr Blythe, thank you for your time. I think, under the circumstances, I would like you to leave now whilst we try to come to terms with this.'

Having also risen to his feet, Henry stepped forward and shook Mr Blythe's hand. 'I'll arrange an appointment to come into the office after the memorial, and we'll go through the paperwork.'

Algernon had joined his wife, who was furiously whispering to him. He looked at her in surprise, then whipped around.

'Wait. I want to contest the will.'

'Oh, darling, please,' said Imogen, 'not now.'

'Yes, now, Mummy.' He looked back at his wife, who nodded vigorously. 'I demand a DNA test. *My firstborn child.* That's the key, isn't it? That's why he didn't say anything, because it's me. I'm Daddy's firstborn child. You, Henry, are not his biological son!'

Henry stared at his brother in disbelief as the others in the room recoiled. 'Why, you little sh—'

His words were cut off as Imogen fell to the floor in a dead faint.

Chapter Twelve

It was the third of January, and for two days straight Mal hadn't seen a single soul in the shop. The shelves were spotless, everything was in order, and the accounts were up to date. Hell, even the drawing pins had been sorted into colour order. Mal looked up at the little blue and white pottery figurine of a fisherman tucked above the window frame.

'Well, Mr Fishy. Is this normal? Are you letting the side down? Shouldn't you be conjuring up customers?'

She was so bored that she often found herself talking to the shop guardian. At least when she spoke to Mac, she occasionally got a meow in return. She had concerns, not least of which was talking to inanimate objects. The problem was, she needed to make money. There was enough to live off if she was careful, but Malachite Peck had always made money. The only time she hadn't was when she was in jail. Even as a child, she was buying and selling, walking neighbours' dogs, babysitting. As a teen, she opened a shares portfolio with her father's help, and during the holidays, she worked in a nearby pub. Making money was what she did. Sitting in a shop reading a book was not making money. And it was worse than that. She wasn't helping anyone in any way. She'd always been useful. Making money was useful. As was giving it away. But in prison, she had neither, so she'd helped the women that needed it, either with their financial situation or their sense of self-worth.

When she first arrived in Golden, she'd helped solve a murder, and honestly, that had been very exciting. But now everything was quiet again. The village didn't need her.

She was restless and uncertain why. Maybe she was lonely. That was an intolerable thought. The phone jolted Mal out of her reverie.

'Good morning. Yaffle Books.'

'Yes, hello. Malachite, is that you?'

Mal didn't recognise the voice on the other end of the call. From the woman's accent, Mal guessed she was someone from her old life, but she couldn't place her. 'Speaking.'

'Excellent. I wonder if you have a moment you could pop up. I need to get rid of some of Lionel's books, and I thought you might like them.'

London voice, but local. Imogen Haverstock. But Mal wasn't in the position to buy any books. She didn't have the funds, and she didn't know the first thing about antique books. The quickest way to lose money was to venture into something you hadn't properly researched.

'Hello, Mrs Haverstock, I'm afraid I'm not currently buying until I can sort out my storage situation.'

That was a nonsense, but you never ever let the other side know you were low on funds or expertise.

'No, you misunderstand me. I want to get rid of them. I don't want any money for them.'

Mal was in a pickle. She was in no position to be turning away free stock, and she might even get some books to sell if she spent some time in research.

'Would this afternoon work?' Imogen continued. 'The family are all out, and it would be nice to see a friendly face.'

Mal paused, wondering at the woman's inability to consider that Mal was at work and incapable of just dropping everything because Imogen was lonely. Then Mal scolded herself. The poor woman had just lost her husband, so of course she was lonely. And the truth was she could just close up shop. It was her business, after all, and the chances of seeing an actual customer were remote.

'That would be lovely.'

'Excellent. I'll send a car for you. Does two suit?'

Mal wondered if she'd ever sounded like that, organising things and moving people around. She hoped not, but suspected she had. That was how one got things done.

'Two will be fine. But I have a car. I'll see you later.'

After they hung up, Mal headed upstairs to change her clothes and fix her hair and make-up. Although the walk up to Jacques' would probably undo all her efforts, she wasn't going to be smirked at for wearing wellies again.

An hour later, she was plodding up the hill to Jacques' house. She was early, to give herself time to catch her breath, and keep an eye on the place. When he went to France, he'd left his keys and asked her to stop the junk mail piling up. It wasn't necessary, but Mal felt uncomfortable simply borrowing the ancient Land Rover, despite his insistence.

As she drove to Liggan Hall, she came in via the main entrance, then had to be redirected by one of the stewards to the entrance for the private house rather than the public gardens. To the side of the house was a small gravel driveway, and Mal drew alongside the collection of Range Rovers and sports cars. Swinging down from the Land Rover, she could see Liggan Hall in all its glory: a large country manor house, three stories tall, and a façade of large glass windows in the Georgian manner. In the centre of the house was an enormous portico large enough for a horse and carriage to drive through, supported by granite posts. It framed the front door, which swung open as Mal approached. Imogen was dressed in a pale grey dress, which suited her complexion far better than black would have done, although Mal noted the cuff, neck, and hemline of the dress had small black bandings. Rather like a Victorian letter of mourning, thought Mal.

Imogen's pearl necklace also sat nicely against the fabric. Mal wondered just how much the woman was actually mourning, and how much she was simply going through the motions. When they last met, Mal had received the impression that the marriage wasn't a happy one.

'Mal, how kind of you to come. Please come in and let me take you to the library. We'll have tea in there.'

Mal followed Imogen, appreciating the works of art hung along the corridor, large paintings meant to dominate and impress. However, they were badly hung. A corridor was a poor place for a painting as large as the seascape to her left.

The library was another matter. Like the corridor, this room had the imprint of one single creator behind it, but they were not the same person. For one thing, the room felt cohesive. Everything, even in its jumble, made sense. The leather armchair and moth-eaten blanket belonged together. An unfinished crossword lay exposed on the folded newspaper. The room smelled of cigar smoke, and Mal looked around for the half-empty cup of coffee and slice of marmalade toast. It felt as though the occupant had only just stepped out.

'Excuse the mess, I haven't been able to bring myself to send the cleaners in yet. This was very much Lionel's room, as you can see. He was a great reader.'

Lionel quite possibly had more books in his study than Mal had in her entire shop. On a leather-topped desk, she saw he'd been reading one history by Montefiore and another by Hastings. It was a comfortable place.

On a side table sat a collection of silver-framed portraits, and one or two more on the desk itself. In one of those, a little baby was tucked up with their teddy bear. In another, three gundogs were all proudly posing for the camera, the spaniel's tail was an unsteady blur. The third photo was of a bride and groom. Looking at the dust on the sideboard, Mal would've laid odds that the wedding photo had only recently been placed on the desk.

'God, it's so claustrophobic in here,' said Imogen, opening a window. 'Which is where you come in. I should very much like you to get rid of these books for me.'

Mal looked around at all the shelves and felt overwhelmed. The collection was far more than she'd envisioned, and she was also worried about Imogen's motives.

'They are very much a statement, aren't they? This whole room has the mark of one man having lived a life in here.'

'And nowhere else.' Imogen bit off the rest of her sentence as the young woman from her previous visit came in with the tea set, and Mal smiled at her.

'Thank you. I'm sorry I didn't catch your name last time. I'm Mal.'

'Chloe,' said Imogen, interrupting them, 'can you make sure everything is ready for the children's tea?'

Chloe flashed Mal a quick smile and nodded at Imogen. 'I'm making them millionaire's shortbread and macaroni cheese.'

'Excellent. Thank you.'

As Chloe pulled the door closed behind herself, Imogen nodded in her direction. 'She's a good cook but smiles too easily at the men, if you catch my drift. But then I suspect you already spotted that. You are very perceptive, aren't you?'

Mal wanted to defend the young woman, but Imogen ploughed on. 'You saw to the heart of my dilemma with Lionel right away. Whilst this room remains like this, he lives on.'

Mal nibbled on the homemade Florentine and determined that if she was going to keep visiting Liggan Hall, she'd better start walking up to offset the calories.

'I've shocked you, haven't I?' Imogen smiled and held Mal's gaze.

'No. Well, yes, maybe a little. I have to confess I don't understand why you would stay with a man you weren't in love with.'

'Have you ever been married?'

Mal inhaled sharply. She could hardly deny it, yet it brought back such bitter memories that she did her very best not to think about it. 'Yes.'

'Happily?'

'No.'

Imogen nodded her head. 'And how did the marriage end? Or is there a Mr Peck living down in the village?'

Mal grinned at *Mr Peck*. People calling him that used to drive Hugo insane.

'No, there is no Mr Peck. Peck's my maiden name, which I never changed when I got married. And the marriage ended when my husband issued me an ultimatum: plead innocent, or he would divorce me.'

'Curious. Did he think you were innocent?'

'Oh no, not a bit of it. But he had his reputation to maintain. It was bad enough that I was flushing mine down the pan, but he'd be damned if he was going to let me drag him down as well.'

'And you weren't tempted?'

'What? No, of course not. I had to do the right thing. But, as an unexpected bonus, I also got rid of my husband!'

Imogen laughed and shook her head. 'You are a very strange woman.' She took a drink, then continued. 'But if you didn't love him, why didn't you leave him before your...' she paused, trying to think of a polite euphemism for a criminal act and jail time, '... episode.'

Now it was Mal's turn to shake her head. All in all, she wasn't warming to the woman, but she had Mal bang to rights. She might think Imogen was a hypocrite, but she was hardly standing on the moral high ground.

'I think the answer is probably complacency,' said Mal. 'We had our own lives, our own careers. He was an art director. We kept different hours and socialised with different groups. We had no children and often spent as much time apart as we did together.'

'Did either of you have affairs? It sounds lonely.'

That was a strangely personal question, and Mal wondered what it said about the state of Imogen's marriage. 'No affairs on my side. I was too busy. Besides, we had a healthy sex life, but that was probably all we had in common. If he had affairs, I never heard of them, which I think is the most you can hope for if you aren't actually in love.'

'I wanted to be in love,' said Imogen softly. 'Lionel was so dashing and so mature. I worshipped the ground he walked on, but over the years, I saw that it wasn't reciprocated. So long as I did my duty and produced heirs, that was all he was after. You were lucky to have a sex life. Lionel wasn't even interested in that. He had some massive feud with his parents in his twenties and went overseas for decades, and only returned when his father died. He had the estate, so then he wanted the family that went with it. Even the children were a disappointment to him. I tell you, the only thing that man ever loved was his bloody garden.'

She took a deep breath and steadied herself, dabbing a handkerchief at her non-existent tears. As a performance, it was a good one, but Mal was unmoved.

'Maybe I should come another day?'

'Oh, please stay. I'll try not to get emotional again. It's just these past few days have been so draining.'

As Imogen paused in reflection, Mal suddenly saw genuine emotion. The woman was tired, and despite the make-up, her complexion was dull.

'Would you like to talk about it?' *Please say no*, thought Mal.

'No, I couldn't.'

Mal relaxed.

'It's just been so terrible. We had to turn Lionel's birthday party into a wake. The boys were fighting over whether the fireworks display should go ahead. Then the will... Oh look, that doesn't matter.'

So much for not talking about it. The mention of the will was interesting, though, especially since Imogen's oldest son had referred to it. Clearly, eruptions had occurred during the will reading. Mal was tempted to employ Imogen's bluntness and just ask, but the issue was probably a bit more raw than her own divorce.

'Well,' said Mal, deciding to steer the conversation onto easier ground, 'these books. I will happily take some of them off your hands, but I suspect some of them are valuable. In all conscience, I should advise you to get a specialist auction house in here to run through them first.'

Imogen stood and walked to the closest bookshelf and hefted out a large leather-bound book with dates spanning five years on the spine. She placed it on the desk and opened it, waving at Mal to join her.

'Can you at least take these?'

Mal walked over and looked at the handwritten pages.

'What are they?'

'Lionel's diaries. He caught me reading one once and shouted at me until I started to cry. He called me every name under the sun and then refused to speak to me for a month. The boys were away at school at the time, and the house had never been quieter. After that, I began to hate him, and he kept this room locked.'

'That must have been horrible.'

'It was. And it wasn't as if the diaries had anything exciting in them. It was just weather reports and stuff about the garden. The odd bit about his lunch club and his golf score. Hardly worth screaming at me.'

'It must have been very hard to stay with him after that?'

'Yes, and no. What choice did I have? Raised up to marry well, and nothing else. The boys deserved a stable family. If I had asked for a divorce, he might have said yes, but I'd lose everything, and the chances were that he would have said no, anyway. So I learnt to carve out my own life: social events, charities, the children, the house. These all became the focus of my attention.'

Mal could see determination in the woman's expression. The house and the lifestyle were hers, and she'd never had the intention of getting divorced, no matter how unpleasant the marriage. Well, she was a widow now, and would, no doubt, make a merry one. Mal doubted she would be single for long. She made a decision.

'Right, then. Let me take these off your hands. I don't know if I can make use of them, but at least you won't have them haunting you.'

'Haunting me! That's the very expression. I knew I could count on you to understand. And if you can help me, find an auctioneer to get rid of the rest of his books. A proper exorcism is what's needed, and then we can cheer the place up again.'

As the two of them started carrying the books out to the Land Rover, Mal wondered if the poor man would even be buried before his wife cleared the house of all traces of him. Finally, the back shelf was full of diaries dating back to the 1960s and a range of other books that didn't strike her as particularly valuable. Mal looked concerned as the axle groaned. Unloading at the other end would take forever, but beggars couldn't be choosers.

'If I find any other writings of his, can I send them to you as well? Out with the old…'

Nodding in agreement, Mal climbed up into the car, eager to get away before Imogen found anything else. She wasn't judging the woman, but everything felt a bit sordid, and she wanted to go home and have a bath.

Chapter Thirteen

Imogen watched her poached eggs slowly congeal. She had to eat. Once the funeral was behind her, she could start to work things out properly. Today, however, was simply a memorial to celebrate Lionel's life. The coroner hadn't released the body yet, but she wanted to move things on as quickly as possible. The day before, she'd begun to get rid of his books. Today would give everyone the chance to pay their respects. Then, whenever the coroners pulled their fingers out and returned Lionel's body to her, she would arrange a small family funeral.

Since the reading of the will, she'd felt sick to her stomach. Every place she looked reminded her of Lionel, and she wanted shot of him. Everything had been a lie. She knew their marriage was a bad one, but until the will was read out, she hadn't understood how much he'd despised her. Thankfully, Algernon hadn't brought up the matter of the will again, or who the rightful heir was. Imogen prayed he had decided to accept the matter.

Henry had said he would take care of her. She didn't need to let her friends know about her shame. More importantly, if she was to get married again, she could not look desperate. She knew a few single men, and she knew others were out there with suitable fortunes. She still had her looks, a good figure, and impeccable social skills. One of her sons was the owner of the Liggan Estate. Her other son had married into a well-connected family. She felt she had a good package to offer. Now she needed to get rid of Lionel and move on.

'Good morning, Mummy.'

Lost in thought, she hadn't heard Algernon enter the room, as he joined her, having piled his plate up with a full English. For a man who'd just been disinherited, he seemed full of nervous energy. Maybe he, too, was waiting for the day to end, to move on with his life.

'Good morning, darling. Did you all sleep well?'

'Dreadfully, I'm afraid. Daisy doesn't know if she can face everyone. She feels the energy of this room is too challenging. Fen is staying with her, but Fred might make it down.'

Imogen frowned. 'Are they still terribly upset?'

'Dreadfully. You know, it's just as well that Daisy took them to the therapist. She believes they were on the edge of a total breakdown. And for what it's worth, Mummy, I think you should see someone as well.'

Imogen laughed. Even to her ears, it sounded brittle, and she made a note not to laugh in public for a while.

'Going to a counsellor? Imagine what your father would say to that.'

'Who the bloody hell cares what he says?'

'Oh, Algernon.'

'Seriously, Mummy, don't defend him. Not after what he did to me. To you. To all of us.'

'Henry will—'

'Henry will what?' Henry asked, walking into the breakfast room. His hair was ruffled and his face slightly wet from the rain. 'I've walked the dogs and spoken to Barry. I don't need to do anything else on the estate today. Today is about honouring my dear father.'

Algernon snorted. 'You've changed your tune since he left you everything. What happened to "He's an old fool. A dinosaur. An emotional vacuum"?'

'Algernon. Henry. I know this has been a very difficult week. But this afternoon, we remember your father, and for the next few hours, I insist that you and your families keep a civil tongue in your heads. Everyone will be watching us, and I want no glimpse of our issues to be apparent. We are one united family, sharing our grief at the passing of a great man. Tomorrow, we can start planning, and as I was saying when you walked in, Henry, you will ensure that things are arranged fairly.'

That was a statement rather than a question, and Henry tilted his head and poured himself a coffee. As he took a sip, he winced, then rang a bell. After a few minutes of silence, he got up and opened the door, and roared down the corridor for attention. A few seconds later, Dougie popped his head in.

'Yes, boss?'

'Do you think you could find someone in the kitchen and see if it's possible for them to provide hot coffee on the day of my father's memorial? If it's not too much effort?'

Moments later, Chloe came in with a fresh cafetière and apologies as Imogen's two daughters-in-law drifted in and ordered more coffee. Neither woman seemed pleased to be in the other's company, and they quickly separated to sit with their husbands.

Daisy opted for a full English. Jocasta looked across at her plate, having copied her mother-in-law.

'I love your attitude, Daisy,' Jocasta simpered. 'I have to be so careful what I eat. I put on weight so easily.'

Imogen tapped the table lightly with her finger. 'Not today, please. I was just telling the boys that this is a day for family unity.' She glanced across at Algernon. 'And really, darling, must you have your phone out at the table?'

Chastised, he placed the phone in front of him, then continued to eat his breakfast as a sullen silence fell across the table.

'Jocasta, where are the children?' asked Imogen.

'Still asleep,' she answered, as she cut her egg. 'They're terribly upset, so I thought it best to let them rest for as long as possible.'

'And Jasper?'

Jocasta shrugged. She'd been his stepmother for over ten years, but unless he did something impressive with his life, she wasn't taking any credit for him. 'Jasper's nipped down to the village to collect a few items. The whole village is closing today as a mark of respect.'

'The whole village is closing today as a mark of no customers,' Daisy sniped.

'Actually, I wasn't talking about the tourist shops,' replied Jocasta calmly. 'I meant the newsagent, greengrocers, those sorts. Jasper also called me to say that the fishermen will cast a wreath onto the sea at the time of the memorial.'

'That's so thoughtful,' said Imogen. 'I'm glad that the village knows how to pay their respects properly.'

'I don't imagine the pubs are closing though, are they?' Daisy continued, smirking.

'Of course not. This is Golden, after all. Jasper suggested we put some money behind each bar so that people can raise a glass to the old man. I thought that was a cracking idea.'

'Great,' said Algernon, looking across at his wife. 'So even the villagers get a free drink.'

'Knock it off,' said Henry. 'I think it's an excellent idea. Makes us look good in the eyes of the locals. It's a tricky relationship between the village and the estate. This is a smart gesture.'

'Stunt is what it is.'

'Oh really, Daisy,' sighed Imogen. 'Do you honestly think Jasper is capable of stunts?'

Most of the room smirked, and even Henry had trouble ignoring the jibe. Jasper didn't seem to have a business bone in his body. His life was a daydream. He'd flinched when his father suggested joining the army, and he showed no aptitude for business. Bone idle and useless to boot, he just liked fishing and drawing.

Algernon's phone beeped, and he snatched it, tapping the screen.

'Really,' said Imogen. 'Nothing is that important today…'

Algernon held a hand up and continued to read the screen as Imogen's voice trailed off. Today, of all days, she would forgive the rudeness. One day, he would inherit his wife's estate, what there was of it, and Imogen would need his contacts and introductions. In fact, maybe she should invite herself to stay for a while and get better acquainted with Daisy's parents. They might know some available men. A title would suit her.

'I am the rightful heir!'

Henry's fork clattered onto the plate.

'What the hell!'

Algernon's face was flushed red, and his eyes glittered with excitement. 'I knew it. I bloody knew it!'

'What are you talking about?'

'Sorry, Mummy, but I had to do this. I thought the will sounded iffy, and then Daisy had an idea.'

All eyes turned to Daisy, who was breathing quickly and looking at her husband with excitement. He passed the phone to her, and a huge grin lit up her face before she tried to smooth it into a respectful and concerned frown. Algernon continued to grin.

'*My firstborn heir.* It made no sense, and then I realised dear old Daddy was trying to spare Mummy's feelings.'

Imogen placed her hands on the white damask tablecloth. If she could just keep focusing on her rings, no one would see her shaking. That Algernon had done this was unforgiveable, and now her world was about to fall apart.

Henry, however, ploughed on. 'Are you drunk, brother?'

'No, but you might need a drink in a minute, *brother*. Or should I say *half-brother*?' He looked around the room triumphantly.

'I don't understand,' said Jocasta. She'd stopped pretending to eat, her head jerking left and right to see if anyone else knew what was going on.

'You know Marcus, has those labs up country. Well, I called in a favour and asked him to rush a DNA test for me. Cost a pretty penny, but oh boy, was it worth it!' He laughed, grinning at Daisy, and continued, 'I had the test and ran it against you, dear brother. We do not have the same father, and that means that I inherit everything!'

Everyone stared at Algernon in astonishment, but Henry was the first to recover.

'And how do you know that it's not you that has a different father?' he asked.

'Because the wording of the will backs me up. Doesn't it, Mother? Tell me I'm right. You know the truth of it.'

Imogen stared at her youngest son in bafflement, wondering how he could've done this to her, exposing her deepest secret without a pause for her feelings. She stood up carefully and looked at him directly. 'I will not entertain this nonsense.'

'Mother,' said Henry. 'Please, can you tell him that I am Father's son and that, for whatever reason, he is not?' He took a deep breath, then sighed heavily. 'We won't judge you. God knows life with Father must have been tough.'

Imogen looked at Henry, her hands gripping the edge of the table for support.

'You are both your father's sons. To suggest otherwise is outrageous.'

Henry had been reading the e-mail on Algernon's phone and paused, glaring at his brother. 'In which case, there's nothing for it. We will both have to have a DNA test against father. The truth will out, and when it does, brother dear, you can consider yourself no longer welcome at Liggan Hall. I'll see you dead before you inherit a penny.'

Chapter Fourteen

The previous day, Mal had attended the most dreadful memorial ever. Lionel's family were remote and spoke to no one. Imogen wore a black veil and left the minute the eulogies were finished. Henry's address was particularly wooden. The reception afterwards was a ragged affair. No music played, and no family members were present. Whenever anyone enquired, the waiting staff said they were overcome, and then invited the person to try the bellinis. The mourners left before the coffee had gone cold. Mal had been to wakes and memorials where the guests chatted and laughed and shared recollections until the small hours. Yesterday, the guests hung around in small, subdued groups, and within half an hour, the house was empty. Mal herself had left after ten minutes. Enough to show her face and then leave.

The following morning, she headed downstairs to the shop floor. Even if no one showed up, she had plenty of work to do processing Lionel Haverstock's books. In total, there were about sixty books; mostly histories, botanical journals, and thrillers by Leslie Charteris and Jack Higgins. She wasn't sure if anyone even read those anymore, but maybe she could try a shelf of second-hand titles and see if there was any interest. As for the diaries, she didn't have a clue. Maybe a local horticultural society would find them of interest.

After her post arrived, she settled down and opened a letter from Charlotte, its thick creamy paper a joy to unfold.

Dear Auntie Mal,

I have some interesting news that might appeal. Please don't kill me.

I was at a dinner party last night with Emily, and I showed Ted your picture of you in his wetsuit. I know your account is private, but I do hope you don't mind. I only showed him that one photo. He loved it! And this morning, he got in touch and asked if I would approach you about becoming a model for their brand!!!

They are all about sustainability and inclusivity. They feel you are a perfect role model for their brand. You'd receive all the gear free of charge! I know!!

I don't know if you would be up for it, but I bet it would be a laugh. Plus, lots of free gear sounds good. Who knows? This could be the start of a new career.

Love, Charlotte

Mal put the letter down and stared up at Mr Fishy. 'Was this you?'

She laughed to herself. Next, she'd be worshipping false idols. Still, becoming more visible was something she wasn't sure of. This would affect more than just herself. Five years inside for stealing over two million pounds had repercussions. The only thing she and her family cared about was that it saved the life of her goddaughter, Miranda. But done was done.

The doorbell rang, and a young man walked in. She recognised him as a regular customer. She had an excellent memory for faces, especially ones that spent so generously. He'd said everyone deserved a book at Christmas. The world was in good hands if his generation thought like that.

Presently, he looked uncomfortable. He scratched his hip, took his woollen hat off and fiddled with it.

'Hello again.' smiled Mal, getting to her feet. 'Did everyone like their presents?'

Oh God, please don't let him be asking about refunds. January would head straight into the red if he did.

'They loved them, although I think my brother would have preferred a rugby ball or maybe just some booze. But my cousin said the writing set was very retro and has made a post about it. She was thrilled.'

'A post about post. How very meta.'

The man laughed. 'Indeed. By the way, I'm Jasper Haverstock. You called on Granny the day before yesterday?'

Oh dear, Mal thought, jumping to a few very quick deductions, although she was surprised this was Jasper. Imogen had dismissed him as something of a disappointment.

'Has your grandmother changed her mind? I totally understand.'

'No. Yes.' He screwed his hat up in his hands. 'You see, the thing of it is... it's a bit awkward. The books aren't hers to dispose of, and I think my father will hit the roof when he discovers what she's done. I only noticed myself because I like to spend time in the library and noticed the gaps.'

'Holy crap.'

Mal wanted to swear more, but she was concerned she might offend the lad. He didn't seem the swearing sort, plus his grandfather had just died, and he was on a covert retrieval exercise. She saw no point in spooking the horses, but she was furious. She could not allow even the slightest hint of stolen goods attached to her name.

'It's alright.'

'No, it's not alright,' said Mal emphatically. 'I had no idea. I don't understand, though. Surely, your grandmother has some say?'

He looked even more uncomfortable.

'Bit of a snafu, actually. Turns out grandfather left everything to Dad, every last blade of grass and teaspoon. Granny's name isn't even on the deeds. It's all been something of a nightmare.'

'Dear God!'

'Well, exactly. You can understand how hurt she is, can't you? And I think she was just lashing out, trying to get rid of his stuff. But she can't, and I know my father can really bear a grudge about things like this. He and Uncle Algernon are already at each other's throats. So when I saw what she had done, I thought I would quietly try to come and undo it. You were my first port of call.'

'That's very thoughtful of you.'

'Purely motivated by self-interest. I'll do anything for a quiet life.' He smiled. 'Holly says…' He stopped abruptly, the smile vanishing. 'Anyway, the thing is… Do you think I could have the books back?'

Mal nodded furiously. 'Of course. I have one or two upstairs. I was reading a history of the village. I'm a bit of a new girl, but let me go and get it.'

'Gosh no, keep it for now. No one is going to notice the odd book. I'll pick it up next time I'm in. How does that sound?'

'I'm not sure.'

'Please. I feel so dreadful turning up and asking for it all back.'

'You feel dreadful asking for your own family's books back?'

He smiled at her. 'Well, shall we both be British and both feel dreadful about it together?'

She returned his smile. 'Very well. If you bring your car around, I'll help you load them back in.'

As he left, Mal shuddered. That was the last time she was going to take in free stuff.

An hour later, Mal considered closing for the day. Other than Jasper, she'd only seen the postie and was dying to head upstairs to catch up on her correspondence and read a few more chapters of her new crime book. It was brilliant, but she was quickly coming to the conclusion that Ruth deserved better than Nelson.

The bell rang again, and she looked up from her book to see Will, Bob, and another man behind them.

'Alright, Malachite. I was wondering if now would be a good time to remove the trampoline?'

Mal looked around the empty shop and grinned. 'I'm not sure I can close right now. Not with all the trade I'd be turning away.'

'Aye. Quite the crowd you've got in here, right enough.'

Laughing, she came out from behind the counter and, locking the front door, invited the three men upstairs. Over a week had passed since the storm, but with all the bad weather, she wouldn't have been using her patio anyway. She didn't recognise the third man, but like Bill and Bob, he removed his shoes before climbing the stairs up to her apartment, so they all gained some brownie points.

After showing them up to the top level, Bill looked at Mac sleeping on her bed and nudged Bob. 'See? Told you the wily bugger would have found someone to feed him.'

'Is he yours?' Mal asked, concerned that she might have run foul again of harbouring purloined items.

'No, maid,' Bob said. 'He's no one's, but he seems quite happy here. Mayhap he's decided to settle. James here was just concerned that we hadn't seen him around the net lofts recently.'

Whilst they were chatting, James had walked out onto the patio and placed his bag of tools on the ground, then pulled out a bolt cutter and a saw.

'It's beyond saving, isn't it?' said Mal, as they joined him on the roof and inspected the wreckage.

'Reckon,' agreed the man. And so began the slow process of breaking down a ten-foot trampoline into manageable pieces and ferrying it down two flights of stairs and out onto the street.

Mac had scarpered after the first piece of metal swung past his head, and now the night was falling along with the rain.

'Well, we got that done in the nick of time,' Bob said, hunched against the downpour. He turned to Mal. 'Next time I'm passing, I'll drop you off some fish, for you and Mac.'

A flatbed truck rattled along the cobbles, and the men loaded the forlorn plaything onto the back and drove off.

Mal pulled the door to the shop closed, locked it, and turned everything off. So far, she'd lost a donation of books, regained a roof terrace, scared off Mac, and gained the promise of free fish. On balance, the day had fallen in her favour. She was just about to head upstairs, then remembered she was out of milk. Dismantling trampolines was thirsty business, apparently.

Scowling, she realised there was nothing for it. She would not forgo her morning coffee just because she was out of milk. It was too late to head up to the farm shop, and the delicatessen was closed for January, which left only the newsagents.

Trying to shrink under the rain, Mal walked quickly over the cobbles, wishing she were in flats rather than her pretty heels. The smart Cuban shoes were sliding on the wet cobbles, and for the thousandth time, she blessed the overlooked wonder of tarmac.

The newsagents was empty of customers except for an old woman in a long plastic raincoat, talking to Phyllis.

The woman looked around at her, then sniffed loudly and returned to her conversation. 'There's too many in this village already. We've more incomers than we have rats, and they're just about as welcome.'

Phyllis sniggered, then replied in a quieter voice. Mal ignored the two women, her cheeks burning, and headed over to the refrigerated units, where she grabbed some milk and checked the date. Phyllis loved to push her luck, selling stock that should have been flushed away. That was another lesson that Mal had learnt, and she chose a pint from the very back of the shelf.

'I'd prefer you didn't mess up my shelves,' Phyllis called out. 'Take it from the front.'

Ignoring her, Mal walked up to the counter, placed the carton there, and pulled some coins from her pocket.

'I said you need to take from the front.'

'The use-by date on that carton is today.'

'So use it today.'

'I don't need it today,' Mal snapped in exasperation. 'I need it tomorrow.'

'So come back tomorrow and buy an in-date carton then.'

Mal paused and stared at her in disbelief.

'I reckon you're the sort that has lie-ins.' Now the older woman had seen fit to join the conversation. She sniffed loudly.

Mal looked at her, then recognised her as Mrs Kitto, the miserable old biddy that had been insulting Holly and her soups the other morning. Well, every village had them, Mal supposed, but Golden seemed to have more than its fair share.

Deciding to ignore her, she addressed Phyllis. 'So, let me get this right. You think it would make more sense for me to come back here tomorrow morning to buy the pint of milk, the very pint of milk, that I currently have in my hand?'

Phyllis stared at her. Her face was hard now, with no trace of a smirk. 'That is exactly what I'm saying. You need to buy the milk from the front.'

Mal thought about that, then took a step back, leaving the milk on the counter. 'This is the most ridiculous thing I have ever heard.' Phyllis continued to stare at her as the woman beside her smiled unpleasantly. 'Forget it.'

'I'll see you tomorrow then,' said the shopkeeper. Smug in her victory.

'Are you going to put that milk back?' interrupted Mrs Kitto. 'Or are you too lah-di-dah? Expect others to do it for you?'

Mal took a deep breath. *This is surely the very epitome of justifying circumstances.* 'I shall leave the milk exactly where I placed it. As Phyllis doesn't wish to sell that to me, I will leave it in her capable hands to reshelve it. I may inadvertently put it in the wrong place.' She turned towards Phyllis. 'And no, you shall not see me tomorrow. I shall ensure that I don't bother you in future.'

'Oh, your money too good for us now, is it?' jeered Mrs Kitto.

'Give me strength,' muttered Mal.

'Sorry. What did you say?' Phyllis asked.

'I said, "Give me strength."'

Phyllis recoiled in outrage. 'Right, that's it. You are banned.'

'I'm what?'

'Go on, sling your hook.'

Mal stared at the shopkeeper in utter astonishment, then with a sharp laugh, she walked out of the shop and found herself standing on the street. Her cheeks were burning, and she laughed at her own embarrassment. She'd faced down entire boards, challenged CEOs, and dominated trading floors. Yet she felt like a piece of dirt just dismissed by two women standing in a newsagent's, united in their disdain.

Chuckling, she headed along the darkening streets, warm glows of light spilling out from the pubs. Tipping her face upwards, the rain cooled her flushed skin.

This round went to Phyllis, but there would be other battles. And those Mal intended to win.

Chapter Fifteen

Heading back home, Mal locked the door and finally made it up to her sitting room. Mac was sitting on the kitchen counter, and as she came through the door, he started meowing imperiously, patting at her arm as she walked towards the fridge.

'Where are your manners?' she asked as she scratched the top of his head. 'Behave yourself, or I'll send you to the shops to fetch your own milk.' She pulled a tin of cat food out of the fridge. 'And trust me, that is not something to be relished.'

Whipping up a quick omelette for herself, she added a green salad then poured a glass of Merlot and settled down into an armchair. On balance, she liked living in Golden, but she was still adjusting to her new life away from the confines of a prison.

Fed up with her own failures, she pulled the history of the village towards her. As she'd told young Jasper, she was enjoying seeing how a place grew. Trying to understand the history of a place like London could be a life's work, but she wondered if a place the size of Golden might be easier to grasp.

And yet she didn't even understand its residents. Why did they stay if they hated so much of their life? Noticing that in the pile of history books she'd included one of Lionel Haverstock's early diaries, she tutted in annoyance. She would need to get that back to Jasper before his father found out. It surprised her how much families could fall out, but if the head of the family was rotten himself, maybe the spreading canker was understandable.

She pulled the diary over and opened the heavy leather-bound volume. Flicking back until she found a January date, Mal wondered if the weather had been as soggy then as it was today. She was pleased to see that Lionel's penmanship was clear and flowed nicely across the page, and she wondered if he'd enjoyed letter writing. From Imogen's descriptions, though, he didn't seem the sort to engage.

January
Today's rain fell as sleet and froze the surrounding roads. The birds were silent under the ominous clouds, and all the heavens stood still in mourning. My life has ended, and whilst I know I will go on, I know now that it will be as a husk, a shell of a man, a puppet that responds only to the tug of his parental strings.

Mal paused and blinked. These were the words of a heartbroken poet, not a cold patriarch. Taking a sip of wine, she read on.

I shall be taking a plane to America in the morning, and then I hope never to return to these shores. I shall step away from my beloved Cornwall, for all I see now is soot. Were I to place my hand on the trunk of the Old Man, my hand would come away blackened. If I grasped the tiller of my skiff, it would be smeared with dust. The blooms in the garden under my touch would wither. I am the despoiler. And so I leave like a whipped dog, too cowardly to stand and fight.

Good grief. Mal took another drink and turned the page, but the last few pages were blank. How old was he when he wrote this? Early twenties maybe? The strength of his youthful angst was impressive. She knew from the stack of journals that he'd continued to keep a diary and that, despite his declaration, he did, in fact, return to these shores. So what exactly had happened? Mal flipped to the front of the book and saw it was dated a year prior. She settled down to read.

Attended a dance at the Frampton's last night. It was alright, although, as everyone's folks were present, it was a sedate affair.

Mal grinned. She remembered parties like that, where she and her friends would try to hide their inebriated states from the gaze of their parents. Poor Gerry had once raised a glass to the host in an attempt to appear sober and had promptly slid under the table. Come to think of it, that was around that time the dinner parties separated along generational lines. She returned to Lionel's plight.

Julia Carter brought her cousin, a girl called Carole. She's ridiculously pretty, although I think she found me something of a dullard. When I get nervous, I talk about fish. You can imagine how that went down. Still, this morning, Mummy received an invitation from Mrs Carter for us to join her for lunch next week. Is it too much to hope that I might see Carole again? If I do, I shall have to think of things to say that don't include herrings.

'Imagine courting a girl with herrings, Mac. Although I imagine that would work well for you.'

Mal stretched and put the book aside. Knowing that his and Carole's blossoming friendship would end in failure had pulled a blanket of melancholia over the evening, and Mal switched on the television. She struggled through the tangle of channels until she found a James Bond film and settled down to an evening of explosions and heroic deeds.

The following morning, Mal padded downstairs and opened the diary again, full of curiosity.

My darling Pearl,

How silly it seems to be to be writing to you when I could be talking to you instead. But even when I am not with you, you are constantly in my thoughts. Besides, an actual letter would be pointless, so I shall pretend to write to you through the lines of my diary.

I thought your explanation of the life cycle of an elver was fascinating. I have never had such an educated conversation with a girl before, and I was mesmerised. You rightly looked at me as though I was a fool. And you were right. I am a fool. Especially where you are concerned.

Mal flicked back a page. The week before, young Lionel had been all about a girl called Carole. Now, Pearl seemed to be the flavour of the month. As she read on, she found only one more mention of Carole. Apparently, they'd gone to lunch after all, but she failed to be impressed by the size and pattern of limpet distribution on the south coast. Mal rolled her eyes at Mac.

Pearl, however, appeared to be impressed by everything Lionel said, and in return, he was clearly falling head over heels in love with her.

Mal settled into her armchair and read on.

Chapter Sixteen

Detective Chief Inspector Hemingstone was in his office, writing up his notes from the previous day's visit. Yesterday, the high sheriff and the police commissioner had called in to congratulate him. He'd also managed to get a photo taken with the high sheriff shaking his hand. That the sheriff was a woman was still disappointing, but he recalled what he'd said to Mrs Hemingstone: *'It's the modern age.'* The high sheriff wasn't even that good looking. But, according to the commissioner, her husband moved in very high circles, so he made sure to spend a bit of time talking to her.

Certainly, they'd been visiting other task forces the day before, but Hemingstone knew the real purpose of the tour. Who else had solved a murder and broken several drug lines? Admittedly, not the main county lines, but that would come. Maybe when that happened, he could get a photo with the Lord Lieutenant, maybe even the young Princess of Wales. He could imagine her laughing as he explained how he'd foiled a drug-dealing ring. Perhaps she would even pause to look impressed.

A rap on the door frame shook him out of his daydream. Hemingstone looked up from his keyboard. DI Williams was leaning in. Ted was quickly becoming his right hand. He was fast at paperwork and good at sorting out mundane issues, and he had a solid clean-up rate. If anything, he was a little too efficient, and yesterday

Hemingstone had ensured Ted was out of the office, interviewing witnesses for a series of bag snatches on Pydar Street. Hemingstone didn't need him on the commissioner's radar just yet. Training up a new DI would be a waste of his time. If he was disappointed not to have met the high sheriff, he hadn't shown it beyond an initial frown.

Hemingstone knew that would spur the younger man on. He himself had never been presented to the higher-ups even when his contemporaries were, but that only made him hungrier. *And look at him now: detective chief inspector and rubbing shoulders with the high sheriff and chief commissioner.*

Ted didn't normally bother him, so he pushed the keyboard away and waved him in.

'You need my wisdom?'

'I've just had an odd call from the Truro coroner. A son asked them to perform an autopsy on his father, Lionel Haverstock.'

'How old was he?'

'Eighty-five. Died in his bed.'

'Natural causes,' said Hemingstone. 'Is the son after some sort of medical malpractice? Trying to claim medical negligence?' He leant back in his chair and placed his hands on the back of his head. 'You know, that's the problem these days. Too many people are trying to sue the last penny out of everyone and dragging us into the bloody process. If it was up to me, I would ban anyone from suing the NHS.' He paused to allow Ted to agree with him.

'Actually, that's not the case here, guv. The old man was as fit as a fiddle, according to his doctor, so a standard autopsy was on the cards, anyway. But it turns out the son was concerned about foul play.'

'Dear God. Do people have nothing better to do with their time? He was an old man. What did you say? Eighty-five? Past his prime. Mr Haverstock's ticker had tocked its last.'

Ted stood still, waiting for him to finish, then continued. 'It turns out that the son was right to be concerned.'

'He was? Oh, that's interesting, medical malpractice, then? Honestly, the NHS is a bloody shambles. You need to keep these doctors on their toes, you know.'

'Actually, sorry to interrupt you, guv. This isn't a medical malpractice case. As I said, he wasn't on any medications. Never had surgery. I'm afraid the coroner was certain. There is evidence of a puncture mark caused by a syringe. The hospital pathologist has requested a Home Office pathologist take over, and the coroner has agreed. I think we're looking at murder.'

Hemingstone unclasped his hands and slapped them on the desk.

'Well, now. That's interesting.'

A murder always had the potential for publicity but had to be handled carefully. Some old boy killed in a care home stank of abuse and stirred up a lot of public outrage. And if there was something he knew about himself, it was that he wasn't best in large-scale enquiries where the public was always interfering. He didn't have the patience for them.

'And who exactly is the victim?'

'Owner of Liggan Hall. Huge landowner, one of Cornwall's leading estates.'

'Is that a fact?' Hemingstone smiled and walked out into the main office.

'Listen up, team. New case. The murder of Lionel Haverstock.'

An hour later, Hemingstone and Williams pulled up in front of Liggan Hall, and a middle-aged man in red cords and a checked shirt met them at the door.

'Henry Haverstock. Before we go through to the rest of the family, could you let me know what this is about?'

Hemingstone looked him up and down, then shook his head. He was in charge.

'Sorry, sir. That's not my process. If you can show me to your mother…'

Henry paused, narrowing his eyes. 'I won't have my mother unnecessarily upset by whatever you have to say.'

'As I said, that's not how we do things.'

'I've a good mind to call Charles, Devon and Cornwall's chief commissioner. See what he has to say about this.'

'That is your right, sir. I was with him yesterday, and he mentioned what a credit to the task force I am. I'm sure he'll be happy to tell you that. He might also be interested in why I've called on you today.'

Henry tilted his head and rapidly recalculated. 'Very well. Follow me. I should let you know my brother is here, as is a friend of my mother's. Mother insisted, and I could see no way of refusing her.'

'That's her prerogative.'

They walked into a large living room, what was probably called a sitting room or something even grander. Paintings covered the walls, and vases and statues sat everywhere. His wife would have kittens about all the dusting. That log fire was probably a nightmare to keep clean. *And who puts that many photos on a piano? Don't these people remember what their family looks like?*

The family was gathered on the three sofas framing the fire. A second man was clearly Henry's brother. Two older women were sitting together on a sofa. Both looked to be in their sixties, neither appearing old enough to be the wife of an eighty-five-year-old. He looked at them carefully and then swore.

'Dammit, Mrs Peck. What the hell are you doing here?'

Chapter Seventeen

An hour earlier, Mal had been minding her own business when Imogen rang up, sobbing loudly. It sounded forced, but she sounded highly agitated, nonetheless.

'You have to come up. Please. I have no one. None of my friends will understand. I just need a friendly face by my side.'

She began rambling about DNA tests and autopsies and that the police were on their way. Eventually, Mal agreed to come up. Part of her just wanted to say yes to stop her going on, but if she was utterly honest, she was intrigued. She'd been in the room when Henry had stormed in, accusing his father of being about to change the will. The next day, Lionel was dead. *Had the will changed? Did police suspect foul play, and what was the DNA test about?*

Mal wasn't fooled that Imogen held her in any high regard. She simply needed an ally who wouldn't gossip. Additionally, Mal had some first-hand experience of the legal system. Mal had discovered, during her own brush with the law, the speed with which many friends abandoned her. Some she'd expected, whilst others had hurt. Oddly, Hugo's rejection of her hurt only her pride. That she'd stayed married to a man she didn't love for so long was a source of irritation to her. Whatever Imogen was about to go through, Mal hoped she had a few genuine friends to help her.

For the moment, she had to rely on a total stranger to show a crumb of human compassion. Mal wondered if Imogen was relying on the wrong person.

She drove the Land Rover down the correct drive the first time and parked to one side. At the front door, Jasper answered and looked at her, concerned.

'Hello, Mal. I'm afraid now isn't a good time.'

'Who are you talking to?' shouted an older man's voice from inside. 'Tell them to sod off.'

Jasper grimaced and apologised when the voice rang out again. 'Is it the police? For God's sake, bring them in.'

Jasper gave Mal an apologetic smile and called back over his shoulder, 'Not the police.'

His voice echoed back down the main hallway, and Mal considered giving up and heading back down the hill. A door banged, and now she could see Imogen's eldest striding down the corridor. Jasper quickly stepped aside.

Before Henry could dismiss Mal, she took a quick breath. 'Your mother asked for me.'

He looked Mal up and down and glanced over at her car. Spotting the battered Land Rover and her designer clothes, he probably summed her up as an eccentric landowner; wealthy and not bothered by appearance— not his mother's normal sort of friend, but certainly one that passed muster. He smiled warmly, and Mal realised he'd completely forgotten about having met her before.

Obviously, Imogen hadn't told him about her criminal record.

'I'm terribly sorry, but now is not a great time.' He looked over her shoulder.

Mal realised he must be hoping she would go before the police arrived. Whatever was going on, the family wanted it under wraps.

'Your mother explained the police were on their way and that she wanted some moral support.'

Henry narrowed his eyes. 'She has her family.'

'Granny might want Mal as well, though.'

He turned and looked at his son in surprise.

'Do you know each other?'

'Yes. I'm sorry. I should have introduced you. Father, this is Malachite Peck. She has some experience in the legal field. Mal, allow me to introduce my father, Henry Haverstock.'

From the way he mentioned Mal's knowledge of the legal world, she wondered if Jasper knew about her past. Dismissing it for now, she stepped forward and offered her hand. 'Mr Haverstock, I am very sorry for your loss. Your mother asked if I could help, and I said I would be happy to.'

Henry was about to challenge her further, when tyres could be heard coming along the drive. Dismissing her, he instructed Jasper to take Mal indoors.

'Sorry about that,' Jasper said. 'We're all in a bit of a state this morning. The police rang this morning and asked to see Granny.'

'Any idea why?'

'It's probably connected to the fact that Algernon, my uncle, insisted on an autopsy on grandfather.'

'Oh, hell.'

Jasper stopped and looked at Mal. 'Hell, indeed.' He turned and continued, 'Through here.'

As she entered the drawing room, the occupants seemed to be preparing for a scene to start. Sitting on one of the sofas closest to the fire, Imogen was dressed all in black and was wearing a three-strand pearl necklace, a diamond brooch, an emerald bracelet, and several rings featuring large gemstones. She was dressed to intimidate. It reminded Mal of little insects that could puff themselves up to look like scorpions or spiders.

Standing by the fireplace, one elbow leaning on the mantelpiece, was a man in his forties. He had his mother's fine features, and a heavy blond fringe swept majestically back from his forehead.

He looked at Mal and blinked. 'Are you the police?'

Imogen stood and walked over to Mal to kiss her on both cheeks. 'Does she look like the police? In cashmere? Mal, this is my youngest son, Algernon. I take it you met Henry at the door. He can be overprotective.'

'Mummy, what is this? Now isn't the best time.'

'It's the perfect time. I need a friend.'

122

'This is a family matter.'

'Algernon, it was your little stunt that has involved the police. The least I can have is a friend by my side. I insist.'

Quelled, her son glared at Mal, then returned to looking impressive by the fireplace. Mal sat down with Imogen, and Jasper went to stand by one of the French doors and looked out over the sweeping lawn. Voices could be heard moving along the corridor. Then Henry walked in, followed by two men. Mal's heart sank.

Chapter Eighteen

'Dammit, Mrs Peck. What the hell are you doing here?' exclaimed Hemingstone.

Henry stepped away from the police. 'Mrs Peck is a friend of my mother's and a guest in our home.'

Mal dipped her head and smiled to herself. She'd always admired the way people closed ranks against outsiders. By being so rude, Hemingstone had forced Henry to accept Mal as 'one of us.'

'Now, maybe you'd like to tell us what this is all about? Please sit.' He waved towards a small two-man sofa that had been added to the seating arrangements. Henry took the armchair by the fire, and Algernon took the sofa opposite Mal and his mother. Jasper remained in an armchair over by the window, watching the entire party. His expression was blank, but Mal noticed his eyes flicking back and forth, trying to watch everyone.

Inspector Hemingstone looked around the room, then turned to the other detective. 'Williams, wait over by the door. I'm not going to have you sitting on my lap.'

Henry was about to protest, but Hemingstone cut him off.

'I'm here today to discuss the outcome of Lionel Haverstock's autopsy.' He looked across at Imogen. 'I understand you gave permission for your son Algernon to request an autopsy.'

'Not exactly,' murmured Imogen.

'What!' Henry jumped to his feet. 'You told me you had.'

'Maybe I had.' She fluttered a hand and glanced fearfully between her two sons. 'I don't remember, and really, where was the harm? Your father clearly died of old age. I just think this fuss is unwelcome. I just want to bury my husband and then get on with things.'

Hemingstone took a deep breath and looked around the room before speaking. 'I'm afraid that won't be possible. This morning, I was informed by the coroner that Lionel Haverstock did not, in fact, die of natural causes, and we are now treating his death as murder.'

Both sons sprang to their feet, shouting at the inspector, whilst Imogen shrank back into the sofa. Mal sat very still and noticed that Hemingstone was observing the family and Williams was taking notes. They seemed to suspect a family member.

'How did he die?' asked Jasper. He was still seated in his armchair, looking troubled. 'I was the one who found him. He seemed completely peaceful. Are you sure?'

'There is no doubt,' Hemingstone said. 'Now, we are going to have to ask you all for your whereabouts on the night of the twenty-eighth. And we will need to understand who had access to the house at night, and who else was staying here.'

'But the will... Who inherits now?' demanded Algernon. 'What did the DNA test show?'

If anyone was repulsed by his question, they didn't show it. Mal looked around the room. They'd just discovered that Lionel had been murdered and that the most likely culprit was sitting amongst them. Yet they all seem more interested in the will.

'The DNA results haven't come back yet. In matters such as this, we suggest you call your lawyers to see what they advise. My job is catching killers, not sorting out probate.'

Henry walked across the room and sat by his mother. 'In which case, we shall continue as before until we know more.'

'Like hell we will,' said Algernon, pacing. 'Mummy, this is ridiculous. Tell him. What if he killed Daddy because he knew he was being written out of the will?'

Henry lunged at Algernon, but his brother skipped back and turned to face Hemingstone.

'Did you know that? My father said he was going to change his will the morning before he was murdered. I think that gives my brother a pretty clear motive, don't you?'

Shouts of outrage arose from the other occupants in the room. Imogen was berating her son, Jasper was shouting at his father, and Henry was calling his brother every name under the sun.

'Quiet!' shouted Hemingstone. 'To whom, exactly, did Mr Haverstock say he was changing his will?'

Imogen cleared her throat. 'I understand he said some such thing to Mr Whitchurch, our estate manager.'

'Then I will need to speak to him. Does he live here in the house?'

'No. He has a cottage.'

'But it's here on the grounds,' said Henry quickly. 'And he has access to the house.'

'And why the hell would he murder Daddy?' sneered Algernon. 'Trying to cover your tracks, are you? You know if you killed him, you don't get to inherit anything. That's right, isn't it? Killers don't profit from their crimes.' He looked expectantly at Hemingstone, who shrugged.

'That's not down to me, sir. Now, if I can just take some details from you all.'

Mal smoothed her skirt and stood up. 'I think it's probably time for me to go, Imogen.'

Henry looked at her and blinked, then recovered himself. Amongst the revelations, he'd entirely forgotten she had nothing to do with the investigation.

'You are not to speak a word of this to anyone.' He stepped towards her and towered over her. 'Do you understand me?'

With her calves pressing into the sofa, she was unable to take a step back, so she looked down at her feet instead; a small woman bullied by a larger man.

'Dad! What are you doing? Malachite won't talk to anyone,' said Jasper. 'You're scaring her.'

Mal tilted her head slightly in Jasper's direction and raised an eyebrow, smiling gently at his gallantry. Henry stepped back, and Mal moved to the side.

'That's obviously not my intention,' said Henry.

Ignoring him, Mal gave Imogen a small smile. 'I shall go now. Please call me if I can help with anything, but I promise you I shan't speak a word of this.' Mal then looked at Henry. 'But if you think you can keep a murder investigation quiet, then you are in for quite the shock. Inspector, do you have any questions for me, or may I leave?'

Williams grinned, then quickly covered his smirk as he continued writing notes in his jotter.

'Mrs Peck,' said Hemingstone, 'here we are at a murder scene, and you are right in the middle of it. Do you have anything you would like to add?'

'No, I'm afraid I never met Lionel Haverstock. I have only ever been in the house three times.'

Hemingstone glared at her for a few seconds, then nodded a dismissal. 'We know where to find you if we need to. In the meantime, Mr Haverstock, I need to interview your estate manager. If you can summon him...?'

Mal headed down the corridor, thoughts swirling through her head. *How had Lionel been killed? Jasper said he looked peaceful, but the coroner was certain he had been murdered? How had it been done, and why weren't the police saying?*

'Miss Peck.'

Mal turned to see DI Williams walking down the corridor to join her as she stepped out into the sunshine. 'Yes, I know. Don't tell anyone.'

He stopped, turning to look down at her. 'It isn't that. I just wondered if you had any observations about the family that you might want to share with me, out of earshot.'

Mal hadn't taken to DI Williams the last time she'd met him. He'd appeared too busy agreeing with his boss, but when push came to shove, he'd listened to what she had to say. That was a point in his favour.

'I don't, except they do seem to be exactly what they appear to be.'

'Grieving widow, distraught sons—that sort of thing?'

Mal looked up at him. His expression was wry, and he'd clearly also marked the absolute lack of sorrow over husband and father being dead.

'Yes. Exactly that.'

'The DCI failed to mention how Lionel was murdered.'

She thought maybe Williams would let something slip. Instead, he thrust his hands in his pockets and sighed.

'Of course he didn't mention how Lionel was murdered. He's not stupid.' He paused and looked over his shoulder, back through the front door to the corridor beyond. 'Look, the thing you need to understand about my boss is that, despite all appearances, he isn't actually stupid. Sure, he's vain, easily swayed by titles, has one of the thinnest skins I have ever encountered, but despite all that, he's pretty good at his job.'

'It's not a glowing endorsement, is it?'

'Being a good policeman isn't all about putting two and two together, reading people, or running across rooftops. Much of it is dreary day-to-day stuff.'

'And he's good at the dreary?'

'Yes. But that's not a bad thing. He supports his staff. If they make a mistake, he takes the flak.'

'And if they get something right?'

Williams laughed. 'Then he takes the credit. Look, I never said he was a saint. But he works hard. He is ruthlessly efficient, never over budget, and is as honest as the day is long.'

'He's sexist.'

'Probably. But he's also a bit scared of you. You made him feel a fool, and it's one of those things he hates. Remember the bit about the thin skin.'

Mal sighed. 'And I'm supposed to care about hurting the feelings of a senior investigating detective?'

'No, I just...' Williams scratched the back of his head. 'Look, he drives me mad most of the time—I get it—but he gets the job done. All I'm saying is that if you spot anything you think is relevant, let us know.'

'Look. Dammit,'—Mal smiled—'you've got me saying *look* now. Okay, if anything occurs to me, I shall contact Sophie. PC Taphouse. Is that good enough?'

Williams stuck out his hand, and with a laugh, Mal took it and shook hands. Williams then turned and headed back into the house, leaving Mal utterly bemused.

Chapter Nineteen

Mal had been tidying the shelves when the shop phone rang, and she picked it up in annoyance. Running a bookshop was irritating. She wished she could ignore the call and all the daft, scammy salesmen. So hearing the familiar tones of Imogen's voice came as a relief.

'Mal, I just wanted to thank you for yesterday. It's all so dreadful. The police kept asking about any medication I was on, any Lionel was on. If I had a medical background. If the boys had a history of drug use. It was so degrading. What do you think they were looking for?'

Mal sat on the stool and thought about it. 'I have no idea, but I suspect it has something to do with his cause of death. Have they told you how he died?'

'No. I asked, and they said they would tell me in due course. But they can't do that, can they? I mean, I'm his wife. Was his wife. Oh God, it's such a bloody mess. Do you know, I think they are deliberately trying to trip us up.'

For the first time, Imogen sounded genuinely distressed, and Mal felt sorry for her. Her outrage and confusion made it clear that she, at least, didn't believe anyone in the family was responsible.

'If they won't tell you the cause of death yet, maybe they hope that someone accidentally incriminates someone else in the family.'

'But that means they suspect one of us. The boys have been at each other's throats, and Algernon has moved out to the Dower Cottage. Won't even stay in the same house. The police even spoke to the children. Can you imagine? Asking where they were the night Lionel died.'

'And does anyone have an alibi?'

'Not really. We were all in the house. Algernon and his family, and Jocasta and the girls, had all arrived the day before. Henry lives in the east wing, Jasper lives in one of the estate cottages. The only people that can vouch for each other are Algernon and Daisy. I thank God Algernon has an alibi. He was so angry at his father.'

Not a particularly good alibi, thought Mal. *If your partner is asleep, would they notice if you woke? Worse yet, they could be covering for you.*

'What about Henry? Can't Jocasta provide his alibi?'

Imogen snorted. 'They don't share a bed. They barely even share a house. It's all so grubby; the police asking where everyone slept, then acting like there were problems. But that doesn't matter. He would never harm his father. Why would he?'

'I'm so sorry... about everything.' She really couldn't think of anything else to say.

'That's so kind of you.'

'So now what happens?'

'Well, that's the ridiculous thing. They say they'll keep us informed.' Imogen's voice was rising in indignation. 'Some lunatic broke into the house, murdered my

133

husband, and now the police have left us to be slaughtered as we sleep.'

'But surely—'

'Henry's spoken to the chief commissioner to get us protection and to speed up the investigation. I couldn't sleep a wink last night. I actually had to place a chair in front of my door. Can you imagine?'

Mal remembered Tabitha Jones, a young woman she'd met in jail. Tabitha had killed her husband in self-defence after he broke down the bathroom door. Mal wondered if Imogen would take any comfort from the fact that her situation wasn't as dire as it felt.

'We pay so much to the police benevolent fund every year. Lionel was always a strong supporter of the force. We deserve to be treated better.'

Maybe if Tabitha had contributed to the benevolent fund, she wouldn't have been arrested and committed. Maybe she wouldn't have lost access to her children. Maybe they wouldn't have ended up in foster care. Mal tried to keep a lid on her rising temper. Imogen was going through a lot. Her life had been a pampered one, and she didn't have the skills to deal with her current situation.

The bell above the door rang, and a middle-aged man walked in.

'Mrs Peck?'

Mal gestured at the phone, then spoke again to Imogen. 'Look, someone's just come in. I'm here if you need to talk, but I'm sure that you are perfectly safe.'

Hanging up on Imogen, she placed the phone back in its handset and stared at the newcomer. She wanted to think on what Imogen had said. She knew about the proposed change in the will, and she knew about the autopsy. But she was certain that Imogen was holding something back, and she wanted to consider what it might be. Algernon had been shouting about DNA, but she hadn't fully grasped what he was referring to. Was this what Imogen was trying to keep secret?

'I'm Clive Sullivan from the Chamber of Commerce.'

Mal shook her head, brought back to the present by this stout little man. As she took in his words, she was suddenly overwhelmed with memories stirred up by the Chamber of Commerce. Gone were the days when she would attend the annual dinners put on by the great Livery Halls in the City of London. The events were black or white tie, depending on the occasion, and women would be in full-length gowns. She would wear a silk taffeta number unless it was a winter event; then she would wear velvet. The halls were vast, glorious spaces raised like golden cathedrals above her head—but they were a bugger to heat!

As toasts were raised, the chandeliers and crystal sparkled; the conversations laughed back and forth, marking another year of successful trade. Ceremonies stretching back centuries were performed, and new members were welcomed into the company. Mal was only ever in attendance as a guest, but she would sit and listen

135

carefully as people chatted about grain forecasts in far-flung countries. And she would be ready to make her move in the futures market the following day.

She smiled wistfully, remembering the pomp and circumstance of it all, until she was disturbed by a cough from the man in front of her. She was dragged away from the taffeta, velvet, and gold brocade, to the man wearing a nylon jumper.

It was a bizarre ensemble. His V-neck sweater was embellished with zigzags in shades of blue and beige. Under his jumper, he wore a blue shirt and a pink tie with some sort of crest on it. Over the jumper, he wore a double-breasted jacket. She wondered if he was a coach driver, then remembered he'd said something about the Chamber of Commerce.

'Mrs Peck?'

She shook her head. 'It's not *missus*—' She was about to invite him to call her Ms Peck—a phrase she loathed, but it beat missus—when he interrupted her.

'Ah, yes.' He gave a little self-important chuckle and tapped the side of his nose. 'Lady Peck, but don't worry. Your secret is safe with me.'

Malachite stared at him. When she first arrived in the village, she'd flippantly referred to herself as Lady Peck in an attempt to avoid being called missus. And also, really, to shut up DCI Hemingstone. However, despite her quickly explaining that had been a joke, a lot of people had taken her at her word and still thought she was incognito, which was frustrating. She felt like a fraud, but the situation was one of her own making, so she ground her teeth and gave the man a tight smile.

'Can I help you?'

He pulled at his jacket nervously and smiled at her. 'I'm here on behalf of the Chamber of Commerce to formally welcome you to the village.'

'I've been here three months.'

He looked uncomfortable, so she tried to smile properly, but he was so unctuous that he was bringing out the worst in her. There was a particular type of person who loved the importance that a title bestowed and puffed themselves up behind the name badge. She feared she was looking at one such specimen.

'Well, it's been a busy time, hasn't it? And we're only a small group.'

Frankly, November had been deadly. Although after her dreadful introduction to the village with a double murder, she was glad of the peace and quiet. She was about to say so, but decided to play nicely instead. After all, she was the newcomer and felt certain forms should be respected.

'Well, it's lovely to meet you. Thank you for calling in.'

She waited for him to leave, but realised he hadn't finished.

'The thing is—and it's totally understandable, what with the changeover and everything, and nothing to worry about—but the thing is…' He paused and looked at her hopefully.

Mal stared back blankly.

'Your subs are late.'

Mal had been a city trader with a book running into the billions. She'd never been late on any financial payment unless she was playing the market for an advantage. The idea that she had been remiss in a payment was an affront.

'My subs?'

'Your annual subscription to the chamber of commerce. Everyone's a member.'

Mal raised an eyebrow and pulled out a notepad and pencil from under the counter.

'I see. And is this obligatory?'

'Gosh, no. Of course not. We're not communists.' He laughed, then stopped when Mal didn't join in.

'Quite. And how much is the annual fee?'

'Five hundred pounds.'

'And how many organisations in the village are members?'

'Well, I don't have the exact number on me.'

'No? Very well, how much are you currently holding in reserve?'

'I'm afraid I don't have those figures on me.'

'Okay, then. What do I get for this investment?'

'Ah now yes, I can help you with that,' he smiled anxiously. 'We send out a monthly newsletter.'

'I've been here three months. I haven't seen a newsletter.'

'Well, as I said, we have been busy. The Christmas lights are sponsored by the businesses in the village. And we are about to launch our rapid response unit in case of shoplifters and the like. We also have a website. And we support the annual Feast Week, which you were part of. If I remember, you raised a fair bit of money that day.'

'I did,' said Mal slowly, 'but those funds went to various charitable organisations.' She thought about it some more and saw the problem. 'So you give funds to the Feast Committee so that they can raise funds to give to charity. Why not cut out the middleman and just give the funds directly to the charity?'

Clive looked horrified. 'I think you are missing the community aspect of the Feast Week.'

Mal paused and removed her business head and sighed. 'Yes, I suppose I am. Tell you what; send me over your accounts for the past three years, including a link to the newsletters and website, and I'll give you my answer within forty-eight hours. Is that fair?'

Clive stared at her, and she wondered if she had sprouted another head.

'Mr Sullivan, I have very limited funds. This investment will bring me no immediate or tangible benefit as far as I can see, but let me look through your proposal and see if I can't be persuaded.' She gave him her full-beam smile and stuck out her hand. 'Thank you for calling in, and I look forward to talking more.'

He shook her hand in a daze, then left the shop, and Mal went to put the kettle on. Five hundred pounds a year was a huge sum of money in her new budget, and one she hadn't been aware of. In November, she'd barely taken two grand.

She'd only just returned to the lower shelves when the doorbell rang again, and a youngish couple walked into the shop. The man rapped his knuckles on the counter and called out, 'Shop!' whilst his wife laughed. Mal considered throwing a book at him, but instead swept the dirt off her knees and walked to the counter.

'Hello.' His false bonhomie filled the shop. 'I'm after a picture of the Nearly Home Trees.'

Mal stared at him whilst trying to understand the question.

'We're a bookshop. There are a few art galleries on the high street. Maybe they—'

'Both shut, if you can believe it. But then someone said you stock greeting cards. So, do you?'

Mal tried to sound friendly as she pointed at the rack of greeting cards. 'But they are mostly of seascapes. I don't think we have any woodland ones.'

'Not woodland, the Nearly Home Trees!' he repeated with emphasis, whilst his wife nodded enthusiastically.

'You know,' she simpered, 'The ones on the A30. The ones that mean you are nearly home.'

Mal shook her head. 'No, I'm sorry. I don't know what you are talking about.'

The couple stared at her in amazement.

'Are you joking?' the man asked. 'Everyone knows the Nearly Home trees.'

'Well, clearly not everyone.'

'But you must know them. How can you live in Cornwall and not know them? We wanted a picture to hang on our wall. We have a house in Chelsea, and it would remind us of a simpler world.'

'And did you think a greeting card would have the same effect?' Mal asked, aware her tone was becoming sardonic.

'Don't be silly! We'd take the image and get an artist to paint it for us.'

'Why not just dig the trees up and have them replanted in your back garden?'

The couple stared at her, but Mal could see for a nanosecond that the wife had considered it.

'You seriously don't know them,' the woman said. 'On the A30, off to your left. Just before the Tamar.'

Mal let out a deep sigh. 'Look, I'm a newcomer. I've been here what, three, four months. I'd never been to Cornwall before. I travelled here by train. I don't have a car. I haven't been on the A30. And I don't think I have what you're looking for.'

The couple stared at her, then left the shop muttering. The man said something, and his wife laughed as the door closed behind them. Mal leant on the counter then, swearing, grabbed her keys and headed out of the shop, twisting the sign to Back in Five Minutes, and walked down to the harbour. She wanted to sit and look at the sea, her back to other humans.

She settled down onto the granite wall and looked out over the water. The sea was a surly grey like the sky above, and small flecks of white capped the waves as they raced towards the land.

'Closed today?'

Mal turned reluctantly but smiled when she saw it was the harbour master. 'Lunch break.'

'It's ten thirty.'

'Is it? It feels like today has already been quite long.'

'Some days can be like that. But I think you have the right solution. Come and look at the sea. Nietzsche once said if you stare into the abyss long enough, the abyss will stare back into you. I think he meant it as a bad thing. But I think there's something to be said for acknowledging your own scale within the universe.'

He nodded and was prepared to walk away when Mal interrupted him.

'Are the Nearly Home Trees special? Have I failed some test by not knowing about them? Maybe an ancient king is buried under them?'

He laughed. 'Nothing like that. They are just one of those landmarks you tick off on a long journey. If you're travelling by car, that is. As far as I know, there's no test for being Cornish.'

'Except for being born here.'

'Aye, well, there's that. And all of your forebears.'

'Of course.'

They both laughed.

'There's a lot of nonsense spoken. Jam First, Nearly Home Trees, no carrots in pasties. These things aren't rules—they're marketing ploys. If you want to settle here, just do as you would be done by, and that will do for most.'

Then he nodded and, smiling again, turned and walked back along the harbour towards the village, leaving Mal to think on his words. Her customers hadn't made her feel ill at ease. She'd done that to herself and was the greater fool for it. The world was full of idiots, and she was the greatest of them all if she was going to allow them to disturb her.

She needed a distraction, and trying to work out how Lionel had been murdered might be just the ticket.

Chapter Twenty

Hemingstone drummed his fingers on his desk and called Williams into his office. Placing a pile of printouts on the table, he sipped his coffee and waited for the younger man to sit.

'These reports show no evidence of regular drug use in Lionel's body.'

Williams nodded and spoke slowly. 'Yes, we can definitely rule this out as self-inflicted.'

'What?' Hemingstone slammed his cup on the table, splashing coffee on the paperwork. 'Were you entertaining that idea? Do we think that after he injected a lethal dose of morphine, he then hid the syringe?'

'No, guv. Sorry, I thought you were just throwing ideas out. You know, a bit of brainstorming?'

Hemingstone rolled his eyes, then pulled a face. 'Is that what they teach at Hendon? "No idea is a bad idea. Let's throw it out there." What we need more of is clear thinking and straight talking.'

'Yes, guv.'

'So...'

Williams paused, then realised he was expected to provide some theories. 'The victim was injected in his bed, presumably whilst he slept. The tox reports aren't back yet, but the pathologist says morphine looks likely. There was no sign of a struggle and no evidence initially of foul play. In fact, without the sharp eyes of the first pathologist, who saw the puncture mark, this crime may have gone unnoticed.'

'Any report of drug use amongst the family?'

'In their interviews—'

'I know what they said in their interviews. I was there. What do your investigations show?'

'No one is on medication. Henry and Algernon both have cautions for erratic driving in their twenties. Algernon had a further caution for dealing.'

'How much?'

'Several bags of various party pills,'

'Just a caution?'

'I suspect friends in high places.'

Hemingstone frowned. He hated discovering poor practice amongst colleagues. A dealer was a dealer, no matter how posh he spoke, and when the police turned a blind eye for friends and family, that brought the entire force into disrepute.

'Follow that lead. Sounds like it might be nothing. Algernon doesn't seem smart enough to be fronting a drug ring, but you never know.'

'Actually, guv, I ran a background check on his finances. He seems to lurch between feast and famine. He has a pattern of spending that makes no sense, given his level of income.'

'He's an art dealer, isn't he?'

'Exactly.'

Both men paused. The antiques trade was awash with loose cash and regularly shipped goods all over the world.

'If it wasn't for the fact that he'd insisted on an autopsy, things would be looking pretty dicey for him right now.'

'What about the elder son, Henry?'

'After a wild youth, he seems to have calmed down. Now playing it up as lord of the manor.' He flicked through his notebook. 'The wives have a clean sheet, although Daisy also has a very extravagant lifestyle. As do both of their children, Frederick and Fenella. Frederick, better known as Fred or Freddie, has been cautioned for drunk and disorderly. Looks like it was touch and go that he'd get an actual bodily harm caution.'

'The same friend in high places?' Hemingstone asked. 'Jesus. Right, what was the incident? If the lad has a record of violence, this might be something.'

'Rugby match. He and friends got into a fight with a group of football supporters whilst out on a pub crawl after a game. There were several arrests made.'

Hemingstone picked at the skin on his thumb. The lead wasn't a promising one.

'What about Henry's children?'

'All three are as clean as a whistle. To be expected with the younger two, but Jasper doesn't have so much as a parking ticket.'

'Too good to be true?'

'Hard to say. But no one, except for his family, has a bad word to say about him. His family seems to think he's a bit wet. It was him that found the body though. Volunteered to go and wake his grandfather.'

'Alright. So he could have gone back to check he hadn't left any evidence before he raised the alarm. Anything of interest in the rest of the household staff?'

'There's a driver, handyman called Dougie. He's up to his eyeballs in debt. Chloe used to work in an old person's home, so could have had access to syringes and morphine. Barry Whitechurch, the head groundsman grew up in foster care, was in and out of remand centres until he started working on the estate in his twenties and has been clean as a whistle ever since.'

'Could Chloe and Dougie be working together? Similar ages.'

'To what end, guv? The will is pretty clear. There's only one beneficiary.'

'No one knew what was in the will, though, did they? Maybe Lionel told Dougie he was in the will. Dougie, desperate for money, goes to Chloe and convinces her to prepare a lethal dose for Lionel.' Hemingstone looked expectantly at Williams, waiting for the younger detective to catch up and run with it.

'Sorry, guv. I don't see it. Are we suggesting that Chloe stole a syringe full of morphine from her place of work two years ago and has just been sitting on it?' He paused. 'Metaphorically. Besides, why would she help Dougie?'

'Because they're sleeping together, obviously.'

'She's gay.'

'What?'

'Gay. She's a lesbian, guv.'

Hemingstone's shoulders sagged. He hated the whole 'gay' business. He didn't care if someone was gay or not, but it just made his job so complicated.

'Right. Well. Dammit.'

'I'll continue to investigate both of them further, but the will is the key, I think. Who knew what the contents were? And which of the boys is Lionel's?'

'Nothing further from Mrs Haverstock?'

'No, she refused to answer any questions on the matter,' said Williams. He wasn't surprised. People lost perspective in murder investigations. They hoarded their own secrets, rather than reveal them to the harsh lights of public scrutiny. The fact was that those little secrets were often irrelevant, but still needed assessing, even if only to be dismissed; but that never occurred to the individual. The secret became more important than the identity of a murderer.

'Well, Mrs La-di-dah doesn't get a bloody say in the matter,' said Hemingstone, leaning back in his chair. 'What does she want us to do? Arrest her for obstruction? Hell's teeth. This isn't a bloody dinner party.'

'Agreed, but the DNA results will give us what we want to know anyway.'

'Right.' Hemingstone leant forward. Grabbing his pen, he stared tapping it on the table. 'Chase those up. Investigate Barry's youth. Dig into Dougie's finances, and for God's sake, find out who the family's connection in the police force is. The last thing I need is the commissioner coming in here reading me the riot act.' He put his pen down and looked hard into his detective's face. 'And for the love of God, keep Malachite Bloody Peck away from the investigation.'

Chapter Twenty-One

Two days had passed since the police informed the Haverstocks that Lionel had been murdered, and everything had gone quiet. Imogen spent most of her time sobbing on the phone. The cause of death had been revealed to be a massive overdose, and Imogen was convinced that everyone would think Lionel was some sort of junkie.

By now, rumours of foul play had filtered down to the village, and everyone had a theory. Whilst Mal wanted to solve the murder, she knew the experts were in charge. Plus, she had bigger issues to deal with. Looking through her figures, she wondered exactly how people ate in winter. Her takings were barely adequate, and according to others in the village, income fell off of a cliff in January and February. Tourist locations like Cornwall prayed for an early Easter. Hoping the day was going to be spectacular, she'd gone around listing discounts and incentives to entice those last pennies out of people's wallets.

The bell rang over the door, and Mal looked up with a welcoming smile, but froze in horror. Swanning into the shop and chattering to each other, barely glancing at her, were Daphne Page and Ginny Danver-Jones. After five years, they hadn't changed a bit.

She tried to recall where she'd last seen them, maybe at a fundraising gala concert or at Charlie's birthday bash.

Mal moved in lots of social groups and had a few friends—fewer at present, disappointingly. So most weren't friends at all, as it happened, but she had many, many acquaintances. The women who just entered were wives of her ex–work colleagues and fell into the acquaintance category. Before her fall from grace, they undoubtedly would've described Mal as a very close friend. After her embarrassment, she was almost certainly referred to as *someone that Anthony occasionally worked with and always thought was a bit suspect.*

The two women barely glanced at Mal and headed towards the shelves, picking books up and putting them down again. Neither had struck her as a great reader. There was no reason they should recognise her. Gone was her sleek blonde bob, replaced by a mane of curly silver hair. Also gone were the power suits from Harvey Nicks. Today she was wearing a floral silk blouse with a cashmere cardigan in tones of pink. It wasn't a colour she was used to, but it worked nicely with her hair. Finally, the last place anyone expected to see Malachite Peck was behind the counter of a bookshop in a Cornish fishing village.

She continued running through her figures whilst keeping a weather eye on the women. Fingers crossed, they would leave the shop without recognising her. She hoped they weren't staying in the village. Tourists were unusual at this time of year, but sailors were not. Ideally, they would be staying on a boat and she wouldn't bump into them. Acknowledging her cowardice, she made a point to stay in after work, forgoing her evening stroll.

Soon, the ladies seemed done with looking at things and headed back towards the front door. They gave Mal a quick glance to say thank you, when Ginny did a double take, then stood still.

'Mal? Malachite Peck!'

Daphne also stared at her. 'Oh, my God. Mal! It is you!'

Mal's smile made it all the way to her mouth and no further. 'Hello Ginny, Daphne. Are you well?'

'Are we well, she asks. Just like that!' Ginny was shaking her head and leant over the counter, tapping Mal on the arm in playful admonishment. 'I heard a rumour that you were running a bookshop, but I didn't believe it. In a million years, I would never have pictured you hiding out in Cornwall.'

Just as Mal was about to point out that she wasn't hiding, Daphne interrupted her. 'I love your bookshop. It's so charming. It's so important to support the high street like this, and reading is vital, isn't it?'

Yes, thought Mal sourly, *I'm running this as a charitable endeavour.*

'It's been an absolute age since I saw you last,' said Ginny. 'Where was it, Charles' birthday?'

The two women stared at her, similar expressions on their faces: eyebrows raised, attentive smiles, no teeth showing.

'That's right,' said Mal. 'Charlie's birthday. That was a fun event, wasn't it?'

'Such fun,' the women said in unison, then laughed.

Just then, the doorbell rang again, and Anthony and Tony-Too walked in, wearing similar sailing jackets, and Mal remembered Anthony liked to sail. Tony-Too hadn't changed either. He was a small man who wore glasses that never seemed to fit him properly. For a while in the banking world, every second man seemed to be called Anthony, Stephen, or David, so a rash of nicknames sprang up. At one point, when more than five Tonys were in a room, it was like a mafia convention. Tony-Too loved his nickname. A nice, quiet man, he loved being one of the boys. Mal rated him as a first-class analyst, but he lacked the killer instinct, unlike his companion.

'Anthony, look!' Ginny exclaimed. 'Magnum Mal.'

That was a nickname she'd picked up years before, after drinking an entire bottle of champagne in under five minutes. Sometimes, the trading floor could be a very juvenile and competitive environment, and if Mal was taking part, she always liked to win. Normally, she rose above it, but would occasionally play the boys at their own games.

Anthony grinned at her in happy recognition. 'Mal the Merciless, more like! Hello, Em. How the hell are you?'

Mal the Merciless was a nickname she preferred as it complimented her trading record. People rarely bet against her, and those that did, lost. Whether the stakes were a bottle of champagne or a company takeover, Mal's instincts were highly regarded. "Em" was a nod to how she would sign off her communications, an *M* with a large flourish.

'Prison has treated you well.'

Both Ginny and Daphne recoiled. The forbidden subject had just been slapped onto the conversational table.

'Anthony. That's so rude. We were trying not to say anything.' Ginny glanced at Mal sympathetically. 'After what poor Mal went through, anyone would gain a few lines and a few pounds.'

Mal took a deep breath and let that pass.

'Not a bit of it.' Anthony leered appreciatively.

He'd always had a roving eye, and Ginny herself had had at least two affairs that Mal knew of. She would not appreciate Anthony's gaze.

'Your hair suits you like that,' he continued. 'Makes you look majestic, and if anything, I'd say you've slimmed a bit.'

He gave her a saucy wink, and Mal laughed. Their working relationship had always been platonic, but she did enjoy a bit of banter now and then.

'Life inside is all about yoga, pull-ups, and healthy living,' she said. 'It was practically a spa break.'

He laughed again, and Ginny narrowed her eyes, regarding Mal closely.

'Yes, actually, now you mention it, Mal has lost weight,' the woman said. 'Maybe that's what's making you look a little drawn. I suppose you weren't able to moisturise inside?'

Mal thought of a very vulgar response, then thought better of it. However, Anthony must've been thinking the same thing as he hooted with laughter. Tony-Too, ever one to spot a change in the marketplace, moved Daphne off to one side to examine the books, soon calling over to Mal about signed editions in an attempt to defuse the situation.

Ginny stared back and forth between the two of them, then decided not to make a scene. 'Honestly, it's just like the good old days with you two plotting and laughing. Really, Mal, if you ever make it back to London, you must come and visit. But do let us know. I'd hate there to be any awkwardness if Hugo and Minty are over.'

Tony-Too and Daphne froze, and Anthony glared at his wife. Ginny had just landed a direct hit, but Mal was determined to ignore it.

'I shall, of course,' said Mal.

Ginny looked disappointed, but carried on. Daphne quickly gathered a pile of books and headed back to the counter, presumably in an attempt to end Ginny's needling.

'Oh, how thoughtless of me to mention Minty.' Ginny ploughed on. 'But maybe you already know?'

Again, Mal smiled back but bit her tongue. Turning to Daphne, she took the books and rang them up, commenting on each title. 'We have his wife's autobiography as well, if you are interested. They were both in here last year.' Mal hoped that mentioning the ex-president's visit might change the course of the conversation, but Ginny was not to be put off.

'Still, I suppose there was no need for Hugo to have told you he'd remarried. You are divorced, after all.'

Mal turned then and looked at Ginny, who'd managed to land the low blow that Mal had been trying to dodge. Referring to her divorce was way below the belt.

'Well, I wouldn't want to make a new bride uncomfortable. Of course, I would ring ahead. Better still, I won't call at all.'

Ginny pretended to look horrified. 'Oh, but you must! Life hasn't been the same since you were banged up.' She waggled her head and said *banged up* in a silly voice as though to make a joke of the matter. Mal wondered if she grabbed Ginny's hair and slammed her head onto the counter whether her nose would break and she would need to get it fixed all over again. The idea of Ginny with blood streaming down her face made Mal smile momentarily.

'We'd love to see you, and I'm sure Minty wouldn't care at all. Girls that age don't, do they? I swear she isn't even in her thirties! Hugo said he really wanted children.'

Mal laughed out loud. 'Hugo wants to be a father? My God. Now, I've heard everything.'

'Oh, he gave us the impression that it was you that didn't want children,' said Ginny, 'didn't he, darling?'

Anthony shrugged, determined not to get involved.

'Certainly right on that score,' said Mal with a nod, not prepared to open an old wound. 'He said that was one of the reasons he wanted to get married to me, because we both saw our careers as more important.' Mal forced a nonchalant laugh. 'Well, good for him. If he's changed his mind, I wish him the very best. Although how he'll cope with being mistaken for his child's grandfather, I don't know. Hugo always was a vain old bugger. Unless that's changed as well?'

'Well, his hair is still jet black,' Tony-Too said with a gentle smile, and he pushed his glasses back up his nose, 'and Minty has him on a vegan diet.'

'No! What about the chateau entrecôte steak?' asked Mal, grateful that the subject was moving away from children.

'It's tofu all the way,' laughed Anthony, relieved that Mal was taking the news in such good spirits. As Mal continued to ring up the books, Anthony added a few to the pile, and eventually, even Ginny picked out a few bits and bobs as standby presents.

Eventually, they left the shop, with Ginny insisting that Mal call in next time she was in London, and Anthony hailing her as Mal the Magnificent. As the door closed, silence fell. She took a deep breath and steadied her shaking hand.

Hugo Bradley, her husband for thirty years, who had divorced, then sued her, had remarried, and was going to be a father. *Well, whoop-de-fucking-do.*

Chapter Twenty-Two

Another week had passed, and Mal had gone for a few dips in the sea and read some books, but failed to engage in the plots. She'd watched some TV, but all in all, the week was a listless one. And the problem was Hugo. She hadn't even read Lionel's diaries, not caring who'd killed him. Husbands weren't worth crying over.

The post had been sitting on the counter for half an hour, and even her sister's handwriting hadn't enticed her to open it.

The fact was that she had wanted children, but she and Hugo had discussed it, and he pointed out that neither of them wanted to sacrifice their career. She'd thought that once she was established, motherhood might be possible, but one day, Hugo came home and declared he'd had a vasectomy. And just like that, the decision was finalised. She couldn't complain. It was his body, after all, and she did very much want a career first. But once denied, she wondered about the road not taken.

She was moping, and knew it. She had no regrets, having loved her career. She adored her godchildren and nieces and nephews; now they were having little ones of their own, and Mal was part of that. She opened her sister's letter, knowing her voice would snap her out of it.

Hello you,

I should warn you that Hugo is trying to get your address. He rang me the other day. The effrontery! Told him to naff off—well, not actually naff off, but you can imagine what I did say.

Anyway, it appears, and I hate to say this, but he has remarried and wishes you to know. I suspect he wants your blessing, but honestly, I also think he wants to crow. Apparently, she's considerably younger, as if that's some sort of achievement. At our age, everyone is increasingly younger. Anyway, thought I'd better let you know that he has somehow found out you're down in Cornwall, and knowing him, he will find where you are.

Catch up soon,
Love, Me

Mal frowned. Her first instinct was to close the shop, but a parent-and-toddler group was due any minute. She'd decided that during January she would only open on Fridays and Saturdays. For the other five days, she would have to start thinking of other ways to make money because staring at an empty bookshop wasn't going to do it. Having flicked the kettle on in the back room, she pulled a new book from the shelves. Last night, she'd thrown her current book across the living room in a fit of utter annoyance. Ruth deserved so much better.

She'd just started a crime book in which the main character was reminding her of Nelson, and she wasn't sure she could continue. If this character was also unable to keep it in his pants, she would bail and head towards

Sherlock Holmes. She was fairly certain infidelity wouldn't be an issue there.

The overhead doorbell rang as Eden Jago came in, ushering little Sam ahead of her. Since her husband had been arrested for the murder of his school friend, and her mother-in-law had been charged with obstruction and was also in jail, Eden was now living up in the big house on her own. Mal wondered how much longer she would live in the village. Protecting Sam from the gossip about his father and grandmother would be impossible. Mal sighed. Children were always the second-hand victims. However, this little lad had a mother who loved him very much. Mal hoped that would be enough.

'Morning, Mal! Am I the first?'

Mal was about to say she was, when another three parents laden with prams and papooses exploded in through the door. The shop was soon buzzing with a cheerful hum as the children's section was quickly overrun with chatter.

The bell rang again, and a well-dressed woman walked in and looked around, frowning. She looked to be in her thirties, and her dress cleverly accentuated her pregnancy whilst not making her look dumpy. Still, with her height and model looks, the woman had likely never looked dumpy. Even at nine months along, she would probably look like the Venus de Milo.

'Hello,' Mal said, smiling. 'Have you come to join the reading club? There's no charge.'

161

Mal wondered if her other children were outside and if her partner was about to turn up. She wasn't a local, or at least she certainly hadn't been in the bookshop before. The woman looked at her again in confusion.

'No. My husband is here to meet someone. Only I think he must have the wrong place. Is there another bookshop in the village?'

'Just this one. Maybe your husband has got waylaid?'

She stared at Mal again and frowned.

'No, he's outside taking a call. You know what men are like. Always working!' She looked around again then smiled. 'I must have made a mistake. Excuse me.'

Just as she was about to leave, the door opened, and Hugo walked in. He hadn't aged a day and, in fact, looked excellent—tall, slim, still bloody good-looking. Even the dyed hair had been well done. Mal felt a surge of fear followed by a bitter loathing.

He walked up to the younger woman and kissed her on the cheek then looked around the shop. 'Is she here?'

The woman shook her head. 'How would I know?'

Hugo then gave Mal a second glance and recoiled. His failure to recognise her had given Mal enough time to recover from the shock of seeing her husband. *Ex-husband.* And his apparently pregnant new wife.

'Hello, Hugo.'

Hugo continued to stare at her, blinking.

'Have you taken a vow of silence, along with a new bride?'

He coughed and laughed. 'It is you. No one else would be so direct.' He shook his head. 'You look so different. Your hair.'

Mal tilted her head and raised an eyebrow. This man had fought to break their prenup, trying to take the house and all her savings following her guilty plea. When that didn't work, he tried to sue her instead. At the time, she was struggling with her own incarceration and had simply instructed her lawyers to fight him all the way. She'd been happy with a fifty-fifty split of their assets, even though she'd been the major contributor. The greed wasn't what hurt her, as much as the utter abandonment. They'd been a good team, and even without an abiding, passionate love, there had been respect and, she thought, friendship. Seeing him again brought all those horrible memories rushing back. The screaming rows and hurled vases, the court case and paparazzi, and finally, the prison cell. She'd let him down by going to jail, and didn't think she had the right to feel he'd let her down. She'd started it.

'I'll let you catch up,' said the woman nervously.

Hugo gave himself a quick jolt. 'Yes, of course. I'm sorry. Mal, I'd like to introduce—'

'Your daughter?'

'Malachite!'

Mal sighed. 'Yes, that was rude of me.' She thrust her hand out towards the younger woman. 'I'm Malachite Peck. I apologise. I was wrong-footed.'

The other woman smiled shyly and stroked her stomach before shaking Mal's hand. 'Araminta Bradley-Fox-Belling, and yes, I imagine this was a bolt from the blue, but Squidgy said you never wanted children?'

Mal bit her lip when she heard her oh-so-pompous husband referred to as Squidgy. 'Indeed. Although I thought he was also happy with that decision. The first I knew about his vasectomy, he came home one day, and just like that—snip.'

She stared at Hugo as Minty looked flustered and excused herself, dashing off to look at the shelves. The children's group were continuing to chat and laugh, but Mal knew damn well that several sets of ears would be listening in.

'What happened to your vasectomy, then? I'm assuming that the child is yours?'

'Jesus, Mal. Of course the child is mine. I had forgotten how sharp you can be.'

Mal sniffed. 'We used to call that honesty.'

'That's what you called it. And for what it's worth, I always wanted to be a father.'

Mal laughed loudly, and a few of the group looked up from the circle, then down again quickly.

'If I remember correctly, children are dirty, snivelling, boring and a waste of money. That's what you said, yes?'

'Clearly, I just needed to meet the right woman. I can think of nothing more exciting that continuing my line in union with Minty.'

Mal gagged theatrically, then smiled sweetly. 'I have no doubt you will make a wonderful father. You will be drawing your pension when they are potty training. Imagine. You'll have so much in common.'

'I don't remember you being so bitchy, Mal.'

'No, neither do I.'

'Prison life clearly has corrupted you. What a shame. I was hoping for a reconciliation, and yet here you sit, hidden away, crablike in the arse end of the country, licking your wounds. What a comedown for Mal the Magnificent, skulking in the shadows, scrabbling to make a penny.'

'Bitchiness seems contagious,' she drawled, and looked over at the poor woman, who'd moved even further away from the two of them, no doubt mortified. 'How old does she think you are, anyway? She seemed aghast when she discovered who I was. So old.'

'I imagine she was expecting someone more impressive, who hadn't let themselves go.'

Mal was ready to let rip, but felt the fight drain out of her. *What was the point?* 'Is there a reason you've come down, Hugo? Only I have work to do.'

He looked around the shop, sneering. 'I just wanted to come down and let you know that I've moved on and that there's no hard feelings between us.'

'There are no feelings of any sort.' She picked up her pen and looked up at him quizzically. 'If that's all…'

'Well, I was also wondering. I think the Richmond portfolio matures this year?'

Mal put the pen down and closed her eyes briefly, wondering how she'd lived so many years with that snake. Opening her eyes again, it was all she could do to keep a civil tongue in her head.

'It's been five years, Hugo. Are you still trying to live off my earnings?' As he was about to speak, Mal cut him off. 'The financial settlement was clear. The court case was clear, and I think I was also pretty clear. You do not get another single penny from me. Now, unless you have suddenly taken up reading, your business here is done.'

Hugo glared at her. The tip of his nose turned white, and a telltale flush appeared round his shirt collar. In all their time married, she'd rarely seen his anger, and why would she? Theirs had been a charmed existence. But her fall from grace and his loss of her income had brought out the very ugliest in him. Again, she was disappointed in how wilfully blind she'd been to his true personality.

'Minty, darling, let's go. We don't want to be late for our reservation at Gidleigh Park.'

He smirked at Mal and wrapped his arm around his young wife's waist and ushered her out of the shop without a backward glance. Mal stared out after the two of them and hoped that Minty had plenty of money. Hugo seemed to have almost run out of what he'd gained in the financial settlement.

Ignoring the glances from the reading group, she picked up her book and pretended to read, praying that her own face wasn't as flushed as Hugo's had been. By the time she'd read the same page four times, the group was beginning to break up. One or two of the parents brought books up to purchase. It wasn't much, but she didn't stay open to make money. She just felt that the parents and children needed the continuity—a chance to get out of the house and a change of scene, surrounded by books and warmth.

Eden pointed at the book Mal was failing to read. 'Oh, are you reading that? I love Tilly.'

Mal looked at her book cover and frowned. 'I don't know. I've only just started it. Is there some sort of romance between Tilly and Poe?'

She could hear Holmes calling, but the woman laughed.

'As if. Tilly would point out the statistical likelihood of that ever occurring would be as close to nil as possible, within acceptable margins.'

Mal nodded. 'I think I like the sound of this Tilly. I'll carry on reading.'

As Eden waxed lyrical about the series, one of her friends went over to the shelves and picked up a copy for herself.

'Let's compare notes next week,' she said, grinning at Mal. 'By the way, if I look half as good as you at your age, I reckon I'll be thrilled. You look amazing.'

A few of the others nodded their agreement, and one of the fathers laughingly pointed out that having her living here was like having a film star in the village. After that, they all proceeded to bad-mouth her ex-husband and point out how fabulous she looked. Eventually, she shooed them all out, smiling and feeling remarkably buoyed up.

Chapter Twenty-Three

By Sunday, the weather seemed to be on the turn. Mal looked out the window and was pleasantly surprised to see a pale blue sky. Grabbing her phone, she pulled up a weather app that suggested the day would be sunny. Although she'd learnt to mistrust Cornish forecasts, she decided to explore anyway. She would find some sunshine somewhere. *Fingers crossed. Maybe.* After yesterday's altercation with Hugo, she'd had a bad night's sleep and found herself worrying about money and what she was going to do with herself. A long walk was what she needed.

The problem with living by the sea was that forecasts were incredibly hard to predict unless a huge band of weather was affecting a large geographic area. In Cornwall, it got even trickier as the county was basically one long peninsula with the sea on either side, roughly eighteen miles apart. According to the locals, if rain was falling on one coast, they could just drive to the other side for blue skies. She hadn't tested the statement yet, but she'd learnt to take forecasts with a massive pinch of salt.

That said, today she was going to get out of the building and explore. When she was first released from prison, she'd been warned that prisoners could find leaving the building difficult. Mal didn't think she would be affected, but she was aware that she sometimes forgot that she didn't need permission to do something. Every time she'd found herself thinking like that, she put on a pair of shoes and headed out, even if it was tipping it down.

Despite being cold and wet, she soon began to appreciate the freedom and fresh air. The best tonic was swimming; nothing was more liberating or better at reminding one of how big the universe was. But swimming was harder in winter when the water was freezing and the waves often unmanageable.

She decided to test her new wellies, which were apparently good for long walks. Mal had been showered with useful and thoughtful gifts this Christmas, a pair of walking wellies being one of them. Finding a flask in the back of one of the cupboards, she made some coffee, then a sandwich, and added another egg to the water. She could have a boiled egg for lunch as well as breakfast.

Having discovered she had no suitable backpack, she eyed up her Louis Vuitton handbag. It wasn't the obvious choice, but it did have a shoulder strap, so she could sling it across her body.

An hour later, the weather looked set to stay fine. She headed out of the village on the coast path, rising higher and further away from the buildings, and up onto the cliffs standing between the sea and the farmland. As she passed the back of Jacques' garden, she looked up to see if there was any smoke coming from his chimney. That was another revelation of moving out of London: people making fires as part of their daily lives, not just on a weekend break to the Cotswolds. Jacques had a smoking hatch on the outside of his chimney, where he hung food and smoked it. A lot of life in the countryside struck Mal as very close to witchcraft. And honestly, the smoked salmon pâté he made was magical. That said, he wasn't due back until February, so there was no point in looking out for him.

Thinking of Jacques summoned memories of Hugo. The two men couldn't have been more dissimilar. Mal started to imagine Hugo smoking his own food or renovating a house, but thoughts of Hugo were banned that day, so she dismissed both men from her head and strode on.

The path was muddy in sections, but the grip on her boots could handle the rough terrain. Over the fields, a bird of prey hovered, and she took a quick photo, hoping to identify it later. At the moment, her skill level was Not Robin, Not Blackbird, Not Gull. But she was getting remarkably good at identifying the gulls after Bob heard her call them seagulls.

Apparently, no such bird existed, and she now knew quite a few of the individual species. In fact, a few of the most popular—the herring gulls—were flying above the sea to her left. Or was that a lesser black backed? She laughed to herself, and the birds all veered away from the madwoman with the fancy wellies and Louis Vuitton handbag striding across the Cornish cliffs.

After a few miles of undulating path, Mal started to look for somewhere to sit. The stiles were giving her more exercise than she'd anticipated, and, as much as it annoyed her, her hip was aching. The path was currently heading through a particularly nasty bush. It smelled of coconut ice and was covered in the prettiest of yellow flowers. However, when she went to pick some to take home, the thorns had drawn blood. She felt she was walking through a cactus plantation. Rounding a corner, she saw a beautiful sandy beach below, with a path leading down to it. To one side, she could see a narrow road winding past the beach with a small parking bay before it rose sharply again to a small hamlet on the brow of the hill.

Though the climb down meant a climb back up afterward, she was drawn to the water. And from what she could see, she wasn't alone, as some figures were walking along the water's edge.

Finally, Mal was on the sand, and her poor knees were relieved to be walking on a flat surface. She headed down to the rocks near the waves and cracked open her egg, only to discover it stank to high heaven.

'You smell.'

Mal snapped her head around and saw a small girl clambering up over some rocks towards her. She was barefoot and had her trousers rolled up to her knees, although the rolled fabric indicated she might've paddled out of her depth. She wore a dark-blue sweatshirt with a

Christmas tree on it, and a woolly hat was failing to keep her long hair in check.

'Actually, my egg smells.'

The little girl stared at her, then her egg, and nodded in agreement. She shoved a hand into her trouser pocket and pulled out a half-eaten cereal bar and offered it to Mal. 'You can have this if you're hungry. I don't like it.'

Mal blinked and wondered how to turn down such a charming offer. 'No, thank you. My mother says I mustn't accept food from strangers.'

Now it was the little girl's turn to blink, and she cocked her head, looking Mal up and down. 'Your mum must be very old.'

'Yes, I suppose she must be.' Mal looked around and could see a woman with a young lad walking towards them. She stood up to join them, keen that no one should take it amiss that she'd struck up a conversation with a strange child. As she got closer, she recognised Sophie and smiled as she waved at her. 'And is that your mother?'

'Yes. Do you know her?'

'I do, as it happens. She is a very clever woman and a nice person to boot.'

The little girl looked doubtful. 'Don't tell her about the cereal bar. She makes them herself, and Jack says I have to say I like them. He gets really cross with me always telling the truth.'

'The truth is tricky sometimes, isn't it?'

'I think it's easy, but no one else seems to understand it.'

The two parties had come within shouting distance, and Mal called over to Sophie as the little girl ran towards her.

'Hello! Isn't the weather lovely?'

'It is that,' said Sophie in agreement. 'I thought I'd make the most of it and bring the children out for a bit of fresh air.' She turned to her daughter. 'What did I tell you about running off?'

'Not to do it.'

'And what did you do?'

'I walked.'

As Mal tried not to snigger, Sophie glared at Mal in exasperation, then handed the little girl a bag. 'Fill this up.' She turned to the young lad that had followed her over. 'Jack, go with Nancy. I'll join you in a minute.'

As the two children ran back towards the rocks, Sophie rolled her eyes at Mal. 'I swear to God those children cause me more stress than any criminal.'

'I think that's the nature of motherhood.' They looked across at the two children, who were picking stuff off the rocks and putting them in the bag.

'What are they doing?' asked Mal.

'Mussel picking.'

'What for?'

'To eat, of course. That's tonight's dinner right there in front of us.'

Mal looked at Sophie with mild concern. 'For real?'

'Yes, of course, for real. Haven't you ever had mussels before?' As they walked towards the rocks, Sophie pointed at the fat mussels covering the rocks in their blue-black shells.

'I have, but I guess I just didn't really think about picking my own.'

'The ones you eat probably come from mussel farms out at sea, grown on long ropes. But these are just the same.'

Jack came clambering back over the rocks. 'Look at this one, Mum.' He held out a huge mussel, nearly the size of his palm. 'Reckon this is the biggest we've found?'

'Reckon so.'

He clambered back to his sister.

'What do they taste like?' asked Mal.

'Identical to the ones you eat in restaurants except better 'cos they're free.'

Having given her a few tips on the harvesting of mussels, Sophie suggested Mal should pick some for her tea.

'Do you know what? That's an excellent idea.' After checking with Sophie that she was picking the right size, she went to put one into her bag.

Sophie shrieked in horror, staring at Mal's Louis Vuitton bag. 'Are you mad? That looks like the genuine article!'

Mal shrugged. 'It is, but if I put them in my pockets, they'll leak all over me.'

After rummaging in her backpack, Sophie pulled out a plastic supermarket bag and flourished it at Mal. 'For the love of God, use this.'

Grinning, Mal took a few photos, then the two women settled into an easy pattern of picking and chatting.

'So, not on duty today?' Mal asked.

'Nope. I had to do New Year this year, so I got a bit of flexibility to cover the rest of the school hols.'

Mal was about to reply when her phone vibrated. She saw it was Imogen and rejected the call. Today was about simple pleasures. She didn't need any more drama right now. The investigation into Lionel's murder was dragging on, and the police seemed no closer to an arrest. According to Imogen, they were either incompetent or corrupt, depending on how she was feeling that day. It didn't help that the matter of the will was apparently in abeyance as the solicitors tried to work their way through the implications of a murder enquiry. The phone rang again and Mal shrugged, shaking her head apologetically at Sophie.

'Hang on.' Tapping her phone, she got as far as hello before she was cut off by a torrent of sobbing and garbled speech from the other end.

As Sophie called her children to her, Mal tried to understand what Imogen was saying. The shock of

Lionel's death and the suspicious nature of the situation had finally caught up to her.

'I know it's very shocking,' she told Imogen, 'but the police are doing everything they can.'

Sophie nodded in agreement.

'There's just so much blood!'

Mal paused. 'Blood?'

Sophie's head whipped around and stared at Mal.

'I don't know what to do. He's dead. The blood is everywhere! My baby is dead!'

'Whose blood, Imogen? Hang on—calm down. I'm with Sophie Taphouse. I'm handing you over to her.'

Mal handed the phone to Sophie, who was already walking back to the car, ushering her children ahead of her. 'Mrs Haverstock. This is PC Taphouse. Sophie. Whose blood is it?'

She paused, listening to the answer.

'Have you called an ambulance? Or the police?'

Even from a distance, Mal could hear Imogen wailing.

'Okay. I'm going to get someone to you now, and I'll be with you shortly. Don't touch anything and don't let anyone into the library. Here's Mal. I'll be with you in a minute.' After handing the phone back to Mal, she scooped her children into her car and started strapping them in.

'Imogen, it's Mal again. Listen. Call your solicitor and don't say anything until he arrives. Do you understand?'

As she hung up, Sophie gave her a dirty look. 'We're not all bent, you know? And she could be guilty.'

'Gut feeling? She doesn't strike me as a killer.'

'No, but that's not your job, Mal.'

Mal stepped back, knowing she'd offended a woman whose company she admired. 'I know. But she's terrified and has just discovered her favourite son has been murdered. For someone like your boss, she's an easy target.'

Sophie slammed the car door and got into the front, then looked up at Mal. 'Sorry, Malachite. I have to go. I need to drop the children off and then get up to the house. And for what it's worth, Hemingstone isn't brilliant, but he works in a team who work bloody hard serving their community.'

As the car sped away through the rough car park and out onto the small lane, Mal felt the joy of the day slither away. Sophie had looked so fed up with her. Turning away from the car park, she headed onto the coastal path and trudged home, her Louis Vuitton bag over her shoulder and a bag of mussels swinging from her other hand.

So Algernon was dead as well—two dead bodies and a will in dispute. If she'd had to make a guess at Lionel's killer, she'd have picked Algernon. He had been desperate to know about the will. Mal had seen that sort of financial desperation before. Maybe he thought the will had already changed and he would inherit everything. The only thing he was inheriting now was the kingdom of God, and she had doubts about that as well.

Chapter Twenty-Four

Back at the house, Mal struggled out of her boots, placed the mussels in water as Sophie had advised, and felt glum. The two women in the newsagents the previous day had been overtly hostile. Sophie was mad at her. She had no real friends in town, and the only woman who kept calling her was ghastly and at the centre of a double murder. She wished Jacques was there.

'Chin up, Mal,' she told herself, as she looked at her reflection in the kitchen window. 'No one said this was going to be easy.'

When she was about to settle down and write some letters, her phone rang again, and she saw it was Imogen. Upon answering, she was surprised to hear a young man's voice.

'Malachite? It's Jasper Haverstock. My grandmother won't talk to anyone without you being present. Not the police or us or anyone. The solicitor is coming from Truro and has got stuck in a traffic accident. It's making a difficult situation dreadful. Can I come and get you?'

Mal shrank, thinking about how mad Sophie must be. 'I'll come up.'

'No need. I'm actually parked outside your shop.'

The last thing Mal wanted to do was get any further involved, but the situation was partly her fault. She'd advised Imogen not to talk until the solicitor got there. She just didn't think she would take it so literally.

Groaning, she slipped on a pair of shoes and her padded jacket, ran a brush through her hair, then realised it was still tangled from the walk and grabbed a hat instead. When she hurried down to the front of the shop, Jasper was indeed waiting outside and she slid into the car.

'Jasper, I'm so sorry. Has your uncle really died?'

His knuckles were white against the steering wheel as he kept his eyes on the road, not turning his head as he spoke.

'He's dead. Granny found him this morning on the library floor. Back of his head covered in blood. The police think it's a robbery, but without any help from my grandmother they are struggling to proceed. My aunt is having hysterics; the cousins are bawling their heads off; Father is on his way back from London; and my brother and sister are trying to calm our cousins down.'

'Are you okay?'

Jasper shot a quick glance across at her, then looked back through the windscreen.

'Bit shaken. Lot shaken, actually, but if I don't stop, I'm fine. Granny found him. Did I say that already? And she won't talk to Sophie. Then Sophie's boss turned up, and a set of crime scene officers arrived. And Granny keeps shouting at everyone to get out. She's got blood on her shoes and started swearing when the police tried to take them from her.' He paused and rubbed his face, his voice trembling. 'Sorry. It's such a shock.'

'Of course it is. Hopefully, I can help calm your grandmother down. She's had to endure two awful events on top of each other.'

They pulled up in front of the house, where a policeman flagged him down.

'I live here. Malachite Peck is my guest.'

The policeman spoke into his walkie-talkie, then waved them through. Inside the house, Mal could hear children crying from upstairs and two women shouting from the direction of the drawing room.

'That's my aunt and stepmother. Poor Daisy is beside herself. She's been trying to get Granny to talk. There has been a lot of shouting.'

'She should be with her children,' muttered Mal, then followed Jasper into the drawing room.

As they entered, all eyes turned towards them, and Imogen jumped up and ran towards Mal. Her hair had fallen out of her chignon, and messy clumps hung over her face. As Jasper had said, her shoes were covered in blood, and the dark liquid marked the cream carpet as she rushed towards Mal.

'I didn't speak to anyone. I did what you said.'

Mal tried to avoid everyone's glare. She hadn't anticipated that Imogen would collapse like this, or that she would take her words so literally.

'Come on, let's sit down. Jasper, could we have a fresh pot of tea? Maybe some biscuits, hmm?' She held Imogen's elbow and gently steered her back to the sofa.

'Now, the crime scene officers need your shoes, so slip them off.'

Imogen sat down and quietly removed her shoes. An officer picked them up and bagged them, then left the room. Mal turned and looked at Inspector Hemingstone, who was clearing his throat, champing at the bit. 'Could we have some tissues please?' Removing her shoes had transferred some of the blood onto her hands, and Mal really didn't want Imogen to start focusing on her son's blood. Sophie came forward and handed Mal some wet wipes, and Mal gently started to clean Imogen's fingers, holding her shaking hand in hers. 'Does anyone know when Mrs Haverstock's solicitor will arrive?' asked Mal.

Sophie looked across at Hemingstone, who nodded. 'He's coming from Truro. They've said he should be here within the next half an hour.'

'Half an hour, during which we are losing precious time!' said Hemingstone.

'Inspector, please,' said Mal. 'I tell you what, Imogen. Why don't we let the inspector here try to get some facts under his belt? No one is getting arrested.'

'I'll be the judge of that,' said Hemingstone.

'Well, we'll just wait for the solicitor then, shall we?' snapped Mal. She glared at the inspector until he sighed.

'No one's getting arrested right now.'

'Well then, Imogen? Let's see if we can sort out what has happened.'

Imogen nodded, and the atmosphere in the room visibly relaxed. Jasper came back into the room, and Sophie took the tray from him and poured Imogen a cup, then retired to the corner of the room to watch everyone. DI Williams took out his notebook, and the inspector sat down opposite Imogen and Mal. Jasper moved over to the fireplace and added a log to the flames.

'Now, Mrs Haverstock. If you could just take us through this morning. Please, just tell us everything you remember.'

Good grief, thought Mal. Imogen really had taken her advice to heart. She hadn't meant for her to take a vow of silence.

'Very well.' Imogen looked sideways at Mal, who nodded.

'Finally!' Daisy sobbed, and Mal grimaced at how badly her simple advice had gone.

Imogen smoothed her hair with a shaky hand, then took a deep breath. 'I came down for breakfast at the normal time.'

'And that is?'

'Ten. We always eat a little later on Sundays.'

Mal looked across at Hemingstone, who encouraged her to continue.

'Did you see anyone?'

'No, Daisy was up ahead of me. She was taking the children into Truro for the day.'

'I came back when Jasper called me,' wailed Daisy. 'Oh, my poor children, to be orphaned so young!'

Jocasta leant across and tapped her sister-in-law on the knee. 'You're not dead, so they're not orphans.'

At this blunt pronouncement, Daisy wailed again, and Jasper came across with a cup of tea, glaring at his stepmother.

'Carry on, Granny, you're doing great. Did you see anyone?'

'No. You'd obviously been up and about as well. Your father is in London, talking to the solicitors, and the rest of your family weren't around.'

'Did you see any staff?' Hemingstone asked.

'Oh, them. No, in fact, I rang the bell, but no one replied. The room was chilly, and I wanted to know why.'

'And who were you expecting to answer the bell?'

'Chloe, or maybe Dougie. Sometimes the kitchen is empty, though. Cigarette breaks, I imagine.'

'Okay. Well, we'll be talking to all the staff in the house shortly. Now, what did you do next?' continued Hemingstone.

Mal patted Imogen's hand, knowing that the hardest part was yet to come.

The woman blinked, trying to gather her thoughts. 'Well, it really was quite chilly, so I got up to see if someone had left a door open. The staff are forever leaving doors open, and with the children in the house as well, it's like Piccadilly Circus here at the moment.' She looked across at her two daughters-in-law, then back at the inspector. 'I could actually feel a breeze coming from Lionel's library, so I opened the door.' She broke off and shuddered.

When Imogen grasped Mal's hand, she gave it a quick squeeze to tell her she was doing brilliantly. 'Now, Mrs Haverstock, tell me what you saw the moment you opened the door.'

Imogen closed her eyes, and large tears rolled miserably down her cheeks, cutting a path through her make-up. Choking off a sob, she took a deep breath. 'The patio door was wide open, and I walked over to close it. I could see some footprints on the grass etched out in the frost. And it looked like whoever walked that way stopped to play with the dogs as well.'

Hemingstone looked across at Williams. 'Did we get photos of that?'

'No, the frost had burnt off by the time we arrived.' He turned to Sophie. 'Can you inform SOCO? They may catch something.'

Sophie nodded sharply and left the room. At least Mal wasn't to blame for that. She'd told Imogen to call the police right away.

'What did you do then?' Mal asked.

Imogen took a deep breath. 'I pulled the patio door closed and turned around, and I saw a pair of feet sticking out from behind the desk...' She broke down, sobbing loudly. For a few moments, the room was quiet as Jasper came and sat by his grandmother and hugged her tightly.

As Imogen's sobs died down, Jasper smiled at her and tucked her hair behind her ears. 'You are being really incredible, Granny. I'm so proud of you.'

That was all the boost Imogen needed, and, patting Jasper's knee, she turned to look at the detective.

'Now, I'm sorry to be insensitive,' said Hemingstone, 'but did you move the body in any way?'

'The body! Do you mean my son? Of course I moved him. I tried to revive him, but there was so much blood.'

She started crying again, and Mal looked around for a tissue to hand her.

'He was so cold,' Imogen said, choking her words out. 'He hates the cold.'

Numbed by Imogen's grief, Mal stared in horror around the room. Sophie stepped forward with a box of tissues for both Daisy and Imogen, having rejoined the room.

'Then what?' asked Hemingstone, earning a glare from Sophie as she tried to calm the women down.

'That's when I heard my grandmother,' said Jasper. 'I came into the room, saw Uncle Algernon, and called the police. There was a candlestick lying on the carpet beside him. It's one of a pair but I couldn't see the other one. Then I called Aunt Daisy. I didn't say what had happened. I didn't want her to crash, just told her to get home. Then I tried to find my father. I didn't know he'd gone to

London yesterday. He's on his way back now. Anyway, that's it. Granny called her friend Malachite here, and then Sophie was with us very quickly.'

'Did you notice anything unusual in the room?'

'It was colder than usual.' He paused as though to say something else, but he stopped and shook his head. 'But I suppose that makes sense if the patio door was open. We had quite a hard frost last night.'

Williams' walkie-talkie crackled, and all eyes turned his way.

'The solicitor is here,' he said.

'Can you get him?' said Hemingstone. 'Explain I'll be wanting to talk to him about the will as well. We're looking at two murders, and I want to know who benefits.'

Chapter Twenty-Five

With the arrival of the solicitor, Mal extricated herself from the room and was escorted to the front door by Sophie.

'Look, I'm sorry about earlier,' she said. 'I was just cross. I'd been looking forward to a day with the children.'

'Entirely my fault,' said Mal, quickly. 'I had no idea Imogen would take me so literally. It's just that I spent time with women who incriminated themselves rightly and wrongly, and the police never looked for an alternative solution.'

Sophie looked ready to argue, but sighed instead. 'Inspector Hemingstone isn't bent, Mal.'

'No, but he's hardly one of nature's brightest minds.'

'I know, but do you think women like Imogen Haverstock get treated the same way as some of the other women you served time with?'

Mal thought about Tina, who'd left school at fourteen, pregnant and in foster care. And Chelsea, beaten black and blue by her partner for not earning enough on the streets, until she snapped. Those women had no voice and no clue of how to use the system to protect themselves. Imogen would never be treated how they were.

'You don't think she's guilty, though, do you?' asked Mal.

'Can't tell. She's distraught, right enough. But she would be if she accidentally killed him.'

'She's tiny!'

'What if she shoved him, and he slipped back and hit his head on the desk?'

'Is that how it happened?'

'No idea. SOCO haven't let us in yet.'

'But surely, if that was the case, she'd have called for an ambulance?' said Mal. Imogen as the killer didn't seem likely.

'I agree,' said Sophie. 'And if there was a candlestick on the ground beside him, and a second one is missing, it's quite probable that he startled a burglar.'

Mal thought two deaths in the same house, and so close together, had to be related. Deciding not to push her luck any further, she apologised again and headed off around the back of the house and towards the little lane that led down to the village.

Could it have been as simple as Algernon falling backwards? Had Imogen simply witnessed the scene of a dreadful accident? But then, what about the footprints in the frost? And the missing candlestick: was this a botched burglary? As Mal walked, she looked towards the lawn at the back of the house. She would've been tempted to have a closer look, but a team of SOCOs were working there, and she knew they would send her away with a flea in her ear. Plus, Sophie would be furious. She could just picture the woman looking out of the patio doors and glaring.

Mal shuddered, then grinned to herself. That young woman took no prisoners when she thought someone was messing around with her precious law. Besides which, the grass was all green now. Whatever Imogen had seen in the frost was long gone.

A breeze picked up, and Mal zipped up her jacket. Her hat was most welcome, but she would've killed for gloves, a scarf, and a pair of boots as well. But she would be home soon, anyway. When she was nearly through the gates, she heard barking and saw Max and Milo bounding across the lawn towards her. She looked over at the gate. Could she run there in time? She was tempted to try, but in her dithering, she wasted too much time, and the two dogs were upon her. However, their tails were wagging as they bounced around, and although her heart was racing, she didn't think they would bite her. And if they did, the SOCO team had clocked her existence and could come to her rescue if need be—or at least scoop up her remains.

'I don't have any treats this time.'

She gingerly held one hand out, which was duly sniffed, then ignored, but Milo promptly fell on the ground and threw his legs in the air.

'Well, I can certainly oblige a tummy rub.'

Goodness, was her voice shaking as much as her hand? They really were very large dogs.

'Hello! Are you lost?'

Mal was about to pet the dog, but at the sound of the new voice, the dog leapt up and raced with his brother over to the gate, where a young man was closing it behind himself. He was properly tall, although his skinniness emphasised his height, and he had a pleasant face lacking any remarkable features. Mal thought he might look the same decades later, his brown hair turned grey. Maybe he would go bald, his nose and ears sprout hairs, and he would stoop: but at present, he was a fresh-faced young man with his whole life ahead of him, his thoughts laid out across his face.

'The dogs clearly like you,' he said as he rubbed their ears and fed each one a treat. 'Normally, they bark and snarl at strangers.'

Mal straightened her clothes and hoped her voice had settled down. 'I've met them before, with Dougie. He said they were softies most of the time.'

'They are that, only,' he frowned quickly, 'don't mention the treat. Dougie says we're not to spoil them. And I only give them one treat, first thing. They know the rest of the day they get nothing from me. They're right smart are these two. Not like Moonlight. He used to follow me around all day, nudging at my pocket. No brains whatsoever.'

He laughed, and Mal warmed to the young lad immediately.

'I'll keep your secret, don't worry.'

'Thanks. Barry is always having to remind me of stuff. I could tell him I forgot. I do that a lot. Say I forget things. I don't. I just say I do. It's easier that way. People tell me not to do stuff, which makes no sense. So I nod my head and do it anyways. Much easier to say I forgot later on.'

Mal thought about that for a moment. 'If people explain why you can't do a thing, do you then do as they've asked?'

'Yes, sometimes. If what they say makes sense.'

'And if what they say doesn't make sense?'

'Then I do it anyways.'

'Do you ever explain why what they say makes no sense?'

'No,' He laughed loudly, the dogs barking happily with him. 'No one pays any attention to Lachlan Jones.'

'Doesn't that bother you?'

He looked at her curiously. 'Why would it?'

God, thought Mal, *to be so happy in one's own skin that you don't care about the opinions of others.*

Deciding that the conversation was at an end, he turned to the dogs and said, 'Bed,' and the two dogs ran back towards the stable block.

'I'm afraid we're closed today, though, on account of dead Mr Haverstock. Can I show you to the car park? I work here.'

Mal shook her head. He was about to get the surprise of his life when he heard another Mr Haverstock had just died.

'It's okay. I was just walking back to the village.' She pointed towards the lane and then, feeling it was appropriate to offer some sort of condolence, she said how sorry she was to hear of Mr Haverstock's passing.

'I suppose it depends which one you mean. Old Mr Haverstock was nice. Always stopped for a chat, and sometimes he gave me treats for the dogs, it was our secret. He told me not to tell Dougie, either.' He grinned conspiratorially. 'Young Mr Haverstock, though, wasn't as nice. There's not so much blood when old people die, is there? Maybe it starts to run out. Do you think I have more blood than you?'

Mal blinked at the odd thought.

'Young Mr Haverstock had loads. Mrs Mullen is going to be so cross. She gets proper mad at me if I walk mud on the floors. I don't know what she'll say about blood. Not that she'd ever tell Mr Haverstock off. He probably can't hear her now anyway, even if she did.'

As Mal listened to Lachlan's odd approach towards death, something struck her. He already knew Algernon was dead and had seen the blood, but that didn't make sense.

'I thought you just arrived.'

'I did. You saw me walk through the gate.' He looked puzzled, then smiled at her. 'You must have been concerned about the dogs and not noticed me.'

'No, I saw you. But if you have only just got here, how did you know about the blood?'

'Oh, I was here earlier as well.'

'And you saw Mr Algernon Haverstock?'

'Yes.'

'Did you tell anyone?'

194

'No.' He frowned again, like he had about the dog treats. 'You won't tell anyone, will you? Only, I shouldn't have done it.'

'Done what?' Mal looked across to the SOCO team. She couldn't believe this strange young man was about to confess to a murder, but she suddenly felt very vulnerable.

'I went to close the doors.'

'The patio doors?'

'Yes. Mr Algernon Haverstock told me I wasn't allowed anywhere near the family side of the house. I couldn't even touch the bloody walls. He didn't say *bloody,* though. He used a different word when I tried to get him to clarify what I couldn't look at or touch.'

'And he said this to you this morning or last night?'

'That would be tricky on account of his being dead.'

Mal knew she should call for Sophie, but she was too curious to stop right now. 'Explain what happened.'

'When?'

'This morning, the first time you got here.'

He thought about it, then nodded his head, some internal decision having been decided.

'I woke early because of the cold and wanted to check on the seedlings, so I walked up here, and when I came through the gate, I noticed the patio doors over there were open. So I decided I had better close them. The sun was rising, and the grass was a lovely white. Someone had walked across the lawn, and I thought they'd be in a lot of trouble from Barry cos he says it damages the lawn. When

I was a boy, I used to make pictures all the time until he explained why I couldn't. But he showed me another lawn I could walk on, the one over by the wild meadow. Do you know it?'

Mal shook her head, desperately willing the young man to stay on track. 'So how did you get to the doors?'

'I walked along the patio. Even though I'm not allowed to even walk on the bloody courtyard or flagstones or even the bloody gravel.'

'More of Algernon's instructions?'

'Yes, that's right.' He gave her a cheeky grin. 'Anyway. I don't normally ignore those instructions because he was pretty cross when he spoke to me. But I thought he'd be even crosser if he woke up and found his house was freezing cold because someone had left the doors wide open.'

'So what did you do?'

'I went to close the door and then saw him lying there. His eyes were wide open, and there was blood around his head. I knew he'd be really cross with me seeing him like that and touching the door. So I left it open and headed back home.'

'Did you check if he was dead?'

'Go into the house? Not bloody likely. I reckon if I'd done that, he'd have risen up and killed me himself, and then there'd be two of us dead there on the carpet.' He laughed again, struck by the ridiculousness of the idea.

'You don't seem very sad.'

'He wasn't very nice.'

'Or shocked?'

'People die all the time. So do animals. And seedlings. I'd better go and check on them. That would be sad, if the frost got them as well.'

'Why do you think the frost got Algernon?'

'Well, his blood was a sort of white shade. So it was obvious the frost had got him.'

Mal tried to think of how best to proceed. The young man was a key witness and had probably also left prints on the door handle. He would need to be eliminated as a suspect. But whilst she didn't think he was responsible for the death, she wasn't sure Hemingstone wouldn't see him as a perfect scapegoat. God knows Lachlan wasn't displaying any pity or sorrow.

'Do you know Sophie Taphouse?'

'The police officer?'

'That's her. She's up at the house. Could you find her and tell her what you told me?'

Lachlan thought about that and nodded. 'Yes, okay.' He walked off towards the stables.

Mal called out after him, 'Lachlan. It's important. This can't be one of those things where you say yes but don't do it.'

He frowned, then shrugged. 'Okay.'

'Lachlan, I'm going to phone Sophie and let her know you are on your way.'

197

The young man frowned and walked back towards Mal. He looked troubled, and she was sorry to be the cause of it.

'But I'm going to get in so much trouble if I do that.'

'No, you're not. The police need to know what happened. His family needs to know. You can help. They don't know about the door or about which way the footprints led.'

'Can't you tell them? Say what I told you.'

'I'm afraid it doesn't work like that. They'll need to hear from you first-hand. But you know Sophie. She's lovely. She'll make sure everything is okay.'

Lachlan looked dubious.

'Mother Kitto said I should always avoid the police. She said I should never work at Liggan. She said no good comes of rich folk.'

Mal paused. 'Is Mother Kitto Margaret Kitto? Older lady, old-fashioned dress?' As he nodded along, Mal groaned internally. 'Well, is she right about everything?'

A small grin crept back onto Lachlan's face. 'No. But don't tell her I said that. Every year, she says the tourists will be the death of her, but every year they come back, and every year, she's still alive.'

'And you like Sophie, don't you?'

'Yes, she's always nice. Although a bunch of us were out once and got a bit daft after a few pints, and she shouted at all of us until we went to bed. And the following morning, she came and knocked on all our doors and marched us down to the harbour and made us pick up every bit of litter on the beach. Connor said she couldn't make him, so she whispered in his ear, and he picked up more than the rest of us.'

Mal would have to ask her about that incident later, but she liked the fact that Lachlan had friends and wasn't picked on for his oddness.

'I am sorry about this, Lachlan. It's not nice when people ask you lots of questions and make you feel bad, but the family need to find out what happened to him. They'll be ever so grateful.'

Lachlan snorted. 'Have you met them? They aren't the grateful sort. 'Cept for Jasper. He's nice.'

'There you go. Do this for Jasper.'

Lachlan nodded reluctantly and headed slowly towards the stables. Mal walked through the gate, then called Sophie and explained what had just happened.

'Oh God. Why did it have to be Lachlan? Leave it with me. And thank you, Mal. Honestly, don't worry. If he's innocent, he'll be fine.'

Relieved, Mal continued downhill. She hadn't warmed to Imogen, but the woman's distress was so raw that Mal felt sick to the stomach. Could she have killed her son? Mal didn't think so, but who had?

Chapter Twenty-Six

Mal was nearing the village when her phone buzzed. She read the text message from Sophie, and her heart slumped:

-Sorry, can't call. Lachlan is heading to Truro to give a statement and have his fingerprints recorded.

Mal stared at the screen in fury. She'd done the right thing. Lachlan had done the right thing. *And for what?* Frustrated, she responded:

-Is he okay?

-Yes. He was quite curious about the whole business. He's rung his girlfriend, she's going to meet him there.

-Has he been arrested?

Mal waited as the three little dots bounced for what felt like an eternity, then the next message came through:

-No. Although you were right, Hemingstone took one look at him and decided it was case closed. Williams pointed out that, so far, it's circumstantial and motiveless. Especially if you factor in the Lionel Haverstock's murder.

-Won't stop Hemingstone.

-Agreed.

As the dots bounced again, Mal decided she would head into Truro, offer her own statement, and be there to help Lachlan if she could:

-I'm going to Truro.

That appeared to stop Sophie in her tracks as the next three messages came thick and fast:

-**No! Don't do that!**

-**Really, Mal. Stay home. You will be asked to corroborate his statement, but he's in good hands.**

-**I've arranged for a solicitor I know to sit in with him. I'm going to owe him big time, but he's the best at what he does.**

-**Who?**

-**Jones is the best in the county. Local boy, often works in London but prefers it down here. Anyway, don't tell anyone I've called him. My sarge will go ballistic.**

-**Why?**

-**Because no one gets arrested when he's sitting beside them.**

-**He can prove Lachlan's innocence?**

-**Don't be naïve.**

Mal bristled and pursed her lips. *Naïve* was hardly an adjective commonly used to describe her. Sophie's text continued:

-**His job isn't to prove Lachlan's innocence. His job is to prove the police haven't got sufficient evidence to make a case.**

Mal grumbled to herself and walked into the village. Sophie was, of course, correct. Mal replied:

-**Okay. When will someone want my statement?**

-God knows. They'll be in touch. It won't be me—conflict of interest. I'm not even on this case, just in the wrong place at the wrong time. In the meantime, go home and enjoy those mussels. I'm doing mine with chorizo and red peppers. I'll let you know when Lachlan is out. Bye.

Mal put the phone back into her pocket and walked through the village and out onto the harbour wall. She sat on one of the bollards and watched the waves roll in until the cold seeped into her bones. Standing up, she slapped her bottom to warm herself.

'I'd pay good money for that!' a man shouted from the upper harbour wall.

Shielding her eyes from the sun, she glared up at the speaker. 'Bob Yates! Did your mother teach you to speak to women like that? And what would your wife say? That's right. Nothing. Because you don't have one. I wonder why?'

Instantly, his smile collapsed, and he rummaged in his pockets, pulling his jumper away from his neck. 'I was just joking!'

'Well, I'm not in the mood for jokes.'

He mumbled an apology and walked on, his hands stuffed into his pockets. Mal winced. In the city, challenging such attitudes had been easy. Often, older men were just struggling to come to terms with a world in which they no longer had the right to offend and abuse others at will. Most of the time, their insults weren't even deliberate, just a total lack of awareness that the other party might have autonomy over their own opinions. She was sharper with the younger men, who had no excuse.

Here in the village, though, the system was much tighter, a closed loop. Bob hadn't meant any offence, and she'd ripped his head off. He was in the wrong, but unwittingly. She was in the right, but had dealt with it badly. She sighed. Village life was the hardest thing she'd ever tried to navigate. Today she'd upset two lovely people, Sophie and Bob, and managed to get a charming if odd young man escorted to the local police station.

She decided the best thing to do was to write it off. Put her feelings down on paper, and thinking of the mussels, she knew exactly who to write to.

Chapter Twenty-Seven

Dear Jacques,

A day of disasters, I'm afraid, mostly of my own making. And one murder that wasn't.

I feel like a thin-skinned fool, and honestly, that is not a feeling I am happy with, although it is merited. I snapped at Bob, and whilst I can cope with his annoyance, I was sorry to have angered Sophie. She is a lovely young woman and a credit to the police force. I wish there were more like her. Maybe the police force should stop employing the same sort all the time and start employing more like her.

The murder was that of Algernon Haverstock, Lionel and Imogen's younger son. The police are obviously all over this as it was a rather violent death, unlike Lionel's, but two murders under one roof... It is very alarming.

They are an awful family, all ready to attack each other over the state of the will. And I know I'm dreadful for saying it, but I find them fascinating. It's astonishing how badly some people behave when they should pull together. For the first time, I felt dreadfully sorry for Imogen. The depth of her pain sucks everyone into it. True grief is like that, isn't it? An all-consuming abyss of pain.

After dinner, I'm going to read a bit more of Lionel's diary. I need to return it to Jasper, but I think right now, that's the least of anyone's concerns.

If I'm utterly honest—and I feel like I can be honest with you— I would be less interested in the family if I wasn't so bored. I need a hobby during these dead months. I've never had one, though, so I'm not sure what to do. Some people, yourself included, I suppose, go abroad. The couple from the fudge shop spend three months in the Philippines, which I imagine appeals to them. I'm enjoying taking photographs. Maybe I could do something with that?

Anyway, I'm now going to cook mussels for the first time. I am following a Jane Grigson recipe, so I should be fine. Nice and simple—white wine, butter and garlic. It will be good to get to the end of the day having done something right.

Well, I shall find something, no doubt.

Yours sincerely,

Mal

p.s. It is now the morning. It appears that cooking will not be my hobby. I started to read Lionel's journal, got carried away, and burnt the mussels dry. My home now smells like the harbour at low tide... if the harbour had also burnt dry.

Mal put her pen down and grinned to herself. The smell was truly awful. Rain was falling heavily outside, but all her windows were still open as she tried to waft away the acrid smell from the previous night's disaster. The shells and the pan had all been deposited into a black bin bag and taken out to the corner bin sacks, ready for collection by the binmen. She could only thank her lucky stars that today was a collection day.

Lionel's journal had been fascinating, and she'd placed strips of paper into the book to mark each section she wanted to reread. A mystery was unfolding, and she couldn't help thinking it had some bearing on current events.

Chapter Twenty-Eight

Friday morning, and the shop was open but also empty. The parent-and-toddler group had come and gone, and the shop was silent. Every single one of them had asked about Algernon's murder, and their theories were as wild as they were numerous. A double murderer was loose at Liggan Hall, and people wondered who would be next. Talk of a mysterious thief was also rife, and people were speculating about what hidden treasures he may have escaped with. Once again, the sunken treasure ship, rose to the surface; lost gold had an unrelenting pull on anything mysterious happening in the village.

Mal refused to be drawn into the gossip, but she couldn't help wondering about it herself. She wished she'd met Lionel. The villagers appeared to respect him, though his family did not. Yet in his own words, he struck Mal as an enthusiastic, carefree soul.

She was losing herself in the blossoming romance between young Lionel and a girl named Pearl. What Mal had established so far was that Lionel was utterly head over heels in love with the girl, and she appeared to be a fellow amateur scientist.

Sitting down behind the counter, she continued to read Lionel's diary. So far that morning, she'd taken the princely sum of £2.75 for a greeting card. The previous day, Lionel had spent five guineas on a new car. She and

Lionel were living in different worlds yet love was apparently what kept the world—and the pages—turning.

August '65

Have dodged the family trip to the Highlands for the twelfth. I have convinced the folks that I need to stay here and oversee the harvest. I may have mentioned that Carole Carter was spending summer in Cornwall. Mother's eyes practically lit up at the thought that I may be preparing to propose.

Of course, I won't be giving her a bell, let alone a ring. That would be rude. How could I give her any expectation of an alliance when I have the wonderful Pearl to entertain me?

My diary is a poor repository for my feelings, but what other recourse have I when our meetings are so infrequent and I am unable to write to her.

I walked across the cliffs today and watched a pod of dolphins playing in the bay. I wonder if she observed them at the same time. Poets talk of lovers staring at the same moon, whereas Pearl and I fix our eyes upon the seas.

The door swung open, and Mrs Kitto marched into the empty shop, startling Mal with her presence. Her handbag hung like a cosh from her wrist, and her face promised violence.

'So, this is where you're hiding, is it?'

'In my shop?' Mal drawled, sensing an incoming fight.

'Your sort should head back to wherever it is you come from. Leave us honest folk to live our lives in peace and quiet. Go make your money elsewhere.'

Mal had been in town less than half a year and had already witnessed three murders. Cornwall didn't strike her as particularly peaceful. And with the jabbering of the crow in front of her, it wasn't particularly quiet either.

'Do you have a point to make? Otherwise, do you think you could leave? You're stopping me from making oodles of cash.'

'Think you're funny, do you? Throwing poor Lachlan to the wolves like that. He's one of God's special children, he is. You should know better.'

'Give over. Lachlan isn't special. He's just a bit different. Any fool can see he's on the spectrum. Doesn't mean you should mollycoddle him.'

'*Mollycoddle*! The nerve of you. I have always looked out for that boy.'

'That man. Who has a girlfriend, mates, a job, and an interesting way of looking at the world. Why treat him like a child?'

'Because he is one of God's children.'

'Oh, spare me. You should be proud of him. Yesterday, he stepped up and helped the police try to uncover a murder.'

'Which had nothing to do with him,' spat Mrs Kitto.

'Except he witnessed an important clue. And because of that, the police will be closer to catching the actual killer of Lionel and Algernon Haverstock.'

'Who cares about that? Maybe the killer had a point.'

Mal raised an eyebrow at the old woman, who paused and realised her words fell short of the Christian values she was spouting only seconds earlier.

'Maybe there's something you know that the police should also be aware of?' Mal smiled sweetly.

'You are the very devil. I've said what I came to say. Stay away from Lachlan, and if you know what's good for you, you'll stay away from Golden altogether.'

Turning, she made to sweep back out of the shop, and Mandz, one of the girls that worked with Collette in the hairdresser, jumped sharply out of her way.

'Morning, Mother.'

She looked up at the young woman and huffed.

'Don't *Mother* me. I saw you throwing up in the gutter the other night. You have strayed far from the path.'

She stormed away along the cobbled lane, and Mandz turned and grinned at Mal. 'If I had strayed much more, I'd have ended up in the bushes!' She laughed and pulled her purse out of her pocket. 'You said my book had come in?'

Mal nodded and pulled the order from the stock whilst trying to shake off Mrs Kitto's words.

'Bet that was about Lachlan. He was telling us all about it last night.'

'Is he very mad at me?'

Mal didn't give two figs for Old Mother Kitto, but she hadn't wanted to throw Lachlan to the police. It was just the right thing to do.

'He loved it. Didn't have to buy a pint all night.'

'She called him one of God's special children.'

Mandz stuck her fingers in her mouth and pretended to gag. 'She's a patronising old cow. Never had her own kids and interferes with everyone else's. Mum said when she was the school nurse, she used to be a proper nightmare. Then she got involved in the church as well, the only place you can guarantee not bumping into her is the pub. Any of them.' She laughed again, tucking her new book under her arm. 'Lachlan's just a bit odd. That's all. And so what?'

She raised her chin slightly, and Mal nodded. A place like this, you probably all just learnt to get along, whatever the personality.

'Telling someone they're special doesn't help, I reckon,' Mandz went on. 'Makes them feel more different. Tell you what, if I could paint like he does, I'd be well chuffed. He got an A for it at A-level. Plus three other As. Everyone said he should go to uni, but he just wants to work in the gardens at Liggan and sell his paintings. He does cards as well. You should stock them.'

After tapping the reader with her card, she sighed gratefully as the payment was accepted then, grinning at Mal, headed back out onto the lane.

Mal laughed to herself. Every time she seemed to piss someone off, someone else turned up and cheered her up. Whatever else she could say about the village, life wasn't dull, and everyone had an opinion that they would share at the drop of a hat.

The door swung open again, and Mal's hope that she might yet break the twenty-pound barrier was dashed when she saw the postie.

'It's alright,' he said. 'No bills in here. I reckon you get the most mail in the village. Keep me in a job, you do.'

He left, chuckling, and the shop returned to silence.

Flicking through the letters, she recognised each hand and was surprised by a brief moment of disappointment at not seeing any French stamps. She decided to start with the parcel from Jasmine, a lovely ninny of a girl, who didn't have a mean bone in her body or a sensible idea in her head. She was well matched with Mal's nephew.

Inside the parcel was a postcard and a second parcel. On the card's front was a line drawing of some flowers. She turned it over and sighed as she took in the handwriting with little circles above the *I*s.

Dear Mal, you mentioned it was quiet in Golden and were considering a hobby. I hope this is the start of something wonderful. Love Jasmine

Mal looked in trepidation at the smaller parcel, wrapped in tissue paper. Happily, this package was soft, so it wasn't another ghastly book full of mawkish sentiments.

She gingerly unwrapped the package, careful to save the tissue, and stared in horror at her present.

Chapter Twenty-Nine

In her hands sat a small embroidery kit for beginners. A robin was sitting on a holly branch with the motto "New Year, New You" underneath. She was still holding it aghast when the door swung open with a ring of the bell, and Sophie swept into the shop closing the door behind herself, then glanced at Mal's gift.

'Stocking a new line?'

Mal shook her head in wonder. 'It's a present.'

Sophie looked at the opened wrapping paper and laughed.

'For you? Have they ever met you? God, I barely know you, and even I know that *that* is not your thing.'

Mal raised an eyebrow. Sophie sold herself short. She was a quick judge of character.

'I'm afraid this is from my nephew's wife. I think she has appointed herself as my personal morale officer.'

'Reckon she needs a new job.'

Mal looked at it again. 'I mean, what am I supposed to do with this? Don't get me wrong—embroidered arts are incredible. Look at the work of Barboza and Jokisalo. There was an exhibition in the V&A, and some of the gowns in there were exquisite. But this? This is a robin.'

'Careful, Mal. Someone might call you a snob.'

'They can call me what they like, so long as they don't expect me to like this.'

'You're just cross because you think she sees you as a little old lady.'

That took the wind out of Mal's sails. Was that the cause of her intense dismay? That Jasmine viewed her as old? Maybe Mal was scared that was how she was viewing herself.

'I'd rather be a snob!'

Sophie laughed. 'Fair enough. But tell you what— hand it in to the church's unwanted-gifts box. Each year, the churches in the area collect up and then swap with neighbouring parishes; then, the following year, regift to those in need without fear of causing local embarrassment.'

'That's smart.'

'Yep. Drop it in at the church, or if you see Mrs Kitto around, hand it to her. She's the brains behind it.'

Mal shuddered. 'If she knew it was from me, she'd likely burn it. She was in here earlier and tore a full strip off me.'

'Lachlan?' Sophie asked, wincing.

'Exactly.'

Sophie looked around the shop, and after satisfying herself that the place was empty, she spoke. 'Sorry. She can be quite...' She paused, then sighed. 'Tricky.'

'Tricky!' Mal snorted.

'Protective, then. Plus, she has a few chips on her shoulders. Outsiders, people with money or land. So a police case involving Liggan Hall and you... Well, it was

215

all her bugbears rolled into one, attacking her beloved Lachlan.'

'What does Lachlan make of having such a formidable champion?'

'Not sure he even notices.' She shrugged. 'You've met him. Anyway, I only popped in to say I'm sorry for being mad with you the other day. I'd been looking forward to spending a day with the children.'

Mal dismissed her apology. She was right to be cross with her, and Mal was annoyed with herself for spoiling what had been a lovely chance meeting. She explained how she'd burnt the mussels and was rewarded with a proper belly laugh from Sophie.

'Bloody hell, woman! How'd you burn mussels?'

Mal explained what she'd done, and Sophie could only shake her head.

'I don't think I've ever been that lost in a book. If I had, the kids would have burnt the house down ten times over.'

For the thousandth time, Mal raised a small prayer to the gods for blessing her with time to be herself, then remembered that the gods had nothing to do with it. It was a choice that had been forced upon her.

'Don't scowl at me, Malachite! I'm not the one that burnt my mussels.' She laughed again and then explained when the next best tide would be to try again. Mal promised she would return, but privately thought her days of foraging had come to an abrupt halt.

Her phone buzzed, and she picked it up to see a text from Imogen:

-**Please come. The very worst has happened.**

Mal gritted her teeth. Where were Imogen's friends, her family? She started typing:

-**It's Friday. I'm in the shop. Hope everything is okay.**

-**The police have released their prime suspect. What if he tries to kill me? What if I'm next? You must come immediately.**

Mal waved the phone at Mac. 'See, this is what happens with her sort. Give them an inch and they take the whole bloody mile, build houses on it, and then charge you rent.'

Her phone buzzed again:

-**You must.**

I must not, thought Mal and, grabbing Lionel's diary, started to read again. *Who was this wonderful Pearl, and what happened to her?*

-**Please.**

Mal ground her teeth and replied:

-**You are perfectly safe. You have two family liaison officers with you. I'm sure if they thought Lachlan a credible threat, they would have charged him. Shall I call on you tomorrow?**

-**There's something I need to share.**

Dear God. Mal rubbed her eyes then responded:

-**You should tell the police.**

Mal was tempted to mention that people who dropped heavy hints about secrets tended to be dead by the time the next scene was aired.

Imogen replied:

-They won't understand. You will. Besides, they are awful. They are only here to spy on us and make dreadful cups of tea. I sent them away.

Mal looked at the cat, currently sitting on a beanbag, watching the pigeons in the gutters outside. He chittered excitedly as his tail swung back and forth. She wished her life was so simple. Picking up the phone, she texted back:

-But I'd have to close the shop.

But she didn't hit send, instead she sighed. 'Mac. I have come to the conclusion that I may not be a very nice person.'

Imogen was grieving and asking for help. Of course it was inconvenient, but at the best of times, Imogen didn't seem the sort to consider her impact on other people. In her pain, she was oblivious to anyone or anything else. Mal tapped on her phone again, deleting the message and starting over:

-I'm on my way.

Going out the back, she grabbed her padded jacket and slipped into her boots. Thankfully, the rain seemed to have stopped. Heading to the front door, she turned the sign to Closed and looked back at Mac, who was now curled up in one of the reading chairs, the pigeons having eluded him.

'If you wish to be useful, the floor needs a hoover. Alternatively, find a job. We need more kibbles in the coffers.'

Chapter Thirty

At the top of the hill, Mal paused and heaved a sigh of relief. At her current rate, she was going to have the most toned glutes in all of London. She expected everyone in Cornwall already had calves of steel and thighs of granite. Sure enough, Cornwall was in no way mountainous, but it was a landscape that felt squidged together. No sooner had a person walked up a hill than they were heading back down. This wasn't a rolling vista—it was a trampoline.

Pulling a hand mirror from her pocket, she touched up her lips and tidied her hair. Calling on Imogen felt like a meeting with a rival investor. Appearances were as important as facts. There was no friendship to be had here, but for now Imogen needed help, and Mal felt unable to deny her.

Happy that she'd stopped wheezing, she headed across the drive and was pleased to see Jasper leave the house and head in her direction. He appeared ready to walk off towards the farm lane, but on seeing her, he paused and smiled. Mal picked up her pace, keen not to delay him but happy for the opportunity to offer her condolences properly. The previous day felt too on the nose.

'Jasper, I'm so glad I've seen you. I wanted to say properly how sorry I am for your losses.'

He rubbed his face wearily. 'It's all a bit dreadful at the moment. Dad is beside himself. I even heard him crying.

Jocasta's buggered back off to London with the kids. She says it's for them, but honestly, it's all become too real for her here.'

Mal felt like giving the young man a hug. He looked devastated. Mal suspected he was the person holding everyone else together.

'Jocasta's probably had a very pampered life,' she said. 'She doesn't know how to respond, and you know this isn't the right place for your brother and sister.'

As tears welled, he looked down at her. 'Do you think I'm being too harsh? I just don't know what to do. Granny is a mess. Dad's worse than useless. You know he threatened to kill Algernon in a big fight they had. It's torturing him.'

Mal sighed. She didn't care for Henry Haverstock, but that was a dreadful thing to have on one's conscience. She patted Jasper on the arm, her diamond rings glinting in the winter sun.

'Don't worry. The police know families fight and people threaten to kill each other all the time. It doesn't mean they would actually do it. Your father has nothing to worry about on that score.'

Jasper rubbed his face as he took a deep breath. 'The police are telling us almost nothing. Granny dismissed the family liaison officers earlier, so now we are having to chase for answers. At least when they were in the house, I could ask them things. Although Dad kept roaring at them as well. Daisy won't leave her bedroom, and the twins buggered off this morning, and I don't know where they are or if they're safe. Their father's been murdered, and they've legged it.' His voice trailed off as he thrust his hands into his pockets and stared up at the sky.

Mal waited until he composed himself. 'Every day is going to get a little easier. I promise. It will take a long time, but tomorrow will be better than today.'

'But how do I manage today?' He sounded like a twelve-year-old boy whose dog had died.

'You just do.'

'Stiff upper lip and all that?'

''Fraid so.'

Jasper gave Mal a weak smile, then noticed a couple over by the farm gate. In the distance, Mal could see a tractor and a herd of cattle being moved from one field to another.

'Jasper?'

As she spoke, they could hear raised voices from the couple by the tractor.

'Is that young Holly from the ice cream shop?'

'Yes. Dammit. I told her to stay away. God knows what my father will do.'

'Trouble?'

'Almost certainly. She and Grandad had a private arrangement about milk supply. Holly always wanted it on a more formal footing, but Dad said it was a waste of time. She wants to make her ice cream purely from our milk. A single-vintage ice cream, she calls it. And it's delicious.

She'd got a great business brain. But when Grandad died, Dad cancelled the supply. Said he wants a sole contract with one of the large milk conglomerates.'

The voices were getting louder.

'I told her to wait until I tried to convince him.' He seemed distracted, looking back and forth between Mal and the scene unfolding. 'Look. Would you excuse me? I'll need to break this up.'

With a quick tip of the head, Jasper headed off the drive and down the lawn towards the farmyard. Mal watched him go and wondered about the concept of a single-vintage ice cream—and local, to boot. It sounded like a good plan to Mal, but maybe it didn't benefit Liggan. Holly was unlikely to be able to take their entire supply. Mal certainly didn't know how those farms worked, but she knew how markets did. Supply and demand were the same the world over. Making a mental note to call in on Holly, Mal headed towards the house, where Imogen was waiting for her at the open door.

'I saw you standing in the drive and was about to come and see if you were alright.'

Mal felt foolish and hastened towards the house, apologising for making her hostess stand in the cold whilst she ruminated on the dairy trade. 'I was talking to Jasper. But he's gone to intercede between his father and Holly.'

Imogen shook her head in rejection of the name.

Mal pushed on. 'She has an ice cream shop in the village?'

'Ah, one of the farm tenants or suppliers.' Imogen waved a hand dismissively. 'There's always someone griping to Henry that they want more. Whoever Holly is, I hope he has the sense to dismiss her contract. How dare she come here to discuss business?'

Mal smiled bitterly to herself. How often she'd met businessmen who complained of a lack of manners, then only to drive through deals that made people destitute and homeless.

'Let's ignore her. How are you doing?' Mal had followed Imogen into the kitchen where she was making coffee.

'Holding up. The doctor prescribed something that sort of makes me feel detached. I know my heart is broken, but I don't care. Does that make sense? Plus, I fired those dreadful spies. Following us everywhere, asking if we needed anything. Smiling sympathetically.' She shuddered. 'I can't handle sympathy today. I have to be strong for the family. My life has been a pampered one. Now, I need to face up to things.'

Imogen had relaxed in Mal's company and was no longer playing lady of the manor. Every now and then, her words slurred. It was almost imperceptible, but the sedatives were playing a role, no doubt. Either way, Mal relaxed in the kitchen's warmth and accepted her coffee. The pair of them settled down into comfortable armchairs to one side of the kitchen. It was a space where the corsets were loosened, the buttons undone.

'So how are you coping?' asked Mal.

'Honestly, I'm numb. I need to leave here, and once I do, I don't think I will ever return.'

'Where will you go?'

She shrugged and sipped her coffee before looking at Mal. 'To tell you the truth, I don't know. It seems I have no money and no property. Henry says there will always be a home for me here, but how can I stay?'

'Maybe one of the estate cottages?'

Imogen shot Mal a look of pure disdain. 'Live in one of them like one of our tenants? No, I was hoping for a small flat in London. Not Chelsea—I fully understand my fall from grace won't allow for that. I thought Henry could stump up for a small house in Fulham, but he refuses.'

Mal blinked and tried to remember that the woman had stumbled upon the bloody body of her favourite son. Her sense of entitlement didn't alter the fact that she was still in a state of shock.

'I know you understand,' Imogen said. 'After all, you're in some flat above a shop, having once been the star of the stock market. I read you had a place in Mayfair. Golden must have been the most colossal comedown after that.'

'I did have five years in between, residing at one of His Majesty's establishments. After that, Golden was quite the tonic.'

Imogen laughed. 'You are always so positive. You always know the right thing to do.'

That Mal had spent five years in jail would suggest she didn't always know the right thing to do. But done was done.

'So what's the problem? Why did you text me?' Mal tugged at her cuffs and settled back into the armchair, observing a range of emotions crossing Imogen's face.

Eventually, the other woman took a deep breath and held out a scrap of paper to Mal. As Mal took it, she instantly recognised Lionel's handwriting and the paper it was written on. It was a scrap from one of his diaries. It appeared to be the corner of a page, ripped off.

'I was hoping you could help me. This is Lionel's handwriting.'

'Yes,' said Mal, trying to reassure the woman. 'I recognise it from his diaries.'

For a moment, Imogen looked confused, then collected herself. 'Of course. You have them. So where did this come from, do you think?'

Now Mal was confused by the question, so replied slowly. 'Well, given the paper, I would say this was from one of the pages in his diary.'

'But you have them!'

'No, I returned them last week. Jasper came to see me and explained that his father might be upset if he found them missing.'

Imogen leant forward, her eyes fixed on Mal. 'And what did you do?'

'I returned them, of course.'

Imogen put her coffee cup down and swore. 'That stupid child. Why did he interfere?'

Mal didn't want to betray a confidence and point out that, legally, the diaries weren't Imogen's to dispose of. 'I don't understand. What is the significance of this piece of paper?'

Imogen gestured for the fragment, and Mal returned it.

'Why are you concerned about this?' asked Mal.

Imogen dropped her head, her hair masking her face as she muttered something.

'I didn't catch that.'

'It was in his hand.' She looked up challengingly. 'This paper was in Algernon's hand when I found him in the library.'

Chapter Thirty-One

Mal threw herself back in her chair and glared at the widow.

'Imogen! How bloody stupid! Why didn't you tell the police? They are currently working on the theory that this was a botched robbery. Oh Jesus, my fingerprints are on it. Damn it, so are yours. What were you thinking?'

Imogen shrank before Mal's tirade.

'I wasn't thinking straight. I saw what was written on it, and I panicked.'

In a flash, Imogen crumpled the paper and threw it onto the fire. She stared challengingly at Mal. 'That fixes it, doesn't it? No fingerprints.'

Mal lunged to intercept the paper but was too slow.

'Are you insane? This doesn't fix anything. I still have to tell the police about it.'

Imogen looked shocked. 'But why would you do that? I thought we were friends?'

'Imogen, I'm a convicted criminal. I'm still on parole. I can't be found to be perverting the course of law. Someone else might have turned a blind eye, but I can't.'

'But you don't understand—'

'I might understand more than you know. I saw the word *vasectomy*.'

She paused, and the silence fell heavily between the two women.

'When did you find out?' asked Mal kindly. The initial shock of Imogen's recklessness had passed, and Mal was overwhelmed with pity. God knows, she knew something of that shock.

Imogen took a deep breath and choked back a sob. 'When I saw that scrap of paper. At least, that confirmed it.'

She sniffed loudly, pushing a knuckle against her nose. Mal stood and grabbed a sheet of kitchen roll and returned, handing it to Imogen, who looked at it, then shrugged and blew her nose. Taking pity on her, Mal retrieved some more roll and passed it over.

'Your mascara's running.'

As Imogen composed herself, Mal compared their griefs. Both had been married to men that had voluntarily deprived themselves of children. Were she and Imogen alike? Had they attracted the same sort of man? Was it something in them or, like two individuals caught in a bomb blast, were they simply unlucky?

'Did you ever suspect?' asked Mal.

Imogen sniffed and shook her head. 'I had two children. How could I have guessed?'

Mal tried to think of a delicate way to proceed. 'But Lionel wasn't the only man you slept with?'

She sniffed again and looked into the fire, unwilling to make eye contact. Her voice was quiet as she talked. 'I had a friend that I used to hang around with in London. It was shortly after our honeymoon, and Lionel wanted to go back to the estate and discuss crop yields or something equally tedious. But he told me to stay on and have fun. He said it would give him a few days to get the boring stuff out of the way, then he'd be able to devote all his time to me.'

She looked at Mal defiantly. 'It was always that way—estate first, me second. So I stayed and played. My girlfriends were so jealous. It was wonderful, and we had the best time, then I bumped into Ralph.' She smiled fondly. 'Oh, you should have seen him back then, twenty years younger than Lionel and so full of life. God, when he walked in the room, all heads turned to watch him walk past, and he had a smile for everyone. There wasn't a face he didn't know, a story he couldn't tell. When he entered the room, the party started. And well, at the end of the evening, we just fell back into old habits. One for the road, so to speak.'

She looked back into the fire and grabbed the brush, sweeping some of the ash back towards the hearth. 'And so I returned to Cornwall, and soon after, I discovered I was pregnant.'

'And you said nothing to Lionel?'

Imogen raised her eyebrow. 'Whatever you might say of me, you can't call me an idiot.'

Mal could say a lot of things but wondered what it was like for a twenty-year-old to marry a forty-year-old man that had barely any interest in her. What a dreadful couple they must have made.

'How did he react?'

'He was cold. I thought he would be delighted—you know, son and heir sort of thing. But he just stared at me for a while, then took the dogs out for a walk. I cried for weeks. Everyone said it was my hormones, but I knew he hated me. He wouldn't have sex with me. Said we needed to protect the baby. All sorts of excuses. That's when I decided he must be gay.'

'So how did Algernon come about?'

'Oh, we had occasional sex, and I still had occasional flings. Algernon's father was a rather gorgeous Chilean polo player. My God, that man could ride.' She laughed, then started crying. 'I must sound so awful—vulgar gags and infidelity.'

Mal wanted to agree with her, but honestly, humans were such a mess. What was the point of making this woman suffer more? She'd lost a husband, lost a son, and now she'd discovered her husband had always known about her infidelities. He hadn't despised her because he was gay, he'd despised her because she was a liar and a cheat.

'You're in shock. It's a lot to take in. Seeing that word on the old scrap of paper must have been dreadful.'

Imogen nodded. 'Although I had suspected Lionel might have known when the will was read out.'

'How so, if you don't mind me asking?' She was certain that the contents of the will were at the centre of it all, but as she didn't know exactly what the will said, she hadn't been able to put things together. She knew DNA was somehow involved and now things were becoming clearer.

'The will was very simple. It basically said, "I leave everything to my firstborn heir."'

'Ah.' Mal tilted her head and smiled to herself. 'So that explains one mystery.'

'Explain,' snapped Imogen, then took a deep breath. 'I'm sorry—I'm raw. Another coffee?'

As she went to reheat the kettle, Mal ran through Lionel's diary entries in her head and began to work out what must've happened.

'So what mystery does it solve?' Imogen asked again when she returned. She nibbled on a biscuit and waved the packet in Mal's direction. 'I shouldn't, but at the moment, what's the point? Algernon's dead and I just—'

She burst into tears again in earnest, so Mal brought the entire roll over.

Imogen smiled weakly. 'Sorry. Distract me. Tell me what you have cracked with that clever mind of yours.'

Mal sipped her coffee, then put it on the table beside her. 'Okay, remember you gave me Lionel's diaries. Well, I've been reading the first one, and I thought how different he sounded. A young man in his twenties, it was the swinging sixties, and he was in love.'

'He was?'

'Oh, very much so.'

'Who was she?'

'No idea. From what he wrote about her, there was some sort of mystery surrounding her.'

'Could it have been a man?'

'Not unless that man had particularly fine breasts and long hair that glowed like embers in the sun.'

'Gosh! Are you sure this was Lionel?'

'Positive. His diaries, his handwriting. Plus, her name was Pearl.'

'Pearl? That's such a pretty name. So what happened to her?'

'That, I don't know. I haven't got that far. At the end of the diaries, he'd somehow disgraced himself and was being sent abroad to America to learn to be a stockbroker or something.'

'He was always good with money.'

'Well, I couldn't work out what he'd done that was so dreadful, but now… I think he must have made someone pregnant, and for whatever reason, he wouldn't or couldn't marry her.'

'Do you think she was already married?'

'Possibly. He did regularly refer to the frustration of their circumstances.'

'Gosh. It's like a novel.'

'There is an entry towards the end of that diary that implies before heading to the States, he was going to London and would thwart his father's plans for a dynasty.'

'Do you think that's when he had the vasectomy?'

'Seems possible, doesn't it?'

Imogen's face was flush with excitement. 'Do you realise what this means? God, Mal, you're incredible. That's who killed Lionel and who killed Algernon. This unknown child.' She pressed her face into her hands and sobbed in relief. 'God, ever since I saw that bit of paper in Algernon's hand, I thought that one of the family must be responsible, but now we know who the actual murderer must be.' She stood up abruptly, catching Mal off guard. 'I'll call the police at once. And Henry. I'll call him too. And you must bring back that diary so we can find out who this Pearl was.'

Imogen was a sudden flurry of activity. The revelation about the will had certainly opened up a new line of enquiry, especially as Mal could provide proof of a potential child via Lionel's diaries. But Mal wasn't certain that the family was in the clear yet, no matter how much Imogen might wish it.

Chapter Thirty-Two

Two hours later, Mal found herself sharing the same air as DCI Hemingstone and feeling all the worse for it. She was back in the drawing room, having walked down to retrieve the diary and then lugged the heavy book back up the hill. She had already promised herself, when this day was over she was going to have a very long bath and a massive glass of wine.

Imogen was flanked by Henry and Jasper. DI Williams was on one side, and an unfamiliar woman was standing near the far wall. Despite her lack of uniform, Mal was certain she was with the police. She was watching everyone, her eyes darting back and forth, and each time she caught Hemingstone's eye, she stood up straighter. Clearly, this was one of the family liaison officers or *spies* that Imogen had dismissed. Mal knew FLOs were supposed to be unobtrusive, but maybe leaving the premises so soon after a murder was the wrong move. She felt sorry for the young detective. It must be a tough job.

Hemingstone took a deep breath and muttered as he watched Mal enter. She was certain she heard 'Miss Marple' and muttered 'Inspector Clouseau' in return.

'I'm sorry, Mrs Peck. What did you just say?'

She raised an eyebrow. 'You first.'

He glared at her, then continued speaking to Imogen. Williams was sitting, taking notes. When he walked in, he'd spotted Mal, rolled his eyes at her and given her a small grin. Well, she didn't want to be there any more than he wanted her there, but at least he was being good-humoured about it.

'So, you found a piece of paper in your son's hand, but you didn't tell us about it,' Hemingstone said. 'Can you tell me why?'

'Because I didn't think it relevant.'

Henry took his mother's hand. 'What's this about?'

She turned towards him.

'It's nothing, darling. At least, I thought it was nothing, but Mal here explained how it could be a clue and that I should call the police.'

Mal wished Sophie was there to hear that.

'Where is it? Can I see what it says?' said Henry.

Imogen pulled a little face. 'It fell into the fire.'

'What!' snapped Hemingstone.

Imogen's voice wavered. 'I'm so sorry. Please don't shout at me. I didn't do it deliberately. Mal will tell you.'

All eyes turned towards Mal, who swore inwardly. Smiling demurely, she shrugged. 'I'm afraid I was helping myself to a biscuit at the time, but yes, the scrap of paper did end up on the fire.'

'So what did it say?' Hemingstone asked, his tone conciliatory. He looked uncomfortable on the sofa, aware that Henry was ready to jump down his throat if he thought he was badgering his mother.

'I'm not sure if I recall what was written on it,' said Imogen hesitantly.

Hemingstone looked fit to explode.

Mal cleared her throat. 'I'm sure if you put your mind to it, it will come back to you.'

It was going to be unpleasant, but if Imogen wanted to expand the horizon of the suspects, she was going to have to spill the beans. Henry clearly disagreed.

'If my mother says she doesn't remember, then maybe we can take her at her word.' Henry's tone was aggressive, and he glared at Mal, wrapping an arm around his mother. 'Do you know what she's been through?' He turned to the inspector. 'Why is she being hounded like this? If she can't remember, surely that's enough? Mrs Peck, did you see what was on the paper? Maybe you can help.'

Mal looked across at Imogen and gave her a sympathetic smile and nodded in encouragement. What was about to take place was going to take guts, but Imogen had endured a loveless marriage for decades, which required a certain sort of courage. Sitting upright, she patted Henry on the knee.

'Henry, I'm so sorry.' Imogen then cleared her throat and addressed the DCI. 'I can't remember all of it, and in fact, it was a scrap of writing from a larger page, so its content was incomplete. However, its meaning was clear.'

As she paused, Williams was scribbling furiously. Mal wondered if he just wrote what was said or if he was also making other observations of everyone. From where he was sitting, he could take in the whole room. Only Jasper had his back to him. Everyone else's faces were clear, and everyone was hanging on Imogen's words. Even if Williams couldn't see Jasper's serious expression, thought Mal, he could infer it from the way the boy was leaning forward.

'Did you recognise the writing, Mrs Haverstock?'

'Yes, it was Lionel's. I believe it came from one of his diaries.'

'For heaven's sake. Why didn't you tell us about this earlier?' barked Hemingstone. Henry inhaled deeply.

'Thank you, Mrs Haverstock,' said Williams, cutting off an imminent explosion. 'This really is most helpful. Now, you mentioned you understood the meaning, and I appreciate this may be difficult, but if you could just let me know what the subject matter of the note was…?' His smile was as calm as his tone, and the tension in the room rapidly de-escalated.

'Thank you, dear. This is painful, but if it helps you catch poor Algernon's killer…' She looked ready to cry again.

Henry gave her a small hug. 'Come on, Mum, let's pull that plaster off, shall we? One quick rip.'

She looked up, cradled his face in her hand. Her pale skin and jewelled fingers seemed tiny against his tanned complexion. 'I fear this will hurt you more than me.'

Mal had enough time to register Henry's puzzled expression before Imogen continued.

'The note referred to the fact that Lionel had had a vasectomy. Given the age of the paper, ink, and handwriting, this event happened some time ago. I was unaware of this and, in fact, looking back over our marriage, I believe he had the procedure before we were wed.'

'But, Mother, he must have had it reversed,' Henry said. 'I don't see the significance.'

Hemingstone had already caught up and spelled it out for him. 'Given the ambiguous wording of the will and the fact that you and your brother were not full blood brothers, it's pretty clear he didn't have it reversed. He always knew neither of you were his sons.'

Chapter Thirty-Three

The room didn't calm down for quite a while. Henry was shouting at his mother, Jasper at his father. Williams was taking notes, and the FLO had nipped out to put the kettle on. Mal sat and watched Hemingstone, who watched the family tear into each other.

This was unbecoming. She stood up. 'Haverstocks!'

All three stopped and looked at her.

'This is not helping you. What happened has happened. You can fight about that as much as you want later. Now, you need to pull together and fight for your family.'

'But this can't be true,' said Henry.

'The sooner you accept it is, the quicker you can move on,' said Mal. 'And for God's sake, stop shouting at your mother. Imagine what she's going through.'

'What she's going through? What about me? I've lost my brother and my father, and now I find out I'm not his son. And if I'm not the heir, then who the hell is?'

Mal rolled her eyes in disgust and sat back down again.

'But don't you see, darling,' implored Imogen, 'Mal thinks your father had a child before I met him. That's the heir, and that darling child is the murderer.'

'Can a murderer inherit?' Henry asked, quick to grasp the situation.

Everyone looked at the police officers.

'That's not our area of expertise,' Hemingstone said. 'I suggest you consult your solicitor, but it sounds like a suitable motive, providing they could get away with it. What we need now is the book the scrap of paper came from. Clearly, your brother and his killer were fighting over it. We need to see what else was written.'

'Mal has those,' said Imogen, completely forgetting that Mal had already told her they had been returned.

'Why am I not surprised?' said Hemingstone, shaking his head. 'And why exactly do you have them, Mrs Peck? The personal diaries of a man you claim to have never met?'

'Actually, she doesn't,' answered Jasper. 'Well, she has one. She texted me the other day that it had got left behind. But that can't be the diary in question as she has it.'

'Hang on a minute,' said Henry. 'The inspector's right. Why the hell does this woman have my father's diaries?'

Mal wanted to sink into the sofa as the three officers of the law looked at her.

'Cup of tea, anyone?' the FLO asked with a bright smile. As Hemingstone glared at her, she refilled his cup from the teapot. 'I thought Mrs Haverstock could do with some refreshment.'

Mal was grateful for the pause and was trying to figure out how to save Imogen from more recriminations when Jasper stepped in.

'Easily explained. Granny asked her friend to have the diaries valued for probate. I explained it wasn't necessary and brought them back up to the house.'

Imogen closed her eyes then opened them, smiling warmly at her grandson as she silently mouthed a quick thank you. The police didn't miss her gratitude, but let it go for the moment.

'And how is it that one was left behind?'

'Ah, now, that *is* my fault,' Mal said. 'I had taken it upstairs to determine its value.'

'And you had a quick read of it, did you?' Henry asked.

'Come on, Dad. That's unfair. How could she assess it for probate without seeing if there was any value in the subject matter?'

'Do you know much about the value of old books, then, Mrs Peck?' asked Henry.

'Maybe you thought you could fence them, Mrs Peck,' said Hemingstone. 'Maybe you kept one back, thinking you could flog it and hope the family wouldn't notice.'

'Come on, Inspector,' said Jasper quickly. 'I'm not sure that's appropriate. Mrs Peck is a friend of my mother's and beyond reproach. I think accusing her of petty larceny is a bit rich.'

Mal winced.

'You are indeed correct,' said Hemingstone, an ugly sneer on his face. 'Petty larceny is miles beneath a woman who spent five years inside for the theft of several millions of pounds.'

Jasper didn't blink, but that was clearly news to Henry, who looked dumbfounded.

'Mother?'

'It's okay, darling. I'll tell you all about it later, but it isn't relevant.'

'But... No wait, I'm sorry.' He looked around in confusion. 'Are you suggesting that my father's diaries were valuable and that Mrs Peck was trying to steal them?'

'Oh, for God's sake, Henry,' said Imogen. 'She wasn't stealing them. She didn't even want them. I was throwing them away. After the despicable way your father cut me out of the will, I wanted to be rid of all traces of him. Those bloody diaries were the first. I told Mal to burn them, sell them, throw them in the sea—I didn't care. I also had no idea that Jasper went to retrieve them. Now, stop accusing Mal of wrongdoing. You too, Inspector.'

'So they aren't valuable?'

Mal removed the diary from her bag and pulled it onto her lap, trying to steady her hand.

'I have no idea if it's valuable; financially, probably not. But if it reveals the identity of the mother or child, then I suspect it's going to be priceless.'

Chapter Thirty-Four

Hemingstone looked positively gleeful as he flicked through her volume of Lionel's diaries. As he closed it, Mal raised her eyebrow and asked if she could leave. As she left the house, she leant against the solid walls until her shakes passed. Taking a deep breath, she told herself to get a grip, then turned towards the safety of her home.

Heading downhill, she tried to work out the age of Lionel's child and decided they now had to be somewhere in their sixties.

God, she would've given anything for a swim right then. Maybe she could join a yoga class? She snorted, then laughed at seeing a squirrel sprint across the path in front of her and skitter up the trunk of a large tree. As she watched, the squirrel ran across one bough and jumped again, headed farther up into the canopy of another tree.

Pearl would know the name of that tree, Mal thought. Hell, Pearl was such a paragon of perfection that she would probably be able to talk to the squirrel as well. The first bloom of young love was a marvellous thing. What did she do? Mal wondered. Pregnant, and the father vanished. Was she married like Imogen? Had she passed the child off as her husband's? The child had clearly survived. Lionel said as much in his will. He had returned to Golden some twenty years later; had he tried to track Pearl down? Was he too ashamed? For the umpteenth time, Mal wished she could have spoken to Lionel. She'd give anything to read his other diaries for clues.

At the bottom of the hill, the trees thinned out. She passed the football pitch and recognised Clive Sullivan collecting cones from the muddy field. She gave him a wave and waited for him to finish his work. After a moment, he saw her and jogged over. He wasn't a man built for speed, yet she admired the fact that he was out there, helping clear up from a training practice. Presumably, the village had a local team.

'Mrs Peck, how can I help you?'

'Malachite, please. And I'm sorry to make you come over here. My footwear.' She pointed at her pale blue leather boots and decided then to buy a pair of walking shoes. Waving that thought away, she carried on. 'I sent my business contributions over to you last night.'

He grinned broadly. 'You liked the figures, then?'

Mal recalled the sheer mess of a spreadsheet. Someone had even selected *comic sans* as the font.

'No, I did not like the figures,' she paused, and tried to take the sting out of her voice, 'but they were far from the worst I have seen.'

'Well, that's excellent. I tell you what—we could always use fresh blood on the committee. What do you say?'

'I say no.'

'You seem quite certain.'

'I usually am.'

Mal paused, preparing to leave and trying to think of a polite way to end the conversation.

'Do you have a child on the football team?'

'Nope. Well, I have a grandson that plays, but he's up in Burnley. The wife and I moved here six years ago, and I like to help out.'

Realising that she didn't care, Mal smiled, muttered that that was nice, and made to leave.

'You know, football's a lot like life. Being part of a team helps you win more. The wife and I found that getting involved helped us settle into the community. Lots of people don't stay, you know. The villagers can be very off-putting until they trust you are going to stay.'

'I don't know that I am.'

His head jerked. 'Not stay?'

The idea seemed alien to him, but then, he'd chosen to come here. Mal had grasped at it as a place to hide and regroup.

'You know, in football—'

'In football, isn't another essential skill knowing when to pass?' She smiled, taking any sting out of her interruption. 'Trust me, I'm not a team player. If I see a problem, I fix it. Doesn't matter whose problem it is. Can't help myself. I don't mind listening to other people's ideas, but when those ideas are wrong, I don't have the bandwidth to entertain them.'

His face lit up as he rocked back and forth on his feet.

'Ah, but that's the joy of a committee.'

'No. I'm going to stop you right there. "The joy of a committee" is not a phrase that should be given the time of day. Listening to someone waffle on about their fabulous idea when you know it won't jump the first fence is an excruciating waste of time.'

'But what if we all brainstormed and found a way to get that idea over the first fence?'

'Oh, dear Clive. You are well and truly infected with the committee bug, aren't you?'

He laughed. 'I have to confess I do enjoy them.'

'Each to their own, I suppose.'

'Well, what about you? If you do decide to stay in Golden, what will you do?'

'Sell books, solve crimes?'

'Golden's caped crusader?'

Mal laughed. Clive was proving to be better company than she'd given him credit for.

'Maybe not.'

'What about writing books? I bet you're quiet in the shop right now. You could write your book over the winter, then sell other people's books during the summer. And, of course, solve crimes by night!'

They were both laughing now. The sound of it set off a few crows, launching themselves into the air, crying in alarm before returning to another roost.

'Look, I'm sorry I can't help,' Mal said, 'but if you ever have a financial query, I'd be happy to have a look.

Unofficially, of course. His Majesty currently takes a dim view of my handling other people's money.'

Clive cleared his throat, and Mal was disappointed to have embarrassed him. She was used to her situation and kept forgetting that it made others uncomfortable.

'Or not. I'll probably be too busy leaping from roof to roof after fleeing villains.'

'In those shoes?'

They both looked at her pretty heeled boots.

'You have a point. Oh dear, I'd better go write a bestseller instead.'

'Well, you have fun with that. And yes, if I have any financial pickles, I would be more than happy to ask you about them.'

As she left, Mal smiled at the idea that he was doing her a favour by bestowing his financial issues on her. But then, in his mind it probably was a big deal, as well as an enormous act of trust.

He was right, though. She had to find a way to settle into the village, but maybe it didn't have to be as extreme as joining a committee. Maybe she could simply learn to be happy there, and that would be enough. As he walked away, a string sack of footballs over his back, she snapped a photo of him and uploaded it to Instagram after adding #notallheroeswearcapes.

She'd just started to experiment with hashtags. As her account was family-access only, they were irrelevant, but she was enjoying the medium.

Which reminded her, she still hadn't replied to Charlotte's letter about a possible sponsorship offer. It would mean money, but it would also bring her back into the public eye.

Chapter Thirty-Five

The next few days followed a pattern of wind and rain. Mal was holed up in her flat, reading books and writing letters. The initial chaos up at Liggan had calmed down, and the police were going through the routine steps: checking alibis; reading Lionel's diaries; searching for the missing one; and trying to work out who Lionel's true heir could be. She could do nothing to help, which was maddening. Nothing about the case made sense. Everyone was convinced a random heir to the estate was running around, killing people. But why hadn't they just made themselves known to Lionel, or maybe they had? Were they local? Were they someone Lionel had always known? Did he know they were his child? If he did, why not acknowledge them or name them properly in his will? Why did he suddenly decide to change his will? These questions plagued her daily and, with disgust, she pushed them out of her mind and picked up a pen.

Dear Charlotte,

A quick note only, I'm afraid, but I wanted to discuss your friend's offer to represent his brand on Instagram. I have spent the last week thinking about it and have to confess the free goodies are incredibly appealing, but I think I shall have to decline.

Given my recent history, I think my association with the brand will prove to be negative. I am also concerned about privacy. Mine in part, but I am concerned that I risk dragging the rest of the family, and Miranda in particular, into the limelight.

That said, please thank your friend. His products are lovely, and I will continue to be a firm supporter of his and, when I earn a bit more, a patron as well. Maybe convince him to have a discount for senior citizens!

Now, on the bombshell of my referring to myself as a senior citizen, I must put my pen down and catch the post.

With love, as ever,

Mal

Popping a stamp on the envelope, she decided to make the most of a lull in the weather. Grabbing her other letters and a coat, she headed out into the village. Despite the cold weather, the door to the post office was wide open, and Mal was sorely tempted to ignore her ban and head inside for her milk.

'Hello, Mal,' said Sophie, walking up behind her. 'Heard you got banned. What did you do?'

'Used logic.'

Sophie laughed. 'That'll do it. Our Phyllis isn't strong on brains or common sense. She just thrives on conflict. Give it a few days, and you'll be fine.'

'As if I'm going to spend my money in there now.'

'What were you after?'

'Milk. But I can get it from the farm shop.'

'Long old walk up the hill. Besides, it's Wednesday. They're closed today. January hours catch everyone out, not just you.'

Mal scowled. Village life was impossible. The delicatessen was closed that week, as were most of the cafes. And those that were open she didn't want to ask to borrow some milk, because saying she'd been banned would be embarrassing.

'Tell you what,' said Sophie. 'Stay there.'

A minute later, she was back out of the shop with two pints of milk, which she thrust towards Mal. 'Yours. Now, how about you make me coffee, because I want to pick that squirrelly little brain of yours.'

Up in the flat, Mal made two mugs of coffee whilst Sophie looked around the place.

'It looks a lot better without the china horses and shell pictures. Who's this?'

Sophie was pointing at a framed photograph of Will, perched atop a horse. He was waving wildly to whoever was taking the shot. It was part of a cluster of photos that Mal had set up on a sideboard, and it made her smile to be surrounded by her family whenever she walked past.

'Young Will. Scourge of teachers and parents alike, but a good sort, really. My godson.'

Sophie smiled as she took her coffee, then joined Mal as she sat down in a high-backed armchair. 'Okay, straight down to business. This morning, Jasper Haverstock was arrested on suspicion of murdering his uncle and grandfather.'

Mal's jaw fell open.

'Hmm.' Sophie nodded. 'Got to admit that was my first instinct as well.'

'What evidence do they have?'

Sophie put her coffee cup down to tick off the points on her fingers. 'He had the diaries in his room, but one was missing; the one covering the year in which Henry was born. It's believed this missing diary will be a match for the scrap of paper that Imogen helpfully threw on the fire. This morning, that diary was found in the dog kennels, along with the missing candlestick, which now firmly rules out a robbery. The diary does indeed have a scrap of paper missing from it and Jasper's fingerprints were found on the diary.'

'Well, of course they were. As are mine. Anyone else's fingerprints there? Are his fingerprints on the candlestick?'

Sophie smiled. 'On the diary there are Lionel, Imogen, Henry, and Algernon's. The candlestick has been wiped clean.' When Mal started taking notes, Sophie shook her head. 'Sorry, Mal. This is strictly off the record, and I'd likely be fired if I was found discussing a case I'm not even on. I'm far too close to too many of the interested parties.'

Mal frowned. No doubt, she was one of the interested parties, but she was pleased that she was no more than that. She put her pen down, knowing she would have no trouble remembering what Sophie told her. She just relished writing things down, as doing so often untangled a problem.

'Fair enough. But if that's the case, why are you here discussing it with me?' The last thing Mal wanted was for Sophie to get in trouble.

'Because this is my village. I grew up with the people involved. I'm the one they turn to when things go wrong and I want,' she took a deep breath, 'I want to keep my people safe.' She stared at Mal, daring her to laugh at her passion or disagree with her. Mal nodded slowly. She could only imagine how frustrating this must be for Sophie.

'That's fair enough. So, why were Henry's prints there?'

Sophie looked relieved and started to tick the points off on her fingers.

'He found the diary. He's shouting blue murder that his son is innocent. There's some fancy lawyering-up going on at the moment.'

'Pretty circumstantial, isn't it?'

'Pretty much. His solicitor is arguing that only a family member, or staff, could have accessed the kennels without upsetting the dogs and drawing attention to themselves. And don't forget, Jasper also found Lionel's body.'

'But what motive does he have?'

'It's the bloody inheritance. There are two options at the moment. First option, there's a mysterious heir bumping people off. If they exist and are guilty, they can't benefit from their crime and thus the inheritance.'

'Providing they don't have an heir themselves.'

Sophie ran her hands through her hair. 'Let's not complicate things. Okay. Second option: the children aren't Lionel's, but there is no missing child. If that is proven, his true heir is his wife as his only next of kin.'

'She'll like that.'

'Indeed. And Algernon was clearly her favourite. Hemingstone, according to Williams, is suggesting that Jasper killed him to ensure she leaves everything to Henry; then, as Henry's eldest son, Jasper will inherit. Who knows? He might even be ready to target Henry or even Imogen herself.'

'This seems an even more far-fetched option.'

'The Liggan Estate is huge. This is a very wealthy inheritance for someone and one hell of a motive for murder.'

Mal drank her coffee and thought about the problem for a few seconds as she pushed ideas around in her head. 'But it still doesn't make sense. Jasper already lives and works here. He already stands to inherit when his father dies.'

'Murderers often act impulsively. Maybe killing his uncle was an accident.'

'And he slipped and stabbed his grandfather with a syringe?' Mal shook her head dismissively. The killing of

Lionel was premeditated, but why would Jasper do it? 'And his alibi?'

Sophie drained her cup, then poured another from the cafetière. 'Well, now, that's when things get tougher for him. He has none. Lionel was killed on the evening of the twenty-eighth. Jasper was asleep in his cottage, alone. Again, his uncle died early in the morning of the fourteenth. Again, Jasper was in his cottage alone. Henry was up in London, and the rest of the family were in the house.'

The more Mal heard, the worse the situation sounded for Jasper. The problem was that innocent people didn't go around making sure they had watertight alibis.

'Okay, the fingerprints. Mine, Henry's, Lionel's, Algernon's, and Imogen's. What if the killer wore gloves? That would explain why their fingerprints don't show on the book.'

'Well, wouldn't that have made Algernon pause?'

'What if he was used to seeing them in gloves?'

'Like Imogen?'

'Imogen was...' Sophie trailed off as both women remembered how distraught she'd been that morning. 'Well, I think we can rule her out.'

Mal shook her head. 'I wouldn't put any money on that. I spent a lot of time with murderers in prison. All incredibly remorseful. But guilty, nonetheless. However, I'm with you. It seems unlikely.'

'What if she was trying to hide her infidelity?'

'I can see that. In fact, I can really see that, but her overpowering Algernon... That is harder to picture.'

'A groundsman, then? They walked in from the garden. It would make sense.'

'But what motive?'

'They are the long-lost heir?'

When Sophie was about to reply, her phone rang. Rummaging in her pockets, she looked at the number, then, mouthing an apology to Mal, tapped Accept.

Giving her some privacy, Mal collected the two empty cups and headed over to the sink to wash them out.

'Goodish news,' said Sophie, popping her phone back into her pocket. 'I asked Williams at the station to let me know how things were going. Jasper was released on bail. He is, however, now Hemingstone's chief suspect.'

'Lachlan was his chief suspect last week.'

'He may be again if they consider the killer might have been wearing gardening gloves and was well known to the dogs.'

'It just doesn't make sense. Either of them.'

'I know. Let's see if the diary they recovered tells us anything more.'

'Fingers crossed. Lachlan, or Jasper, as the murderer just doesn't feel right.'

'Agreed. One mark against Jasper is the lack of an alibi. Williams said he was cagey about it.'

'You think he's hiding something?' said Mal.

'It's a murder investigation. People always hide things. Liggan has a murderer hiding on its grounds, and murderers like to stay hidden, tangled within the secrets and lies. If Jasper is hiding something, he might be Liggan's next victim.'

Chapter Thirty-Six

Mal opened the curtains in her bedroom and smiled at the blue sky. It was Saturday, and she hoped that the fine weather would bring people out of their houses and into her shop.

A couple of hours later, she flipped the sign on the shop door to Open and wandered around the shelves, choosing titles to display. Today was going to be a good day and, within the first few hours, she racked up a decent number of sales. Some people even bought books on her recommendation. Only one couple asked where the harbour was, and so far, no one had asked why the loos were closed.

She also received a note from Miranda calling her a ninny. An actual ninny, which made Mal laugh. According to her goddaughter, if Mal wanted to be an influencer on social media, she should go for it. Clearly, Charlotte had been in touch with her and told her of Mal's concerns.

Miranda had her own account where she shared her journey through her illness and subsequent recovery. Mal was a follower and loved the overall tone of positivity. Her posts rarely, if ever, touched on her illness, but instead on a young woman just having the time of her life. Jasmine also had an account, but her posts were all about sunrises and profound quotes. Mal followed her as well, grudgingly. And she resented it every time the platform showed her similar posts. She was also discovering more about companies from their CEOs' social media posts than their LinkedIn accounts and was happily taking notes. So many nuggets of gold showed up in the comments section. Mal was not allowed to trade, but she could pass on tips to friends and family.

The bell above the door rang, and she put her book down and looked up, smiling. The day suddenly lost its appeal as her smile slid off her face. She glared over at the little pottery figurine who was supposed to protect the shop, and then turned back to her ex.

'Hello, Hugo.'

'Hello, Mal. I thought I'd come back without Minty. So we can talk properly.'

'Did I mumble last time? I said no. What else is there to say?'

Hugo looked around the shop, then leant towards Mal, snarling. 'Don't you think you owe me?'

Mal was grateful there was a counter between them. Hugo had never been violent, but she still felt deeply uncomfortable. That said, she refused to lean back.

'Owe you?' She too looked around the shop, then dropped her voice. 'Tell you what. I'll give you the bond—in its entirety—if you give me my child.'

'What?' Hugo spluttered, recoiling. The look of horror on his face was perfect as he took a full step back. 'Are you saying you want Minty to hand over our baby? Are you insane?'

'No, Hugo. But I am a long way from calm right now. And you suggesting that I owe you something may be the absolute straw that breaks the camel's back.'

'So, what are you saying?' He pulled at his shirt collar, easing his neck as he rolled his head. 'Minty would never agree to giving up her baby.'

'No, but you might.' Mal stopped and stared at him in horror. 'You would, wouldn't you? I can see from your expression you're considering it. My God!'

'Of course I'm not. I don't know what you are talking about. Living down here has twisted your mind. Why would you even want a baby? You never wanted one before.'

'Yes, I did.'

'What?'

'A baby. When we first tried, I did want one. Of course, once it became apparent that wasn't going to happen, I retrained my expectations.'

'You never seemed that fussed. When I mentioned the vasectomy, you said you might as well ditch the pill. And look at the life you had. Do you think you could have got to where you did with a brood of children attached to you?'

Mal pictured the scene and shrugged. 'Why not? With the right partner, I think anything is possible. And maybe if I had had children, I wouldn't have wanted my career. Who knows? All I know is that the option was taken from me. You just waltzed into the flat and told me it was a done deal. Have you any idea how much that hurt me?'

'Hang on, that's not quite—'

The doorbell rang again, and Mal looked across in fury. Then her face broke in delight.

'Jacques!'

Aware that she sounded like a teenager, she tried to wipe the grin off her face as she tried to recover. Instead, she continued to grin at him as he looked between her and Hugo.

'Hello, Mal. Is this a bad moment?'

Hugo cleared his throat. 'It is, actually. I'm trying to have a word with my wife.'

Mal stopped beaming and glared back at Hugo. 'Ex-wife. Your current wife is somewhere around with a sore back, swollen ankles, and a disappointing future ahead of her.'

Jacques looked between the two of them in confusion. 'Maybe I should call later?'

'Not at all. In fact, what about lunch?'

'That's a great idea, Mal,' said Hugo. 'I can explain everything. Maybe we can come to some sort of understanding.'

Mal turned and looked at Hugo in derision as she gathered up her keys and wallet.

'I wasn't talking to you. Jacques, I believe The Lugger is open for lunch?' She checked her watch. 'Yes. Shall we?'

'It would be my pleasure,' grinned Jacques, as Hugo blustered, and Mal walked out of the shop behind him.

From the street, she looked back into the shop, where Hugo was standing defiantly, his arms crossed.

'I'm not leaving,' he called out.

'Stay for all I care, but I'm locking the door.'

She waved the keys at him, and he sped out of the shop. Mal never made false promises.

Jacques offered Mal his arm, and with a twinkle, she laid a hand on it as they walked towards the pub.

'This isn't over!' shouted Hugo, standing outside the shop. 'I'll destroy you, Malachite Peck!'

Chapter Thirty-Seven

Jacques paused to look over his shoulder, then turned towards Mal. 'Would you like me to have a word?'

'Certainly not. But give me a moment. I need to cauterise this.'

Mal removed her hand and walked back towards Hugo. Years of anger fuelled every step as she strode back to where he stood, puffed up and scowling.

She jabbed a finger into his chest. 'It is over, and if I ever hear from you again, I will ask for a restraining order. Is that clear? And if that doesn't work, I will start putting the word out regarding your financial situation.'

Hugo stared down at her in silence, his face contorted into an ugly grimace. Aware that he wouldn't reply, she turned and walked back to Jacques.

'Sorry about that. Now, we don't have to have lunch. I just said that to get rid of him.'

'I think lunch is an excellent suggestion. Or we could just stand in the cold.'

Smiling, Mal led the way and opened the door, waving Jacques into the warmth of the pub.

Settling herself into the corner table, Mal smiled at Jacques' retreating back as he headed to the bar and was greeted warmly.

The scene with Hugo had been ugly, and she hoped she wouldn't hear from him again. She pitied Araminta. That young woman was about to have a very rude introduction to the path of poor life choices. Mal wondered what she would do. Imogen's marriage had quickly deteriorated, but she'd stayed for the money and the lifestyle. She'd been miserable but secure. But that was decades before. Society had changed, and Hugo was not a wealthy man. Motherhood was another factor, though. Mal had little insight into that, beyond the fact that many women made incredible decisions and sacrifices when the lives of their children were involved.

She turned to look outside and watched the boats on the water. Fishermen were tidying up their nets and crates on the jetty. Gulls hung overhead, ever hopeful of random scraps. As she watched, the scene exploded into a riot of noise as hundreds of gulls took to the air. Mal had never seen so many birds in the sky at one time. The fishermen looked up but then returned to their work. As the door to the pub opened, she could hear the intense racket of hundreds of gulls screaming in alarm. Jacques sat down, placing a Virgin Mary in front of Mal.

'What's going on out there?' she asked, gesturing her glass towards the skies before enjoying a sip of the sharp drink.

'Buzzard, most likely,' Jacques said, as he scanned the skies. 'Yes, there he is.' His finger indicated a large brown bird perched on the roof of one of the warehouse sheds. 'Bold as brass.'

Mal could see the bird was indeed the focus of the gulls' alarm. After a moment, he launched himself off the roof, accompanied by a mob of birds diving at him as he flew inland, unconcerned by the screaming chaos around him. After a few moments, the gulls returned to the harbour and settled down to their scavenging again.

'That was quite the sight,' Mal said, putting her phone away.

'One for social media?'

Jacques was one of a handful of friends and family that had access to her account under her privacy settings, although he never posted himself.

'I've been considering making my account public.'

Jacques sipped his small, dark drink and sighed with satisfaction. 'My God, that is good. France has many great strengths, but stout isn't one of them.'

'Just a half?'

'I have to drive up to the house.'

'You drove down?' Mal mocked him with a smile.

'I drove from the ferry and have just parked up,' he contradicted her, staring at her thoughtfully.

Mal blinked. 'You haven't gone home yet?'

'No, there were a few tasks I wanted to complete before going home. Then I will likely sleep for the day. The crossing was dreadful.'

Mal wasn't sure how to respond, but she was delighted that he happened to be walking along her street when Hugo showed up.

'Oh hang on, you came into the shop. I'm so sorry— were you after a book?'

'A bookseller, as it happens.'

Mal took a sip and tried not to blush.

'I've been reading your letters with increasing alarm. Burning the *moules* was the tipping point, and I had to hurry back before a further tragedy unfurled.'

Chastised, she grinned at him, then looked at the menu. 'Do you actually have time for lunch? I rather kidnapped you back there, but you might need to go home and unpack.'

'Lunch would be excellent, and Jan said they have their chowder on the menu today. Which I would highly recommend.'

As he returned to the bar to place their order, Mal wondered why she'd felt a moment of delight at thinking he'd come just to see her. She wondered what his other tasks were that had been so urgent. He wasn't due back for another month.

'I presume you are concerned about your family's privacy,' he asked upon coming back.

Mal nodded, pleased that he'd been thinking about her earlier comment about social media but hadn't given a knee-jerk response. She enjoyed conversations in which the other person could think, reflect, and keep up. Her thoughts often raced, and she became frustrated when people couldn't follow her.

'Yes. Although Miranda, my goddaughter, sent me a letter this morning to crack on and, in her words, not to be a ninny.'

'I think I should like to meet the person who calls you a ninny and makes you smile as you recall it.'

'She is a treasure and is happy to speak her mind. Even when uncalled for. I love her very much.'

'So your reluctance is closer to home?'

Mal sighed and looked down at the table. 'I think I'm scared. Which is stupid. I doubt anyone will even notice me.'

'Maybe it's more than fear. You've had no privacy for the past five years. These last few months must have been a very special time.'

She hadn't looked at it that way, but as she was about to comment, their soup arrived. She wasn't one for navel-gazing, but perhaps Jacques could be onto something. Maybe she could expand her online account slowly and just see how it felt. She certainly didn't expect to be an overnight success.

'Doing something new always creates tension. Now, enjoy your soup. Raymond makes a lovely chowder and almost never burns the mussels.'

She returned his grin, grateful for the change in topic, and wondered if Jacques was ever going to let her live that down. She blew on the spoon, then sipped cautiously. Instantly, her taste buds were overwhelmed by the smoky, fishy creaminess of an excellent chowder. She'd have paid a lot of money for a meal this good in London and wondered what they charged here. She hadn't eaten out once and was uncertain of the prices.

'This is delicious.'

'Told you. Only young Holly's soups come close.'

He nodded out the window to where Holly was walking along the harbour in front of them. Spotting them, she stopped in her tracks, returned to the pub's entrance, and walked in.

Mal looked at Jacques, who shrugged in denial.

'Hello, Mal. Hello, Jacques,' said Holly, looking flustered as she bumped into one of the dining chairs.

Mal put her spoon down and waved at Holly to sit down and join them.

'No, I won't stop. It's just... Mal, when you're finished, could you pop over to the shop? Just for a minute. If you've time. If you don't, that's perf—'

'I have time. I'll call in after my lunch.'

'Right. Good. Thank you.' She turned quickly and hurried off.

'Is everything okay?' said Jacques, watching her dash out of the pub. 'I don't think I have ever seen the lass in such a state.'

Mal had taken another sip of the soup and was enjoying picking out the flavours of lemon and fennel. She didn't know what Holly wanted, but she could guess. She dabbed her lips with her napkin. 'I suspect it's to do with the Liggan deaths.'

'In what way?'

'I think—and please don't think I am gossiping—but I think she may be involved with Jasper Haverstock.'

'Nice lad. Quiet, thinks before speaking. Not a skill he learnt from his father. And you think he and Holly are dating?'

'Just a hunch.'

'Your hunches seem pretty accurate. So why is she looking so flustered?'

Mal looked around. There was no one sitting nearby, but she lowered her voice, nonetheless.

'He was arrested yesterday.'

'My God.'

'Exactly. Poor girl.'

He picked up his spoon again. 'Well, it's no business of mine. I hope you can help her.'

'I don't see how.'

For a few moments, they enjoyed their soup.

'This really is delicious,' said Jacques, smiling. 'It is so lovely to be here, sipping soup, watching the boats in the harbour, seeing all the familiar faces and enjoying the company of a new friend.'

Mal paused, her spoon hovering above her bowl.

'Is friend too bold?'

She laughed. 'Not at all. I think at my age, it seems preposterous, like I'm back in the schoolyard.'

'Shall I pull your pigtails?'

'Only if I can box your ears.'

He roared with laughter, causing those at the bar to turn around. Jan called out that if he carried on

270

interrupting the peace, she would have to throw him out—again.

Mal carried on eating her soup and smiled. 'That sounds like there's a tale attached to it.'

'Let me tell you about it tomorrow?'

She raised an eyebrow. 'What did you have in mind?'

'A walk and a cooking lesson. The weather is fine, so we'll go and pick some mussels and then have them for lunch. If you like? You don't open on Sundays, do you?'

'I don't, and I can't think of a nicer way to spend it.'

Smiling at each other, they continued to eat and plan the following day. As she left the pub, the cold air and noise of the harbour refreshed her, and she laughed just for the sheer pleasure of her senses.

'Right,' said Jacques, swinging his jacket back on. 'I shall see you in the morning. Give my regards to Holly.'

Mal watched as he strode away towards the car park. Then, smiling, she turned and walked along the harbour to Holly's.

Chapter Thirty-Eight

It was a short walk to Holly's and as she pushed the door open, she could see Holly had a customer, so she waited to one side. As she looked around the shop, she noticed Holly also had a shop guardian in the other corner. Hers was a rough-looking teddy bear with a blue flower stitched in his ear. He appeared to be suffering more than her own pottery figurine, but a soft toy probably struggled in a food shop and right by the sea air. The views from Holly's takeaway were glorious as the building sat right on the harbourside.

When the customer left, Mal pointed up at the bear. 'Tell me. Do all the shops in Golden have a guardian?'

'Most do. We call them Watchers, mind. Some newcomers come in and get rid of theirs. Coincidentally, their businesses don't last long. Newcomers add them if they don't have one.'

'Do they all have a significance?'

'Yes. But some have lost their story.'

Mal nodded and explained that hers had been gifted to the owner when a potter came to stay in the twenties. If it hadn't been chipped, it might have been valuable.

Holly pointed up at hers. 'Teddy there was Nan's. When she moved to Cornwall with Grandad and turned this building into an ice cream shop, she added her teddy. Sprinkles, the shell shop next door, has a jam jar lid. No one knows the significance of it as the original owner took the story to their deathbed. But the new owners kept it in place, and they've been trading some twenty-plus years.'

'How can a jam jar lid watch anything?' asked Mal, trying to unfurl the village superstition.

'Don't need eyes to be a Watcher,' said Holly, as though that was obvious. 'There's shark teeth, cow bones, snow globes, toy cars, straw dolls, all sorts.' She shrugged. 'Just a village thing, I reckon. I suppose you think we're daft.'

'Are you kidding? You'll never meet a more superstitious bunch than bankers. I think they'd give the fishermen a run for their money. Special socks, lucky gonks, ways to start their computer, set walks to work. Most traders have a little tic that they'll laugh about and dismiss as nonsense, just a whim. But my God, they stick to them religiously, and if the door is touched with the wrong hand or the milk is poured first, then the end of days is upon us.'

Holly laughed.

'Do you know the fisherman, Max? He always goes to sea with mismatched socks and a pebble in his pocket. Says he knows it's daft, but does it anyway.'

Mal agreed, and Holly cleared her throat, eager to move the topic of conversation along to whatever was on her mind.

'Look, what I wanted to ask, if it's okay, what with you being friends with Mrs Imogen Haverstock, is why do the police think Jasper's involved? If you can say. I mean—'

'It's alright.' Mal quickly brought Holly up to speed. 'And of course, his lack of alibi for the night is a problem.'

Holly froze and looked at Mal. 'He has an alibi!'

'He says he doesn't.'

'But he does!'

'I thought he might.' Mal smiled at the young woman, who sighed.

'Yes. I'm his alibi. But why the hell hasn't he said?' She frowned, then opened her eyes wide in alarm.

'It's me, isn't it? He doesn't want his family to know. He's ashamed of me.' Holly was wavering between anger and despair and started vigorously wiping down her countertop as tears welled up in her eyes. She furiously pushed jars aside, scrubbing behind them, her cloth flicking back and forth.

'Is that what you think of him, then?' asked Mal.

'No, of course not. Or at least I didn't. What other explanation is there?'

Mal shrugged, waiting to see if the girl would come to the conclusion of her own accord.

'I run my own business. So what if I don't have loads of money or a fancy house and a posh name? I'm just as good as any of them.'

Mal remembered just how stupid and insecure youth was. 'Maybe he thinks you're not as good as them.' She shrugged. 'Or maybe he thinks you're better. Maybe he doesn't want you dragged into this mess. Maybe he's trying to protect you.'

Holly stopped scrubbing. Her jaw fell open, and she spoke slowly. 'There is no way Jasper Haverstock is that stupid. No way.'

'I believe the correct response here is "Way."'

'But that's the dumbest thing I ever heard.'

'Love usually is.'

'Jasper doesn't love me,' mumbled Holly, blushing.

'Well, all I know is he needs an alibi, and I need to get back to work.'

She walked towards the door and looked back at the very confused girl. Holly was barely more than a teenager and reminded her of Miranda.

'Jasper's a nice lad, isn't he?' she asked as she opened the door.

Holly nodded shyly and Mal wandered back to her shop, humming to herself. At least Jasper's situation was improving, but someone had killed his uncle and his grandfather. The two main suspects so far were Lachlan and Jasper, but neither felt right to Mal. That said, she didn't have any idea who might be responsible.

As she opened the door to her shop, she looked across at her pottery fisherman and remembered Jacques appearing out of the blue.

'You're forgiven.'

Laughing at herself, she went out back and put the kettle on. Then spent the rest of the afternoon wondering what outfit to wear for the following day's expedition.

Chapter Thirty-Nine

The morning rain had dampened Mal's spirits. She had no doubt Jacques would cancel the expedition, but at ten o'clock, he pulled up outside the shop and rang the doorbell. After leaning out of the first-floor window like a teenager and giving him a quick wave, she headed downstairs. She locked up and slid into his car. It was a two-seater Mercedes soft-top with cream leather upholstery and navy trim. Today the roof was up, which was the right choice, given the weather. In fact, owning a convertible in Cornwall was a very brave move in any month.

'I do like the Land Rover, but this is a much nicer ride,' said Mal, smiling as she pulled the seat belt on.

Jacques looked across at her. 'You look very nice.' He paused as he turned the corner and headed up the hill. 'Are they your waterproofs?'

Mal looked down at her Aquascutum gaberdine trench coat and beret. 'The coat is waterproof. My boots are in the bag.'

'Are your boots made by Dior or Chanel?' he asked, his mouth twitching into a smile.

'Le Chameau, actually.'

'Well, they'll do, but I'm just going up to the house to get you a spare raincoat. Your lovely outfit will be ruined, scrambling across rocks.'

'It's all I have.'

'We can take care of this.'

Ten minutes later, they were heading along country lanes with a yellow sou'wester and a wax raincoat stowed in the boot.

'I thought we'd go to Porthluney,' he said. 'The tide's good, and the mussels are nice and fat.'

'Is it far from the car park to the beach?'

Mal didn't mind walking in the rain, but she was worried the coast path would be too slippery for her to manage in wellies. Going base over apex would be too embarrassing to contemplate.

'Best part about this beach is that the car park is right by it. Course, that means in summer, it's a heaving mass of people, but today, it'll be perfect.'

As they scooted along the road, Mal was convinced that if she leant out the window she could touch the hedges, and she said as much to Jacques.

'Come spring, you'd be able to pick a whole bouquet of flowers. Cornish hedgerows are some of the most beautiful sights in springtime. You wait.'

Today, the hedges were sullen lumps of grass and twigs growing twisted out of towering banks. Mal had been told enough times that Cornish hedges were full of rocks, more like earthen embankments than coppiced bushes; she pitied anyone that ever hit one. Through the windscreen, Mal caught a glimpse of the sea before the road headed downhill. Then she caught her breath as

Jacques drove past a sprawling castle sitting above an ornamental lake.

'That looks like a movie set.'

'It's been used enough times as one. You probably recognise it from TV. Now, here's the beach. Belongs to the castle, so the car park is always in good repair.'

As he pulled up, he muttered crossly to himself, and Mal tried to work out what the issue was. Ahead of her, a wide bay of sand was framed by hills on either side, creating a sheltered bay. The tide was far out, and the waves didn't seem too large.

'What's wrong?'

'A parking meter. Look at that. Never had to pay to park here in winter.'

He drove across the hardcore and parked at the far end, where sleepers marked the edge of the beach.

'I have money,' said Mal, scrabbling in her pockets and hoping to hell that she did actually have some loose change.

'We're not paying.'

Jacques got out of the car and, before Mal could object, nipped around to her side and opened the door. 'Stop scowling. Now, grab your wellies. Let's go picking.'

As Mal struggled into the ridiculously heavy wax raincoat Jacques had rustled up for her, she wished she could access a full-length mirror. She wanted to elicit shades of Joanna Lumley exploring new continents, but she suspected she looked more like Paddington.

'Is this coat a little large on me?'

Jacques looked across and her and grinned. 'A little. But you'll be glad of it if that cloud comes any closer.'

As they walked towards the waves, Mal looked back at the car. 'Aren't you worried you might get a ticket?'

'No. If any idiot is fool enough to ticket me, I'll have a word with Andrew. Now, let's head for that section.'

Pointing to a line of rocks by the shoreline, they headed across the sands. As they passed through some of the deeper puddles left in the wet sand, Mal had to hitch up the bottom of her coat. She couldn't see what she looked like, which was probably just as well; suspecting it would mortify her. She also wanted to know who Andrew was; maybe the local ticket warden or the owner of the castle? Jacques seemed to know everyone and treated them all equally.

As they set to work, Mal happily led the way, making it clear she knew what she was doing, and sent several prayers of thanks to Sophie for her diligent instructions. She was determined to not be a total city slicker in Jacques' eyes, although he roared with laughter when she stumbled over the pronunciation of *snakelock anemones*, which Sophie's daughter had taught her the week before.

'If it helps, I can't say it either.'

He laughed then mangled the pronunciation, his accent becoming more and more pronounced as he struggled with the syllables.

'What about the "Pheasant Plucker's Son?"' asked Mal mischievously. They roared with laughter as the two of them tried to race through the tongue twister, swearing as they did. Where the waves were breaking, a flock of oystercatchers took offence at the foul language and flew across to the other side of the bay, calling out their disgust as they went.

'Now look,' laughed Jacques, 'You've offended the oystercatchers with your vulgarity.'

'Are there oysters here?' asked Mal, suddenly alert to an even finer lunch.

'Nothing worth bothering with here. Ah, and here's the rain.' He looked at her plastic bag laden with mussels and nodded. 'We have enough. Let's head back to the car.'

By the time they were halfway back, the heavens had truly opened. The wind was whipping Mal's hair around, slapping tendrils across her face and blowing the hood of her coat off her head. She wrapped the heavy wax jacket tight around her, and whilst her hair and face were being buffeted, the rest of her remained warm and dry.

'I need a cap like yours next time,' shouted Mal through the wind.

'I'd give you mine, but I suspect it would just blow off.'

Each time Mal raised her arm to hold her hood on her head, rain trickled down the sleeve, and in the end, she gave up the fight.

By the time she got back to the car, she was a windblown mess, grinning wildly at the elements. After throwing wellies, coats, and bags into the boot, Mal dashed into the car and pulled down the mirror from the visor.

Jacques closed the door behind her, then sprinted around to his side. He shook his hair as he pulled on his seat belt.

'Look at me!' exclaimed Mal, pointing at the mascara running down her cheeks. She grabbed her phone and snapped a quick selfie, then ran her red, raw fingers under her lashes. 'Even Paddington looks better than this!'

'You look fine to me,' said Jacques. 'Now, how about lunch?'

Chapter Forty

Mal emerged from Jacques' bathroom, still towelling her hair. The sea spray and rain had turned her silver curls into an explosive tangle, and the towel was doing nothing to calm it down. Sighing, she accepted that her days of coiffured perfection were long behind her. Added to that was a complete lack of hand cream by the basin, and Mal apologised to the dry skin around her nails.

Draping the towel over her arm, she padded through to the kitchen in her bare feet. She'd only been here twice before, but the view over the bay still took her breath away, even as the rain lashed the window. Maybe, because the weather outside was so vile and inside was so warm and welcoming, it made the storm all the more dramatic. She wiggled her toes and looked at Jacques, who was already prepping the shells.

'Do you have underfloor heating?' She'd expected the slate tiles to be cold, but her feet were warming up instead.

'The joy of having to gut a house is that you can remake it exactly as you wish.'

Holding out a glass of wine, he exchanged the drink for the towel and hung it on the Aga's rail.

'Well, I certainly feel more human now. Thank you.' Mal looked at the countertop where Jacques had assembled bits and pieces. Whilst he seemed to be in his element, moving between pan and chopping board, Mal felt obliged to offer her help.

'It's all under control, but why don't you bring me up to speed with what's been going on at Liggan? Your letters sounded so breezy, but by my reckoning we're at a body count of three, and I sincerely hope there won't be any more.'

'No, just two.' Mal frowned. *Had she missed a dead body?* That felt careless.

'Lionel, Algernon, and the bones under the tree?'

Ah. She shook her head in relief. 'No, they were old, old bones. Pre-Conquest, apparently.'

'Ah, before we civilised this island?' Jacques asked, twitching his lips.

'Did you watch the match last Sunday?' said Mal innocently, in an apparent non sequitur.

'Bof. That was a disgrace.' Then he waggled a finger at Mal, who'd deliberately drawn his attention to the English drubbing of the French rugby team at the Stade de France. 'Let's call that even. No more insulting the other side, then.'

Mal stuck out a hand, and they shook, agreeing to play fair.

'So just two bodies, then. And you haven't solved it yet? I am shocked.'

'Oh, stop it. Sophie has been teasing me as well, but honestly, everything about this seems off.'

As she settled herself onto one of the stools, she watched Jacques work and brought him up to speed. She liked the simple way in which he prepared everything.

There was no rushing around or grandstanding, just a sense of calm that relaxed Mal. At one point, he knocked over his glass of wine, startling both of them, and she realised just how relaxed she was in his company.

'Ah, my nephew would berate me for spilling this. It's one he's particularly proud of.'

'He made this? I mean, is it his vineyard? It's delicious.'

'It's the family vineyard, but he's in charge. And by the taste of what he's producing recently, he's doing us proud. His children are all in the business as well, even young Hortense, although she appears to be drinking more than she's selling. But what do I know of young girls these days?'

'In my experience, they are much the same as young girls of any age. They're just not hiding behind veneers anymore.'

Jacques seemed unconvinced, but Mal left him to it. It wasn't her place to convince him that some teenager she'd never met wasn't going off the rails.

'And the police have stopped hounding Lachlan Jones, I hope?'

Clearly, Jacques also didn't want to dwell on his family any further as he poured himself a fresh glass and spooned the mussels into bowls. The smell of butter and garlic wrapped around the salty air of the dish, and Mal could swear she was drooling. It was a long way from the

285

smell of burning shells when she'd attempted the same meal.

'Yes. Poor Lachlan. A perfect example of wrong time, wrong person, wrong place. I felt dreadful when he told me what he had seen.'

'But why?' asked Jacques, as he placed the bowls on the kitchen island in front of Mal and settled down opposite her. Between them was a large bowl of buttered bread and an empty bowl for the shells.

'Because it was me that told him to talk to the police.'

'But he had to. He was a witness. He must have had vital information.'

'Oh, I know. But how odd it must have sounded to the police when he explained how he had seen the dead body but done nothing.'

Jacques dipped a chunk of bread into the mussel broth.

'Well, he has a very clear set of rules, and he already knew he was in trouble, from what you said, by approaching the house.'

'But his lack of concern over the fact that Algernon was dead…'

'An unusual but honest response. Still, it's understandable, I suppose, why the police wanted to question him further.'

'I know. He was just so clinical. The way he described the blood turning from white to red as the frost lifted…'

Mal paused. Something about that sentence was wrong. She fell silent, frowning as she tried to shuffle out the problem. The steam from the dish lifted the scent to her nose, and she absent-mindedly pushed her shells around the bowl.

'Is everything alright?'

Mal shook herself from her reverie and focused on Jacques. 'Yes, no. Sorry, the food is incredible. I'm amazed I had anything to do with it. No, it's what Lachlan said. Something's niggling me.'

'Let it go. Enjoy your food, and when the thought is ready, it will announce itself.'

'How very French of you.'

He shrugged and smiled at her, his eyes twinkling.

'Well, yes. Food is to be enjoyed, not worried like a dog with a sheep. So tell me—what else have you been doing? Have you been in the sea yet? I must confess, whilst I was skiing down the slopes, I thought how brave you were, even in a wetsuit.'

'I think I would draw the line at swimming in the snow, but I don't think that's much of an issue here, is it? Mostly, I've been settling into village life or trying to avoid it, if I'm honest. Walking, writing letters, reading books— entirely unexciting.'

The steam caught a rare shaft of sunlight, and Mal saw that the rain had passed.

'Oh, bloody hell. That's it.'

Jacques looked startled and twisted round to look out the window. 'What is? What have you seen?'

'Blood. The blood was white. That's what Lachlan said.'

'Yes, you said there was frost on the ground. It was very cold.'

'Yes, but don't you see? Everyone assumed Algernon had died that morning.'

'And?'

'But his blood would have been hot. It wouldn't have frozen—not indoors, even with the patio doors open. He must have been lying there a long time for his blood to have got cold enough to freeze.'

Mal was speaking quickly as she waved her spoon in the air, frantically tucking her hair behind her ear as she tried to marshal her thoughts.

'He didn't die that morning. He died the night before! The police have the wrong time of death. I have to tell Sophie.'

Jacques stared in sorrow at his half-empty bowl of mussels as Mal whipped out her phone and tapped away frantically. Then, with a satisfied smile, she slid her phone back into her pocket and, picking up her spoon, scooped it into the bowl.

'You don't have to leave?' His voice was hopeful and Mal shook her head, smiling. A week before, she would've been grabbing her pencil and jotting down all the variables about whose alibi was affected and who had night-time access to the house. The time of death changed so many factors. Yet here she sat in a warm kitchen, eating a delicious bowl of lunch in engaging company.

'No,' she said warmly, placing a shell in the bowl, 'I don't have to leave.'

Jacques was about to speak when Mal's phone rang, and she winced an apology at him. So few people had her number that it was only ever used if someone important needed her urgently. Her shoulders slumped when she saw Sophie's name on the display.

She answered. 'Hello, Sophie. A statement?'

Jacques stood and gave Mal a rueful grin and went to collect his car keys.

'Ten minutes?'

She looked across at Jacques, who raised his thumb.

'Yes. I'll see you then.'

Ending the call, she frowned. 'I'm afraid Sophie wants a statement right away.'

'Of course. I shall run you down there now.'

'I'm so sorry.'

'Nonsense. Besides which, I can see that you are dying to find out more about the case.'

'You're not wrong, but I was having such a lovely time.'

Jacques opened the front door, and they hunched up under the rain, which had picked up again as they dashed to the car.

As they drove down to the village, he spoke again. 'How about oysters next time?'

Mal looked across in surprise. She'd assumed that, since she'd cut and run, Jacques wouldn't extend a second invitation or would at least wait for her to suggest something.

'Oysters? Really? That sounds fun.'

'Excellent. Leave it with me, but in the meantime, may I ask a favour?'

'Anything,' said Mal, as she pulled her keys out of her pocket.

'Please don't do anything rash. The last time there was a death in the village, you were being shot at by the coastguard.'

Mal laughed. 'I promise. All I'm doing is giving a statement.'

'I don't know. You see a bone, and you can't let go.'

She shook her head, laughing. 'The only bones in this case don't count.'

Chapter Forty-One

The car pulled up outside the shop as Sophie headed down the lane in the opposite direction. Mal jumped out of the car before Jacques got out and, thanking him profusely, waved to Sophie.

The two women watched him drive away as he stuck his arm out the car window and gave them a friendly goodbye wave.

'Jacques is home early,' said Sophie. 'We don't tend to see him before spring.'

Mal shrugged. 'I think he had some business to take care of and needed to come back sooner.'

Sophie watched the car as it slowly made a right turn along the cobbled lanes, then drove out of sight. Mal had unlocked the door and called out to Sophie to come on in, and the two women headed upstairs.

As Mal recounted Lachlan's conversation, Sophie added her statement into her works tablet, a clever gizmo that immediately updated the entire team.

'So, are you a formal part of this investigation now?' asked Mal, knowing that Sophie would rather remain a police officer than a detective.

'I've been drafted in again. Local knowledge. Hemingstone thinks it's good PR to have female faces on the team. Like that's a thing. He's about twenty years behind the curve on what he thinks the job needs.'

'What about DI Williams? He struck me as being more switched on.'

'Oh, yes. He's going to go a long way. He enjoys playing the game, the schmoozing and whatnot, but he also enjoys having a good clean-up rate. And in fairness to Ted, he's also a really firm believer in community engagement.'

'So he's a good guy?'

'Nah, he's still a prat,' she laughed, 'but many shades above Hemingstone, so you have to work with what you've got. He might be in touch with you after this.'

Mal gave Sophie an old-fashioned look.

'No, don't worry,' said Sophie quickly. 'He spoke highly of you to me after the Trebetherick case. Like I said, he likes results, and he isn't proud about how he gets them. Remember, he has to work directly with Hemingstone, so whatever we think of Ted, we do also have to feel sorry for him.'

Sophie's pad beeped, and she had a quick glance. 'Okay. That's been actioned. Looks like Williams is off to talk to the coroner. See what effect thawed blood would have on the time of death.'

'Get them to ask if the study has underfloor heating. That might affect things. I was up at Jacques' just now and realised how warm it was on my feet. That would affect a body lying on the floor, depending on when it switched on. If they had it.' She trailed off as Sophie grinned at her. 'What?'

'Oh, nothing.' She smiled to herself, then paused. 'Hang on.' Grabbing the pad, she tapped on the screen and pulled up some photos. 'Don't tell anyone I showed you this, but have a look at the study. Can you see anything that indicates underfloor heating?'

Sophie passed the pad to Mal, revealing a few photos of the study but not of the body.

'I'm limiting what you can look at,' said Sophie as Mal flicked back and forwards. 'Can you see anything that suggests underfloor heating?'

Mal zoomed in and out of a few images but couldn't see anything. However, she honestly didn't know what she was looking for. But being part of the team just felt good. As she flicked through, one image caught her eye, and on the third pass, she looked at it for a while.

'Have you seen something?'

A group of photographs was sitting on the sideboard. Similar in style to the ones in the sitting room; family groups and individuals in silver frames all stared at the photographer. Unlike the collection in the sitting room, these were of an older, more formal generation, some in colour, others in black and white. In his robes, Lionel. as a young man, was receiving a degree in something or other, a red and blue sash lining his cape. In a younger photo, he sat smiling at the camera with a group of fellow rowers. Other than himself, the other photos were of formal aunts and uncles and parents; wedding photos; babies staring solemnly into the lens; young men in military dress looking proud and eager and so terribly young.

'Mal, what have you seen?'

Mal scratched her jaw thoughtfully. 'It's probably nothing, but something strikes me as familiar.'

'Care to share with an officer of the law?' said Sophie, eyeing Mal carefully.

'Not yet. Let me see if my hunch is correct, then I'll call you immediately. Can I take a picture of this?' asked Mal, nodding at the photo displayed on the tablet.

'Christ, no. I'd get bollocked for that,' said Sophie in alarm. 'If I were to knowingly share evidence with an unauthorised civilian, I could get fired.' She paused and glanced upwards, lost in thought. 'I mean, it's not like you haven't already been in his study anyway and seen this for yourself. In fact,' she said carefully, 'you could have even taken your own photo.'

She put the pad down on the table, carefully making sure the image was exposed, and zoomed in on the photos Mal had been interested in. 'Right. I'd better go to the loo then and leave you to it.' Slapping her thighs, she stood up and walked to the bathroom. 'I shall be about two minutes, I reckon.' Then she closed the door.

Mal looked after her in astonishment, then laughed as the penny dropped. Pulling out her phone, she took a photograph of the screen, then tucked her phone out of sight and went to wash the cups.

When Sophie returned, she made a pantomime of retrieving her pad and placing it back in its wallet. Then she headed to the door as Mal walked with her back to the front of the shop.

'Now, I can't say this clearly enough. If something occurs to you, what do you do?'

'I do nothing.'

'Correct.' said Sophie, beaming. 'And then what do you do?'

'I call you.'

'And if you can't get me?'

'I call DI Williams?'

'Perfect. Now, enjoy the rest of your afternoon, and apologise to Jacques for me.'

'To Jacques? Whatever for?'

Sophie shook her head.

'You know, for a bright woman, you are a little bit dim. Now, remember what I said. Don't do anything without speaking to me.'

Mal watched, perplexed, as Sophie walked off down the street. A little thump from the ceiling announced that Mac had woken up and was probably on his way down for food. As she fed him, she studied the photo she'd taken and tried to understand what the connection was. There were some curious coincidences, but they made little sense to the murders. Deciding to push it to the back of her mind, she put some music on and settled into her armchair.

So far, she'd had a most pleasant day. Running in the rain back to the car as she and Jacques traded tongue-twisters had been very silly, and the moment when they shook hands had surprised her. For so long, she had been without the touch of another human. His hand had been warm and strong, although, from the calluses on his fingers, he clearly had never heard of moisturising lotion. Looking at her own hands, she was relieved they were no longer red raw, but she squeezed some Clarins onto them anyway. He'd probably thought her hands were old and skinny. The skin was no longer tight like it used to be, and her freckles were joining up into larger freckles that she refused to call liver spots.

It had been a good day, and she had oysters to look forward to as well. Her wine at lunch had made her feel oddly lethargic. As she curled up in the armchair, she fell promptly asleep, Jacques' last words to her about old bones running through her head.

Mal woke with a start and a groan. She'd woken up in the chair. The room was dark and cold, and she ached all over.

'Idiot,' she mumbled to herself. Standing up, she stumbled over something on the floor and kicked her book out of the way. She didn't fancy doing anything as energetic as stretching, so she limped over to the kitchen, slowly unknotting her body. After turning on the light, she filled the kettle for a hot water bottle. The flat was freezing, and she would never get back to sleep if she was shivering under her duvet.

'Mac?'

In the silence, Mal shrugged. No doubt, Mac was off terrorising the local rodent population. She yawned and, having screwed the stopper into the bottle, headed upstairs. As she fell asleep again, she dreamt of cats and old bones.

Chapter Forty-Two

'Sophie, I think I know who the killer is!'

Mal could hear Sophie shouting at her children in the background, trying to get them ready for school after the weekend.

'I'm sorry to call so early, but I woke up and saw that I had been asking the wrong questions. Started at the wrong place.'

As she explained her theory to Sophie, she could sense the younger woman becoming increasingly wary.

'I don't know, Mal. That seems like an incredible stretch. And without evidence, we're going to need a confession.'

'I have a plan for that.'

Mal had been working on this all morning. The moment she woke up, a fog seemed to have lifted, and everything was down to the burial of a little girl with her pet dog over a millennium before.

'No. Not those shoes. Mal. Listen to me. Don't do anything. Yes, those shoes. Ugh, Mal, sorry, this is a bad moment. Danny's on nights, and Billy has chickenpox. Look, I'll call DI Williams. Do nothing. Don't talk to anyone and don't do anything. No, those are your sister's.'

Mal tried to separate Sophie's mangled conversation, and promising that she would stay put, she hung up.

She then went out for a quick walk.

Half an hour later, she'd had a few interesting conversations and was heading back to the shop when her phone rang. She didn't recognise the number and answered cautiously. The last thing she wanted to do right now was tie up her number with a telesales pitch.

'Hello, Malachite Peck speaking.'

'Good morning, Malachite, this is DI Williams. I believe you have a theory.'

Mal unlocked the shop door and sat down in one of the reading chairs as she explained her deductions to the detective.

From time to time, he interrupted her to clarify a point, then let her continue. At no stage did he dismiss or denigrate her theory. Eventually, she ran out of steam and waited for his reaction.

'Some of what you said ties into our suspicions, especially as time of death has now been revised and we can throw some of the main alibis out of the window. But without a full confession, I think we're going to struggle to get a conviction.'

'I agree, but I think I know a way to do it.'

Two hours later, Mal walked up the Liggan drive alone. She'd called Imogen and told her she had some news on the case and asked her to gather the family. With Imogen agreeing, she then made a few more phone calls and began to slot things into place. DI Williams had made it very clear that he thought her plan was dreadful, but he couldn't stop her. He also warned her that no police could be involved. If any confessions were made, no hint of entrapment could exist.

Even then, a confession wouldn't be enough, but it would strengthen the police's case.

And after a month with no developments, the police were getting desperate.

As she came down the driveway, she nodded at Dougie, who smiled nervously at her. 'You understand what you have to do?'

He nodded.

'And on no account let them into the living room until you hear my cue.'

Content that he knew what to do, even if he didn't know why, Mal headed towards the house. As she knocked on the door, Henry flung it open and glared at her, and she smiled benignly back. This was going to be difficult for him, so she tried to quell her dislike.

'Did your mother tell you I had some news? About the heir?'

'She did. Who is it? Do they exist? The police said the diary entries gave no further clues than Dad got some girl called Pearl pregnant. Not even if the baby was born. I mean, Christ, she could have had a miscarriage. That's why he was so upset.'

'Who are you talking to?' Imogen called out from within the house.

Flustered, Henry apologised and invited Mal indoors. As she entered the sitting room, she was grateful for the fire roaring in the hearth. Though anxious about the next few minutes, she was certain she had the right of it. That Sophie and Williams agreed with her was reassuring, but she knew she was a harbinger of doom, which chilled her bones. She really could've done with their presence, but Williams had been dreadfully clear on that point.

As she followed Henry into the room, Imogen saw her and jumped up. 'Mal, what's going on? Do you know who the murderer is? I knew you would solve this.'

The woman was flustered, and Mal felt chilled by the warmth of her welcome. Looking around the room, she saw Henry was sitting alone on one sofa, Daisy was sitting beside Imogen, but the children were absent. Jasper was sitting on a two-seater sofa, and Mal was glad to see Holly sitting next to him. Mal had contacted her earlier and suggested that she be with Jasper. Given the hostile glares she was receiving, her addition to the family was not going down well. But then, this wasn't the best of circumstances to meet potential in-laws.

Mal cleared her throat, and everyone stared at her. 'Thank you all for gathering here. I just felt it would be easier to tell you what I found, all at the same time. As you know, Imogen asked me to help her the day the Old Man fell down in the gales, and ever since, I'm afraid I've been somewhat drawn into your current situation.'

She paused. She was playing for time and had no idea how long she might need to spin this out. Until the first domino was in place, the rest couldn't fall.

'I had been reading one of Lionel's early diaries and found a man who seemed very different from the man you all knew. This man was a dreamer and full of enthusiasm.'

Jasper was leaning forward.

Daisy looked angry. 'What does this have to do with the murder of my husband? And why are we listening to you, anyway? Where are the police?' When Holly tutted, Daisy rounded on her. 'And who the hell is this, Jasper? This is a private moment. We don't need village gawpers in here.'

Jasper had been holding Holly's hand and gave her a quick smile before turning to Daisy. 'Auntie Daisy, I love you, and I know this is a dreadful time for you. But you're going to have to get used to Holly. I love her too.'

'Oh, for the love of God,' roared Henry. 'No, you don't. You've just fallen for some village gold-digger.'

'Dad! Don't you bloody dare speak about Holly like that!'

Mal's phone buzzed. She looked down and saw the short text from Dougie. *Perfect timing*, she thought. The room was already pretty explosive.

Raising her voice, she caught everyone's attention. 'In which case, I have no option but to inform the police and have them arrest Lachlan Jones for the murder of Lionel Haverstock.'

Everyone in the room stopped arguing and stared at her in confusion. Imogen was about to speak when the door flung open, and Mrs Kitto hobbled into the middle of the room.

'You can't arrest Lachlan. I killed Lionel, and I'd do it again. The boy is innocent.'

Chapter Forty-Three

As Mrs Kitto's confession hit Imogen, shock and grief washed over her. She let out a pained cry and attempted to stand up, but her legs buckled under her, and she collapsed back onto the sofa. 'Henry, what's going on? I don't understand.'

Henry stared at the intruder, his face blossoming with rage. 'Who the bloody hell are you?'

Most of the room looked at Mrs Kitto blankly. Only Holly stared at her in amazement and whispered to Jasper, who then looked puzzled.

Mal held her nerve. So far, her plan had worked like clockwork, but she still had a way to go and was desperate to keep the show on the road.

'Malachite,' said Jasper, his voice cold with anger, 'would you explain?'

Mal looked at Margaret Kitto with pity. The old woman was visibly shaking, and Mal was concerned for her state of mind as well as her body.

'Mrs Kitto, would you care to sit down?'

'Now, hang on a minute,' Henry interrupted. 'This is my house, and I say who sits down.'

'Unless you want another dead body in this house, I suggest you permit Mrs Kitto to sit before she falls.'

Mrs Kitto sneered at the assembled room. 'I'm fine standing.'

'No, you're not.' Mal waved at Jasper to get a chair, then addressed the woman again. 'You've just confessed to murder. You've saved Lachlan. Now, for once in your life, do as you're told. Or do you want to embarrass yourself by fainting on the floor of Liggan Hall?'

Mal watched the struggle on the old woman's face. Clearly, the idea of making a fool of herself set fire to her resolve, and she made a point of sitting down on the edge of the seat. As she straightened her back, she made it clear that she took no comfort from the chair or any implied hospitality from the occupants of Liggan.

'Now, do you want to explain why you killed Lionel?' asked Mal.

'I do not.'

'This is ridiculous,' said Henry. 'How the hell could she have even got into this house? I've never even seen her before.'

'Mrs Kitto knows this house inside out,' said Mal.

'That's impossible.'

'I never thought Lionel's son would be so stupid,' the older woman said.

'He's not Lionel's son,' said Mal, 'but we'll come to that.'

Margaret Kitto narrowed her eyes as she looked at Henry, then back at Mal.

'Mrs Kitto used to work here many years ago,' said Mal to Henry. 'Decades ago, in fact, long before you were born.'

305

'But why would she wait decades to murder my father?'

Mal rolled her shoulders. She was working on a hunch and wanted to make sure she had it right. As she began, she turned to address Margaret directly. After all, the story was hers, and Mal wanted to watch her expression. She wanted to stay on the right path, but she also didn't want to hurt the old woman.

'Ever since Imogen asked me to get involved, something about the murder of Lionel made no sense. Everyone was so fixated on his will and then, with Algernon's murder, that was the focus of everyone's attention. But what was it that had triggered Lionel's declaration to change his will? It was the discovery of a grave. We all overlooked that because what could a Saxon burial have to do with current events? But for a few critical hours, no one knew the bones were ancient. It was the discovery of those bones, *those child's bones*, that set two chains of action in motion. Lionel declared his will invalid, and Margaret Kitto decided to murder him.'

'I don't understand,' said Imogen. 'Why would you want to kill my husband?'

Margaret remained closed faced. She blinked occasionally, but her mouth was a thin, hard line, her lips bleached white, and she stared straight ahead.

'Because she was once in love with Lionel,' said Mal, 'and he was very much in love with her.'

Margaret's lip curled slightly as she sneered. Mal tried to keep the pity out of her voice as she spoke to the older lady, knowing it would be unwelcome. Plus, she thought her own heart would break if she allowed herself to show any compassion. Their story was pitiful and had ended in despair.

'He kept a diary, Mrs Kitto. All his life. Jasper, there, asked me to dispose of the books, and I read the first diary and discovered a young man very much in love with a girl called Pearl. In his diary, he hinted that there was some barrier blocking their relationship, and it had to be kept quiet. As I read it, I thought he was somehow at fault, that he wasn't good enough for Pearl as he was protecting her.'

'Reckon it was the other way round. I wasn't good enough for him. Or his family.'

All eyes turned to Margaret as she fell silent again, but her face had twisted into disdain as she met their eyes.

'Whatever Lionel's parents thought of you, he adored you. His love for you sang off the pages. He would record all your adventures as you counted whales in the bay, tracked the herring shoals, recorded the birds. He admired your knowledge and intellect. Lionel loved you very much.'

The weight of Margaret's furious expression fell heavily on Mal's shoulders, but she carried on.

'It was the little girl buried with her dog that made me see it all anew. All those centuries ago, that little girl had been well loved, so much so that when she died, she was buried with her pet to keep her company. The archaeologists think they both died in a fire. It's a very rare burial, but reminds us that people a thousand years ago are no different from us today.'

Mal paused, and Dougie brought her a glass of water. The room was silent as everyone waited to hear what she had to say next.

'If I had children myself, maybe I would have seen this quicker. If Lionel had referred to you by your Christian name of Margaret rather than your diminutive Pearl, I might have seen it sooner, but in the end I realised. You were the girl that got pregnant in his diary. It was your child that you thought was buried under that tree. And it was your love for your child and your anger at Lionel that drove you to murder him.'

Margaret inhaled, her nostrils flaring.

'They promised me they would send her to live with nice people. Lionel had run away and left me to the mercies of his parents. They paid me off and stole my baby. All these years, I prayed for her and hoped she'd had a good life, but they killed her and buried her. When Holly there said a child's bones had been found, I knew immediately whose they were.' She dipped her head, and when she looked up, her face was transformed with rage. 'All these years, they had played me for a fool. A stupid village girl spread her legs for honeyed words. Not worth spit to them. I knew all the ways into the house. A scullery maid knows all the ins and outs, and I headed for his bedroom using the old priest's way. I had a syringe full of morphine, a leftover from when I did a bit of community nursing. I was ready to stab him in his sleep, but he was wide awake.'

She paused.

'And?' whispered Imogen.

'And nothing. That's between me and him.' She glared around the room.

There was silence, then Henry stood up. 'Right. Jasper, don't let her out of this room.' Pulling a phone from his pocket, he tapped the screen three times.

'Police, please.'

Everyone stared at him in silence.

'Hello, yes. This is Mr Henry Haverstock at Liggan Hall. A woman has just confessed to the murders of my father and brother. Please send an officer to arrest her.' After closing the call, he stared at Mrs Kitto. 'Maybe you'll explain to the police what you and my father discussed, or maybe not. But either way, you are going to jail for a very long time for the misery you've caused this family.'

Jasper looked at his aunt and grandmother, who were both crying, then turned to Mal. 'So that's it? His death had nothing to do with his will?'

Mal cleared her throat and got to her feet again. Since the police had been called, she had to work quickly. 'Margaret,' she said softly, aware of the pain she was about to inflict. 'Do you know what Lionel's will said?'

The old woman shrugged.

'He said that he left his entire estate to his true heir. Like you, Lionel truly believed his child lived.'

Margaret opened her handbag and pulled out a white handkerchief and gripped it fiercely in her fist, but didn't raise it to her eyes.

Mal continued, 'It was all in his diary. He was so ashamed that his parents had forced him to leave you and your child that he swore an oath to himself and to you that he would never have another child. And he didn't. He went and had a vasectomy as revenge against his father's obsession with the family line and then left for the States. He believed you had asked for your child to be adopted, and he respected your decision and left. You were the love of his life, and he never forgave himself for betraying you. When he returned to Liggan, he avoided you, as much as you avoided him.'

Imogen sobbed and buried her head in her hands.

'What are you crying for?' snapped Margaret, her hands wringing the handkerchief. 'You never lost a child. You lived your life up here, a Barbie doll in the big house.'

Her words were whip sharp, and Imogen flinched.

'That's enough, Margaret,' said Mal. 'Imogen lived a loveless life, and she *has* lost a child. A little compassion all round is what's needed right now.'

'Why are we letting this woman speak?' barked Henry. 'Where are the bloody police?' He paced over to the window, hoping to conjure a police car heading up the drive.

Imogen watched him, then turned to Margaret. 'He never loved me.' After Henry's outburst, she sounded frail. 'I never knew why, and here you are sitting in front of me. He never even told me he'd had a vasectomy.'

'Made a fool of you right enough, then. God, he must have hated you for your deceit.'

'My deceit?'

'Mother. This is unnecessary. She's confessed to the murders. That's enough. There's no real heir, which means that, as his wife and next of kin, the estate goes to you. I spoke to a solicitor, and while there's going to be a ton of paperwork to settle, it's all quite clear. Liggan Hall is yours.'

'Except it's not,' said Mal.

Chapter Forty-Four

Once again, everyone stared at her. She wasn't done yet, but she needed to tread carefully.

'We're all forgetting the bones. We know how Margaret reacted when she heard about them, but remember how Lionel reacted. He changed his will. Both Lionel and Margaret believed the bones belonged to their child. It was another day before the truth was revealed about the burial. The fact is that their baby didn't die but grew into adulthood and had a child of their own.'

Margaret's breathing had increased, and Mal tried to move carefully through her story.

'The baby didn't die?' said Imogen. 'She killed her lover for nothing?'

Mal frowned, noting that grieving widows were clearly lacking in tact. 'What's important is that, as the will stands, there is an heir.'

'Complete rubbish,' said Henry. 'I should have been his heir. That's what he was going to change his will to say.'

Mal took a deep breath and spoke softly. 'You're probably right. Is that what you said to Algernon before you killed him?'

'What? How dare you! I didn't kill my brother.'

'Not deliberately, I'm sure. Did he slip as you snatched the book out of his hands? Hit his head on the table?'

'It was a robbery. The candlestick.'

'The coroner has concluded that the blow to the back of the head matches the coffee table, not the candlestick. Which means the body was also moved to make it look like a robbery gone wrong.'

'Well, so what? I wasn't here.'

'When would that be?'

'Whenever the robbery took place, I was in London. Tell him, Jasper.'

'That's right, Mal. My father called me that morning on FaceTime. He was in London.'

'But Algernon was murdered the previous evening. Plenty of time for your father to make it look like a break-in, then drive up to London.'

'Don't talk rot. The police said time of death was in the morning.'

Mal shook her head. 'Apparently, they had been unaware that the body had been exposed to freezing temperatures. It threw the time of death.'

For a moment, fear flashed across Henry's face, then was gone as he scoffed at her. 'Rubbish. I phoned Jasper that night as well to say I had arrived. And I called him the following morning too.'

Jasper squirmed uncomfortably. 'I must have missed that first call.'

Mal smiled kindly. 'Don't worry. Your phone will have a record of the missed call.'

'Unless he wiped it,' said Henry desperately. 'Look, can't we go easy on the lad? If my son had anything to do with the death of his uncle, I'm sure it was a tragic accident.'

'Dad! What are you saying?'

'Look, son. The diary was hidden in the dog kennels. Your fingerprints are on the diaries. You knew what was in them. Maybe you thought your uncle was going to inherit. You were trying to protect me.' Henry's words rushed out in a wild heap of explanations.

'Dad, I have an alibi. The police confirmed it. I was with Holly.'

'In the morning. But what about the night before?'

'Dad.' Jasper's voice cracked as he realised his father kept trying to suggest he'd murdered his uncle and covered it up. 'I have the same alibi for that entire time frame.'

'Jesus Christ, Jasper!' shouted Henry, making everyone jump. 'It was an accident. You'll be out in five years. You'll still be a young man. What about me? Do you want me to go to prison? Want me to die in there?'

'Dad!' Jasper almost wailed.

'Are you seriously asking your son to confess to your killing?' asked Holly. She'd been silent the entire time, but was clearly incensed.

Good girl, thought Mal. *You'll need more of that if you're going to be part of this family.*

'Henry.' Imogen's face was ashen as she gripped Daisy's hand. 'Tell me it's not true?'

Henry turned, snarling, 'What? That I killed your precious son? Your snivelling waste-of-space son? Never once did he do anything to earn his money. He either waited on you like a lapdog or married what he'd hoped was a cash cow. I didn't mean to kill him, but I'm not sorry I did.'

Daisy had been sitting, sobbing quietly for most of the time, listening to Margaret's confession in growing alarm and confusion. Never once had the old woman mentioned Algernon, and now Mal seemed to be accusing Henry of murdering him. Mal watched her struggling to keep up, but when he referred to her as a cash cow, something in her snapped.

'Daisy!' shouted Mal, as much a warning to the younger widow as an alert to the others in the room.

Daisy wasn't listening. She leapt onto the coffee table in front of her and launched herself at Henry. Slashing her hand across his face, he fell back in surprise, stumbling. With Imogen shrieking, Jasper sprinted forward, knocking a side table over as he tried to pull his aunt from his father. Blood was running down Henry's face from three long nail scratches. Daisy was kicking and beating him as he tried to push her off, her hair coming undone as she thrashed at him. Imogen was pleading with her to stop, but Daisy's screams of 'murderer!' were drowning her out. Eventually, Jasper pulled her off his father and pinned her arms to her sides. The room fell silent. All Mal could hear was Daisy panting and Imogen sobbing.

315

Henry climbed to his feet and leant on the mantelpiece as he glared around the room. He was panting heavily and attempted to smooth his fringe back off his forehead with a trembling hand.

'Leave. Now. All of you,' he all but snarled, as his eyes darted wildly about the room. 'Get out of my house.'

'It's not your house,' Mal said calmly. When Henry made his confession, she had sent a quick text to DI Williams. With only minutes before the police arrived, the time had come to play the last card. Whilst everyone was staring at Henry in stunned horror, Mal only had minutes to finesse the last revelation. 'Dougie, could you bring in the items we discussed?'

'What the hell sort of nonsense are you playing at, Mrs Peck? I insist you get out now.'

The blood on his face was drying, smeared and flaking, across his flushed face. He shoved his dishevelled hair off his face again and kept glancing at the window. The police would be arriving any minute, and he was in serious trouble.

'Henry, how could you?' Imogen moaned. 'Your own brother?'

'It was a bloody mistake!' yelled Henry, the mottling around his neck was now spreading to his face. 'The stupid fool tried to snatch the diary from me. I yanked it away, and he fell backward. I didn't kill him. He did it to himself.'

'Then why not say so?' pleaded Imogen.

'Are you stupid? After I had said I would kill him before he inherited a penny? With the entire estate left to an unknown party, if everyone thought it was the mysterious heir, we'd get the estate back.'

'You tried to blame me, Dad.'

'For Christ's sake, Jasper. Man up. I was doing this for the family.'

At that moment, Dougie returned to the room holding two picture frames and brought them to Mal. He was watching the whole room, and Mal was very glad to have another man present. Henry was already beyond reason, and the next few minutes could be disastrous.

'Can you show them to Imogen, please, and ask her who's in them?'

'I don't understand,' said Imogen. 'Why are we playing parlour games?'

'Please, Imogen,' said Mal. 'I know you are going through agony, but a grave miscarriage has taken place, and you can help fix it. Who's in the photos?'

Imogen looked at the couple and child. It was an old black and white photo.

'That's Lionel with his parents. Jemima Haverstock was a beautiful woman. Presented to the Queen, you know. Could have been a lady-in-waiting. So beautiful. And his father, such a handsome figure. Just like Lionel.'

'And in the other photo?'

That picture showed a baby in a pram with a teddy bear. From the age of the photograph it was a more recent image.

'Oh, I don't know. Some cousin, I believe.'

'Where was it taken?'

'Here, clearly. You can see the steps to the orangery in the background.'

'And would you say it's the same teddy as the one that the young Lionel is holding in the first picture?'

Imogen examined both photos carefully.

'Yes. Although the teddy in this picture has something blue stitched in its ears.'

'Forget-me-nots,' said Margaret Kitto. Everyone turned and looked at the old woman who had been sitting in silence, lost in thoughts.

Mal stood up and removed the photo of the child and handed it to Margaret. The old woman looked at the photo, her fingers gently caressing the image as a tear splashed onto the glass. Wiping her eyes, she looked up at Mal. 'They said the baby should have something of its mother before she was adopted. I had nothing to give her, and so I embroidered forget-me-nots in the teddy's ears in the hope that my daughter would always know she was loved.' She wiped her eyes again. 'Where was this photo?'

'On Lionel's desk. He looked at it every day.'

'The baby was his daughter, not a cousin?' asked Imogen, now also crying. 'All those years he mourned her loss?'

The silence was acute as everyone contemplated the loss that both Lionel and Margaret had endured. Separated by society's expectations and forced to abandon their baby.

'So the heir survived,' said Henry, grasping at straws. 'That has to be who killed Algernon. Well, their child anyway. There are lots of men around here. Dougie, for example, has access to the house. Fought with Algernon and then, when he killed him, made it look like a robbery and hid the diary in the kennels.'

Poor Dougie shook his head in amazement, then laughed. 'Are you having a laugh? You just confessed. We all heard you.'

Henry ignored him and turned to Mal. 'Are you done? The police will be here any minute, and they need to arrest these two. I suggest you leave now.'

Imogen continued to stare at her son in horror. Not five minutes before, he'd confessed to killing his brother, and now he was making wild accusations, blaming others.

Mal cleared her throat. 'I'm almost done. Dougie, I wonder if you would pass that photo to Holly. Please? And Holly, the item I asked you to bring with you when you came to support Jasper, could you hand that to Mrs Kitto?'

Holly looked reluctant, but she stood and walked over to Mother Kitto. Looking down at the old woman, Holly spoke cautiously. 'I know you don't care much about us incomers, but this is very precious to me. I don't normally let outsiders touch him, so please be careful.'

As Holly opened her bag, Mrs Kitto tightened her grip on the picture frame. She had no intention of releasing the image of her child. From the bag, Holly gently pulled out the small teddy bear that sat in the corner of her shop, protecting all within. In each ear was a blue stitched flower.

The room was silent as Margaret's gnarled fingers gingerly stretched out to take the teddy, the same soft toy as featured in the photograph. Almost absently, she released the picture frame to Holly as she held the teddy again for the first time in sixty years. Gently, her fingers stroked the small ears as she stared at it, a distant smile pulling at her lips.

'How?' Imogen sobbed.

'Holly's grandmother was adopted. Her adopted family told her she was Cornish, but never said any more than that,' said Mal. 'Holly's grandmother moved here when she was expecting Holly's mother. Isn't that right?'

'Yes,' said Holly, as her voice wavered. 'Granny said they came here one day and fell in love with the place. She said she felt an instant attraction.'

'That's because she was born here,' said Mal, smiling. 'Holly, allow me to introduce your great-grandmother to you. Mrs Kitto, this girl is your great-granddaughter. You can do a DNA test to guarantee it, but I think you'll find you're family.'

'Bloody hell,' whispered Jasper.

'Yes,' said Mal, staring at Henry, 'Holly is the true heir to the Liggan Estate.'

Chapter Forty-Five

Margaret Kitto sat on her chair, lost in the past. When Mrs Peck announced that the young girl from the ice cream shop was her great-granddaughter and also the heir to Liggan, Henry had started screaming. He punched his son, who was trying to protect Holly. Dougie, in turn, punched him straight in the face and then threw him to the ground. As Henry fought and kicked to free himself from the younger man, several police officers burst into the room. As they got Henry to his feet, he promptly punched one of the female officers in the gut and threw a vase at another officer.

It had taken a further two officers to restrain him, and now Margaret sat waiting for another police car to come and take her away. A police officer waited with her, but what did they think she was going to do? Make a sprint for it? No, the old woman sat on the chair and watched.

As she looked around the room, Lionel's wife and daughter-in-law were sobbing. Holly was trying to staunch the blood from Jasper's nose. The furniture was knocked over, and the fire in the grate had gone out. That would never have happened in her day. She remembered cleaning it and rebuilding it every morning before the family woke, then heading to the kitchen to help prepare breakfast. Once all the morning chores were done, she headed back down the hill to work in a local café. In the evening, she worked a shift in the pub. Weekends she had to herself, except for her morning shift at Liggan. It was the sixties and household staff were almost a thing of the past, but she liked her job, especially since Lionel had returned from university. Most weekends, after breakfast, the two of them would sneak away together and talk about the clouds, the seas, and the wildlife. But most of all, they would talk about building a future together.

'Mrs Kitto?'

Margaret looked up and saw that Holly had approached. Jasper was talking to his grandmother, and Holly had pulled a seat over. Looking at the young girl's red hair, she remembered her own mother's red hair; it was the exact shade. She had a sweet temper, though, and was happy to help Margaret raise her baby.

'Lionel's father came to see my parents. Told them the baby would have a better life if it was adopted. They also offered them a huge sum of money. Mum said no, but Pa was always about the money, and he said yes.'

'But what about you?'

'Me?' Margaret blinked in astonishment at Holly. 'What choice did I have? I wasn't like you modern girls. I couldn't raise a child by myself.'

'But what about Lionel?'

'He left. They shipped him away the minute they found out. It was only when I last saw him that he told me they'd said I wanted the adoption and had sold our baby to them.'

'They lied!'

Margaret scoffed. 'Look at the people in this room. Are you surprised? That's what this lot do. They lie and cheat to get what they want.'

'Not Jasper.'

'Maybe.'

'No, Jasper's different.'

Margaret shrugged. She was still trying to come to terms with the fact that this incomer, this upstart, was in fact her great-granddaughter.

'How come you and Lionel never met up again?'

'You know how it is here. That lot don't come down to the village. We don't go to the same places. And as far as I was concerned, Lionel had betrayed me. Why would I search him out?' She let out a deep sigh. 'And he thought I had sold our baby and wanted nothing to do with her.' She straightened her shoulders and looked Holly in the eyes. 'I know I have no right to ask this of you, but now you own Liggan, can I ask that you don't fire Lachlan? He's always been very dear to me. I liked to pretend he was the family I'd never had. I thought God put him in my path to take care of and look out for him. Will you do that?'

Holly tilted her head and sighed. 'I haven't even got my head around the fact that this is all mine. But yes, Lachlan's job is safe. Of course it is. I really like him, besides which, I wouldn't be firing anyone. That's not me at all.'

'Just like your great-grandfather. He was always fair-minded, no matter what I came to believe of him. I should never have doubted him.'

'I can't believe we're related,' said Holly, timidly.

'On that, we agree. Although your hair is the same shade as my mother's. What would she be? Your great-great-grandmother, I suppose. She's been gone a long time. It would have been nice to tell her about you. She always said it was a sin to let the baby go.'

'You believe in God, don't you?' Holly asked. 'Maybe you can tell her in your prayers.'

Margaret sat up in her chair and gave Holly a stern look. 'Are you telling me you don't believe in God?'

The young woman looked uncomfortable.

Margaret straightened her spine, drumming her crooked fingers on her handbag. 'Well, we'll see about that.'

'I can't wait for you to meet Gran. She says the same thing.'

Gingerly, in case her gesture was rejected, Holly offered her hand to Margaret. Her fingers looked old and bony, wrapped in the soft embrace of Holly's hands.

'I may never get the chance to meet her again,' said Margaret, her voice breaking. 'I don't believe prison is the place for family reunions.'

Holly chuckled and carefully patted Margaret's hand. 'I believe, in the words of a wise old woman, we'll see about that.'

Chapter Forty-Six

Mal was sitting at a window table of the St Mawes Hotel restaurant, overlooking the sea. Smiling, she gently ran a finger across the white linen cloth and took a sip of wine.

'And he really tried to ask Jasper, his own son, to take the blame?' Jacques' voice was laced with astonishment.

'Even I didn't expect that,' said Mal. 'Of course, when DI Williams arrived, he retracted his confession. Down at the station, however, Sophie said all the evidence against him was overwhelming. The cameras on the M4 clocked his car in the early hours heading towards London. There was no phone call made to Jasper. His confession in front of the others, plus Daisy's rather savage attack, all weighed against him, and eventually, he confessed. His solicitor is going for manslaughter, which I suspect is probably the right call.'

Jacques refilled Mal's water and offered her some more wine.

'After the oysters. It's been so long I don't want anything to mar the taste of them.'

He raised his glass and toasted her. 'You are a clever woman, indeed. And tell me. What of Margaret Kitto? Did she retract her confession?'

'Not a bit of it. She said it was important to set an example for her family. You know, she smiled when she said that. Holly called her mother and grandmother, and Margaret has been reunited with all of them. Her solicitor is saying her hands are too arthritic to have been able to inject the syringe properly. According to Holly, they are arguing that Lionel did it himself. Margaret still won't say what happened in that bedroom.'

'What do you think happened?'

'No idea. But it's a valid theory. She came to kill him but wasn't physically able. In his grief and shame, he killed himself. Remember, that night they both thought their child had died and her body had been buried up by the Old Man. It would mean a reduced sentence for Margaret. She may even be allowed to spend time with her daughter and her family.'

'And what of Holly? Isn't it her grandmother who is the heir?'

The conversation came to a halt as the oysters arrived. With intense delight, Mal tipped her first oyster down in a glug of salt water and lemon juice, then laughed out loud.

'My God. That tastes good.' She grinned at Jacques, who followed suit and grinned back.

'Falmouth oysters really are the finest.' He swallowed a second oyster, then continued, 'So... Holly?'

'Yes, it's her grandmother's, but both she and her mother have said that Holly should treat Liggan as her own.'

'And the Haverstocks?'

Mal shrugged.

'It's all rather dreadful for them, isn't it? Holly said Imogen could stay on in one of the cottages, but she promptly packed her bags and moved up to London. I don't know what's happened to the rest of the family. Holly says Jasper says they are all back in their homes, trying to work out what happens next. Daisy has lost her husband. Jocasta's husband, Henry, is facing prison. And Jasper is still getting used to the fact that his girlfriend has the power to evict him. It's all a bit upside down.'

'Young love. They will find a way.'

'I do hope so. Something good has to come of decades of pain and misery. Lionel and Margaret spent their lives in bitterness. I hope this generation finds a way to overcome it.'

Jacques carefully dabbed his napkin on his beard to remove any crumbs from the bread. 'And what about you? Is it back to the peace and quiet of the bookshop, or are you looking for more adventures?'

Mal had just swallowed an oyster and found herself choking as she spluttered a protest.

'Absolutely not!' She drank some water and wiped her eyes, noticing mascara on her finger; she really had to get a waterproof version. 'But I am going to have to find a better way to spend my time. I've decided to try my hand at Instagram, sharing my new life with anyone who's interested. And...' She paused and grimaced. 'And I've also thought I'd try my hand at writing a book.'

She looked across at Jacques, waiting to see if he would laugh. Instead, he raised his glass again, and she lifted hers in response.

'Good for you. What will you write?'

'Don't laugh, but I thought a crime story. I think it would be good if I could keep the body count within the pages of a book rather than my day-to-day life.'

Jacques laughed as he put his glass down and asked the waiter for some more bread.

Taking a sip of wine, she looked around the restaurant. The crystal and linen, the silverware and beautiful furnishings, all felt very familiar and welcoming. It was a place where she knew how to behave. This was where she felt at home. Today, her hair was held back in a chignon, a style she hadn't quite perfected and the odd curl kept escaping, but it went well with her outfit and jewellery. She looked out across the sparkling sea and thought of her other outfit, neoprene and seaweed, and laughed.

'A penny for them?'

'Just thinking. I somehow seem to have found a second home, a second life. And I like it. Even if I'm still finding my way.'

'So you think you'll stay?'

'I think so. Yes.'

A Letter from Anna, and a Gift

Dear Reader,

This has been an excellent adventure to write. The inspiration for this story starts from a real event. I was working on an archaeological dig in Dorset, and our leader told us of an old oak that had fallen over in a recent storm. When the roots pulled out of the earth, it pulled up the bones of an Anglo-Saxon burial. This story has always stayed with me and this felt the perfect time to revisit the event.

Once again, I am hugely grateful to the assistance of my early readers: Bernadette McGrath, Ruth Goddard, Sharon White Gilson, Amanda Graham, Angela Nurse, Carrie O'Donoghue, Colleen Fullick, Mags Farquhar, Marcie Whitecotton-Carroll, Sarah Sullivan, Stuart Lovell, Alexandra Warsop and Susan Hallard. I would also like to thank my very hard-working editors, Andy Hodge and Kelly Reed.

In particular, I should like to thank Deputy Chief Constable for Devon and Cornwall Police, Jim Colwell. He was good enough to spend time with me, going through my manuscript and offering insights and guidance over several scenes. We worked out where dramatic licence was fine, and fixed some out-and-out errors. All mistakes left in, are, of course, my own. I enjoyed my time with him and learnt so much more about my local police force. It's not an easy job, but I think our local force is excellent.

You may be interested to know what Mal is reading in this book. She has just finished The Secret History by Donna Tartt. The book featuring Ruth and Nelson is part of Elly Griffith's excellent Ruth Galloway series. She then moves on to read The Puppet Show by MW Craven, featuring Tilly and Poe.

Now, I always like to offer a little something extra at the end of each book and this time I thought I might share the short story that Malachite is working on. I'd love to know what you think of it. Drop me a line and let me know.

https://dl.bookfunnel.com/eoh3lbwk5c

Yours sincerely,
Anna Penrose

Printed in Great Britain
by Amazon